# DISRUPTING THE DUKE

### Dukes Done Wrong
### Book 3

## Alexa Aston

Dragonblade Publishing, Inc. is an imprint of Kathryn Le Veque Novels, Inc.
P.O. Box 7968
La Verne CA 91750
ceo@dragonbladepublishing.com

Produced in the United States of America

First Edition September 2021
Trade Paperback Edition

## ARE YOU SIGNED UP FOR DRAGONBLADE'S BLOG?

You'll get the latest news and information on exclusive giveaways, exclusive excerpts, coming releases, sales, free books, cover reveals and more.

Check out our complete list of authors, too!

No spam, no junk. That's a promise!

### Sign Up Here

www.dragonbladepublishing.com

*Dearest Reader;*

*Thank you for your support of a small press. At Dragonblade Publishing, we strive to bring you the highest quality Historical Romance from some of the best authors in the business. Without your support, there is no 'us', so we sincerely hope you adore these stories and find some new favorite authors along the way.*

*Happy Reading!*

*CEO, Dragonblade Publishing*

# Additional Dragonblade books by Author Alexa Aston

## Dukes Done Wrong Series
Discouraging the Duke
Deflecting the Duke
Disrupting the Duke
Delighting the Duke
Destiny with a Duke

## Dukes of Distinction Series
Duke of Renown
Duke of Charm
Duke of Disrepute
Duke of Arrogance
Duke of Honor

## The St. Clairs Series
Devoted to the Duke
Midnight with the Marquess
Embracing the Earl
Defending the Duke
Suddenly a St. Clair
Starlight Night

## Soldiers & Soulmates Series
To Heal an Earl
To Tame a Rogue
To Trust a Duke
To Save a Love
To Win a Widow

## The Lyon's Den Connected World
The Lyon's Lady Love

# CHAPTER ONE

*Hillside, Surrey—June 1796*

DONOVAN MARTIN STUDIED the chessboard in front of him, his fingers hovering above his ball. He hesitated and withdrew his hand, resting it in his lap as he thought over the move he wished to make.

"Your instincts are good," his brother said encouragingly.

He glanced at Sam. "You aren't trying to trick me, are you?"

Sam laughed. "No. You're only a beginner. I wouldn't do that to you. Now, after we've played a few years? I would do everything in my power to lead you astray."

He knew it was true. Though six years older, Sam always looked out for Donovan, taking him under his wing and teaching him to ride and swim. He had made Donovan wait until he turned ten before bringing out the chessboard, saying that it took an older boy to understand the intricacies of the game. Sam was right. Chess was hard. Thinking about your next move wasn't good enough. It was all about thinking several moves ahead. Anticipating what your opponent would do. Working out those scenarios.

Going with his gut, he moved his ball. Seven moves later, he gleefully called out, "Checkmate!" for the first time since he and Sam had begun to play.

"That was terrific, Donovan," Sam praised.

"I hope you didn't let me win."

"I didn't. You earned this win all on your own. However, I think I did let my guard down and my mind wandered a few times." He beamed. "I will know in the future not to do that again. You will master this game in no time," Sam praised.

"What were you thinking about? A girl?" Donovan teased.

Sam's cheeks turned pink. "No," he said quickly. "At least, not too much. My mind was on what Father is going to quiz me over later today."

"Why does he do that all the time?"

"Because I am the heir to the dukedom. Father wants to make sure I am prepared to be the Duke of Haverhill when the time comes."

He snorted. "I am glad it's you and not me. I would hate to have to listen to all those stuffy lessons." Left unsaid was how Donovan was uncomfortable around their father, who probably spoke to his younger son a handful of times in a year. If that.

"They're not too bad," his brother defended. "And if they will help me to be a good lord to our people, they will have been worth it. What will you do while I am busy spouting all my knowledge?"

He shrugged. "Probably see if Mama wants to take a walk."

"I envy you," Sam said. "You are so close to her. She waited a long time for you."

The words struck him as odd. "What do you mean?"

Sam lifted his queen from the board and toyed with it as he said, "She had other babies between you and me."

That was certainly news to him. "How many? Where are they?"

"They didn't live," his brother revealed.

"Why haven't you told me this before?" he demanded.

"You were too young to understand," Sam said. "She had three miscarriages that I know of. That's when something goes wrong inside and the baby doesn't grow right. Each time, she had only been with child a few months. She would have to stay in bed after she lost one. She did have one the year before you were born but it was stillborn."

Donovan frowned at the term. "I don't understand."

"Again, something went wrong. This time, the baby was born but it was still. Dead. They buried her in the family plot."

It astounded him he hadn't known about these babies. He and Mama talked about everything. He wondered if he should ask her or if this was something she wanted to keep private.

Sam reached across the table and ruffled his hair. "When she knew she was carrying you, the doctor had her stay in bed so she could rest the entire time. She was so happy when you came out perfect, all ten fingers and toes. Mama cherishes you, Donovan."

He knew his mother loved him. She told him all the time. But he never remembered her telling Sam that.

"Does Mama cherish you?" he asked quietly.

Sam grew contemplative. "I think she does. As the heir, though, it seems there is an unspoken rule in society that somehow I belong all to Father. Mama doesn't have much to do with me and never did."

"And Father has nothing to do with me. I guess I am luckier than you are. Even if you will be the duke someday."

A polite knock sounded at the door and a maid entered. "His Grace wishes to see you, Lord Samuel."

"Thank you." Sam rose. "Off to another quizzing session. Have fun with Mama."

Donovan watched Sam leave. He was glad he didn't have to spend time with the duke. If truth be told, he was terrified of his father. He barked orders at everyone and always wore a sour look upon his face. The servants walked on eggshells, all afraid they would lose their positions with a single mishap. The tenants eyed Haverhill carefully anytime he went out on the estate.

Hoping that Sam would pass whatever test set before him today, Donovan went in search of his mother. He found her in her parlor, embroidering next to a window.

"Hello, my darling," she said as he crossed the room and

kissed her cheek.

"Would you like to go for a walk, Mama? It's a very pretty day."

The duchess set aside her sewing. "I would love to. Let me fetch my bonnet. I don't want any freckles to spread across my nose or cheeks."

Donovan didn't think a few freckles would detract from her beauty but he waited patiently for her in the foyer. She joined him, slipping her arm through his, and they strolled out the front door.

They walked for a good hour. The sun, which had been hidden behind a curtain of clouds, came out. Its heat seemed to sap Mama's energy.

"Shall we cut through the woods?" he suggested. "The shade will help cool you."

"That's a wonderful idea, my dear."

They ducked into the nearby copse and continued into the woods until they reached a small brook, following it for half a mile before starting through the forest again. Mama asked to stop and rest. They sat on a fallen log. He wanted to ask her about the other babies she had lost but didn't want to see the smile fall from her face. She was so happy today and he couldn't bear to cause her pain.

Helping her to her feet again, they continued strolling through the woods.

Suddenly, a loud shriek erupted.

"Something's hurt!" Mama cried, lifting her skirts and racing toward the sound.

Donovan hurried after her. He stumbled on a tree root and went sprawling. Quickly righting himself, he ran to catch up—and then heard an unearthly scream. It pierced his ears as much as his soul. He knew it came from his mother.

"Mama!" he shouted, hurrying toward the blur of pale blue satin to his left.

He reached her and came to an abrupt halt, his jaw gaping.

She lay on the ground next to a doe who had been caught in a poacher's trap. The animal's panicked eyes frightened him. But what he couldn't understand was Mama also with the same look in her eyes. He glanced down and saw she had also stepped in a similar trap when she came to the doe's aid. She'd hiked up her skirts enough so he could see the steel teeth biting into the flesh just above her ankle.

She sobbed, "Help me."

He fell to his knees and pulled as hard as he could. The jaws of the trap which encased her leg refused to budge. His gaze met hers. Her lips trembled. Her whole body trembled in pain.

"I'll bring help, Mama."

Donovan scrambled to his feet. "I'll hurry. You will be fine," he promised as he took off, not knowing if she would be.

*Help her, God, help her, help her, please, help her.*

The thought echoed over and over in his head as he ran as fast as he could. He reached the stables and a groom started to speak to him.

"Send for the doctor. Now!" he shouted. "Mama's leg is caught in a trap in the woods."

The groom's face went white. "Yes, my lord," he managed to utter.

Donovan continued to the house. As he reached the front door, he saw the groom race by on a horse.

He entered the house and stood in the foyer.

"Father! Father!" he yelled at the top of his lungs. "Father!"

Servants appeared from several directions, including their butler. Donovan ran to him, grasping his lapels in desperation.

"Mama's hurt. She's in the woods. She stepped into a trap. I can't get her out."

The butler snapped his fingers and two footmen raced out the door. The butler sent a maid to the stables for a horse and cart to bring the duchess home. She rushed from the foyer as Donovan stood helplessly, turning in circles.

Then the duke appeared, Sam right behind him. "What is all

this shouting about?" He glared at Donovan. "You are never to disrupt this household in such a manner again or you will be severely punished."

Out of breath, Donovan placed his hands on his knees, bending over and trying to catch his breath. He heard the butler relay the news to the duke regarding the duchess.

Suddenly, he was jerked upward.

"Where is she?" his father demanded.

"I'll show you."

Donovan took off, running out the front door and across the lawn, Sam on his heels. They reached the woods and he shouted for the footmen. They didn't answer and he pushed further into the forest. He saw the two servants ahead, bending to Mama, and hurried to hold her hand.

"It will be just fine, Mama. I know it hurts."

She didn't respond. Her eyes were glassy. Tears streamed down her cheeks but she made no sound beyond a whimper.

Sam took her other hand and squeezed it as the two footmen pried the steel apart. Sam went and stood behind Mama, lifting her under her arms and dragging her back a few feet as she was freed from the trap. Blood gushed from her ripped skin. Sam whipped his coat off and wrapped it around her leg. Almost immediately, the fawn-colored jacket was soaked.

Donovan pulled his coat off. Sam removed his coat and flung it away, taking Donovan's and wrapping it around Mama's lower leg.

By now, his father had arrived, looming over them. Donovan saw the duke's lips purse in displeasure.

"The doe," Mama murmured as she began to moan. "Help it," she pleaded.

Donovan looked and saw the animal nearby, still trapped and quaking.

"Damn the doe!" his father roared, going to the trapped beast and stomping hard on its neck.

The animal's soft keening ceased. The deer's eyes were wide, its neck broken. Donovan looked away, a sick feeling spreading through him.

"The cart is here, Your Grace."

"Get her to it," the duke said impatiently.

The two footmen lifted her, Sam helping to raise her leg. Donovan held her hand as they carried her to the cart, trying to reassure her. Mama had lost all color. She didn't seem to know where she was.

The servants placed her in the cart and both boys climbed in next to her, taking her hands and stroking her hair. As the driver started the wagon up, Donovan's gaze met that of the duke's. They watched one another as the cart pulled away.

Everything was a blur after that. The servants carried Mama to her chambers. He and Sam were told to stay out as Mama's lady's maid began to fuss over her. The doctor arrived and was in the bedchamber a long time as the father and both sons waited in the corridor. When the doctor emerged, Donovan knew the news wouldn't be good.

"May we speak privately, Your Grace?"

"No," Haverhill said flatly. "Say your piece here."

Flustered, the physician swallowed and then said, "Her Grace's leg is nearly severed. The best thing to do would be to amputate the lower part, beneath her knee."

Disgust filled the duke's face. "Amputate? I don't want half a woman. Sew the blasted limb back on, Man."

Horror filled Donovan. He glanced to Sam, who wore an equal expression.

"That wouldn't be best for the duchess, Your Grace. She is in shock now. I have also given her laudanum for the pain. It would be easiest to remove it quickly, while she is more numb to pain. It is her best chance of survival," he added quietly.

His father shook his head. "You heard what I said. No wife of mine will be less than whole."

The doctor looked at him beseechingly. "Even if I could attach it again, Your Grace, infection is likely to set in. She could die from that. Gangrene could eat away at her."

Haverhill sniffed. "Then at least she will be buried with two legs. Not one."

With that, the duke turned and strode away.

"Save her," pleaded Donovan. "Don't listen to him, Doctor. Please."

The physician shook his head. "Your father has legal rights here, my lord. A wife is the property of her husband. His Grace has made his decision." He paused. "I am so sorry. There is nothing more I can do for her. Prepare yourselves, boys."

"Can we be with her?" he asked.

The doctor nodded.

With great reluctance, Donovan and Sam entered the bed-chamber. The maid sat beside the bed, weeping.

"Go," Sam said softly. "We will be with her."

The servant left, leaving them alone.

"Why would he do this?" Donovan asked, his eyes flooding with tears.

"Because he's a vile man," Sam replied. "He never loved her. He doesn't love anyone."

They sat with her for several hours. The fever grew worse. Mama grew delirious as her body heated like a furnace. The maid returned, bringing bowls with cloths. He and Sam dipped them in the water, bathing Mama's face and limbs, trying to calm the raging inferno within her.

The pain returned and she began howling, a guttural noise that stripped him until he was raw. The leg continued to bleed, soaking the bedclothes. Donovan thought if the high fever didn't kill her, the great loss of blood would.

"I will go get Father," Sam finally said as night fell and the room began to grow dark.

"Why?"

"I think she hasn't long to live."

"He should have been here, comforting her," Donovan hissed. "He's probably eating dinner and sipping port."

Sam didn't reply. His brother slipped from the room.

Donovan took Mama's hand again. "I love you," he croaked as her eyes opened.

"I love . . . you," she gasped and then her jaw went slack. Her eyes stared at the ceiling. Her breathing ceased.

He wailed, punching the mattress with his fists. Then he calmed and brushed his hands over her eyes to close them.

Minutes later, his father entered with Sam.

"She's dead," Donovan told them dully, a vast emptiness inside him.

Tears coursed down Sam's cheeks. The duke remained stalwart. Donovan couldn't help but compare the two as they stood next to one another, both short and thin, blond-haired and fair complexions.

"She always favored you," Haverhill finally said. "Said you were her little miracle. You look just like her, you know."

He glanced at the still body on the bed and knew his father spoke the truth. Donovan had his mother's thick, black hair and piercing, blue eyes. She had told him he was built like the men on her side of the family. Tall, sturdy, and muscular. A fresh wave of tears poured from his eyes, like a dam bursting.

"Quit your crying," the duke barked. "She coddled you far too much. I don't need a spoiled, pampered boy for a son."

"I won't quit crying!" Donovan shouted. "I loved her."

"Well, if you'd loved her, you wouldn't have taken her walking in the woods and gotten her killed."

Guilt rose within him. Rationally, he knew it wasn't his fault but his father's words lingered in the air.

"You've cost me a wife," the duke said plainly. "She never had a thing to do with me once you came. You look like her. Sound like her. Walk and talk like her. If she hadn't humored you, she would still be alive."

Shaking his head, Haverhill continued. "I can't stand the sight of you. You will be a constant reminder of her and I certainly don't need that in my life. Get out," he ordered.

"Where am I supposed to go?" Donovan asked, feeling as if he'd been punched hard in his gut. He wanted his mother. He wanted Sam to comfort him.

The duke wrinkled his nose as if Donovan stank. "I'll send you to my cousin for now. Then you'll be off to school." He pursed his lips, a sure sign of his displeasure. "You can stay there. I have an heir in your brother. I don't ever want to lay eyes upon you again."

# CHAPTER TWO

*Turner Academy—September 1796*

DONOVAN ENTERED THE ballroom with his four companions, boys he had just met minutes ago. Emotionally, he felt as if he had been forced through a washerwoman's ringer and hung out to dry. He blinked several times, hoping the tears that kept filling his eyes would go away and not embarrass him as he attended his first school assembly at a place unfamiliar to him. He missed his old school and friends. He missed Hillside and Sam.

Most of all, he wanted his mother.

He had been delivered to Turner Academy less than half an hour ago by his father's cousin, whom he had lived with after his father exiled him from Hillside. Donovan was led by a talkative servant to a room with four boys inside it. They were to be the ones he shared his living quarters with for the next school year.

One had sat mute on his bed as the other three introduced themselves. One by one, they told him why their families had enrolled them at Turner Academy. Donovan had been told the school was a place for naughty, depraved boys. He knew he didn't belong here. He had told himself over and over again that it wasn't his fault Mama stepped in the trap. That it was the poacher who had encroached upon their lands and set it who was to blame.

Donovan had yet to forgive himself, however.

As the boys, all new to the academy as he was, briefly told their tales, he was struck by the fact that they seemed innocent of any wrongdoing. Three of them were sons of powerful dukes, just as he was. The fathers all had their heirs and found these sons dispensable, treating them as rubbish to be tossed away. Miles had lost his younger brother in a shooting accident his older brother refused to take responsibility for, claiming Miles had pulled the trigger. Wyatt's older brother had burned down the family's stables and all their horses inside had perished—but he accused Wyatt of setting the fire. Hart's brother had shoved the youngest brother into the water and the boy had broken his neck and drowned before Hart could reach him. Hart was blamed for the death.

At first, Donovan hadn't wanted to say why he had been sent to a school full of troublemakers. As each of these boys spoke up and candidly explained their presence at the academy, though, Donovan decided he must do the same. He was no longer welcome at home. This school would be his entire world. If he were to make friends and have a chance at any bit of happiness, he needed to be honest.

So, he had told them of Mama's death and how, since he favored her, his father couldn't abide the sight of him. Instead of judging him, the three boys had openly received him. Relief had filled him—as well as hope. Perhaps he could build a life here, among the misfits.

As the five boys seated themselves, he found Finch on his left. He was the only one who had refused to share his past with the other four. Finch had cursed, shocking Donovan but, at the same time, Finch had said he didn't care what any of them had done. Together, they had joined hands and Miles had proclaimed them the Turner Terrors.

The thought caused him to smile, the first time he had done so since that last day with Mama.

Donovan glanced around the semi-circle in which he sat. Besides the Turner Terrors, he counted ten other boys, for a total of fifteen. A few of them looked like the troublemakers they had been branded as. One older boy, about fourteen, glared at him and Donovan looked away.

"Don't do that," Finch said. "Look back at him. Keep doing so until he turns away."

"Why—"

"Just do it," Finch hissed.

He raised his head again and stared at the boy who sat across from him. Though he itched to look away, he didn't want to be seen as weak in Finch's eyes. Finally, the other boy gave him a disdainful look and glanced away.

"You did it," Finch said quietly, his voice laced with praise.

"I did, didn't I?" asked Donovan, who was pleased with himself.

"He's a bully. It's important to stare them down or stand up to them. Never show any sign of weakness with anyone. Here or anywhere else," his new friend warned. "If you do, they'll go after you. I might not be around to help you the next time."

Donovan had never been bullied before. He had liked his school and always made friends easily. Something told him that Finch had been bullied.

Badly.

"Did you ever have to stand up for yourself? With other boys?" he asked.

Finch gazed away, silent. After waiting for a reply, Donovan decided this was something else that Finch would never answer.

It surprised him when Finch finally said, "No. No other boys ever bothered me." He sat up straighter. "And they won't here, either. None of the Turner Terrors will ever be seen as weak. We are strong. We are united."

His vehemence startled Donovan. He wondered if he would ever figure out this boy. At least he seemed to have claimed William Finchley as a friend. Finch seemed fully accepting of the idea that he was a Turner Terror and Donovan was, too.

At the head of the semicircle sat a group of several men. One rose, catching Donovan's eyes, and he sat taller in his seat.

Conversation came to a halt as the fifteen pupils turned their attention to this tall, thin man who stepped toward them. His bald pate gleamed. Donovan had never seen a pair of eyebrows as black or bushy. The eyebrows seem to have a life of their own.

"Greetings. To those of you who do not know me, I am Nehemiah Turner, co-founder of Turner Academy, along with my brother, Josiah."

He indicated a man who was also in his mid-forties. While tall and thin like his brother, Josiah Turner's head was full of white hair and a snowy beard covered the majority of his face. The man stood briefly and nodded before taking his seat again.

"Since there are two Mr. Turners, you will address me as Mr. Nehemiah. I will tutor you in the sciences. My brother will teach you history, philosophy, and art."

He turned and gestured to a third man. "This is Mr. Whitby. He is in charge of languages. You will study both Greek and Latin, as well as delve into the fine intricacies of English, from grammar to composition to literature."

Whitby inclined his head. Donovan thought he would be a hard taskmaster from his expression.

"Finally, Mr. Morris will instruct you in mathematics. He will challenge you to stump him with an equation but I have found no student has ever come close to doing so."

Morris beamed at the boys and Donovan found himself drawn to the tutor.

"I would also like to introduce to our newcomers the two who truly run Turner Academy. Ladies?"

All the boys turned and two women who hovered in the doorway to the ballroom stepped inside.

"On the left is Mrs. Nehemiah, my wife and the academy's housekeeper. She is the one who keeps all of us in line. The other is Mrs. Josiah, Turner Academy's cook. I believe you will find the food to your liking."

The only thing he had disliked at his former school was the

food. Everything seemed bland, boiled, or both. Anything would be an improvement in his eyes.

"Several of you know Mr. Smythe," Mr. Nehemiah said as the servant entered the ballroom and gave a friendly wave. "Mr. Smythe usually becomes your best friend during your time at the academy. Don't let his geniality fool you. He is a former soldier in His Majesty's army and has the battle scars to prove it."

The two women curtseyed and Mr. Smythe bowed before they vacated the room.

"Shall we speak of why you are here? I think it is important to do so. Josiah?"

The other Turner came forward as the first took a seat. He gazed over the small crowd before speaking. When his eyes met Donovan's, he thought Mr. Josiah saw straight through to his heart.

"Hello," he began. "You most likely have been told you have been sent to Turner Academy as a punishment. That it is a school for difficult young boys. Ones who are troubled. Annoying. Boys who are vicious or nasty. Bad to the bone." He paused. "Let me squash that thinking right away."

"It is true that a handful of you have done something very wrong. Heinous. Even criminal. Others of you merely are victims of family politics. Some of you come from venerable, powerful families and are the sons of dukes. Other students may be sons from wealthy, titled gentlemen. The point is you have all been sent here for a reason that doesn't matter."

Donovan shifted in his chair and glanced about surreptitiously at the boys seated in the semicircle.

"I speak from experience," Turner continued. "My brother and I were the sons of a solicitor's clerk. Father emphasized the importance of a good education. Nehemiah and I studied hard and both of us won scholarships to Oxford. Before our last term, while we were at home, our father was murdered.

"Nehemiah and I were taken into custody and sentenced to death."

A chill rippled down Donovan's spine. He wondered how these two men had escaped such a punishment and now stood here as founders of a school.

"We were absolved at the last minute. At university, we had been befriended by the Earl of Marksby's son and had gone home frequently with him to visit during holidays. Lord Marksby, who was quite fond of us, paid for our legal representation. When we were found guilty, he did not stop but pushed on, hiring men from Bow Street to investigate. They discovered the true murderer, a man Father had worked with. Thanks to Lord Marksby's intervention, in a rare move, the court overturned the verdict and we were set free, allowed to complete our education."

Donovan sat mesmerized by the tale.

"Upon our graduation, though cleared of any crime, Nehemiah and I found ourselves unemployable. No employer wanted the taint of scandal attached to us. Though Lord Marksby had passed on by this time, his son—our friend—took a chance and gave us the funds to start a school. This school. We have deliberately kept enrollment small, wanting to give personal attention to every pupil. We take in boys from ages seven to seventeen. Sometimes, for a year. Sometimes, for the remainder of their education.

"If you know your Latin, you are familiar with *tabula rasa*. Loosely translated into English, it means clean slate. *That* is what you have here. No one will question you about why you are here. You will be provided with competent instructors and a rigorous curriculum. You will be challenged. Supported. Embraced. All for being you. Take advantage of your time at Turner Academy and every opportunity which arises. You may remain only for this term. You may complete your education here. Either way, you are—each one—important. Valued. Trusted."

The stirring words bolstered Donovan.

"You will respect our staff and one another. We do not tolerate prejudice, nor do we believe one boy is better than the next. That is why you will all be addressed with the title of *Mister*, followed by your Christian name. Make wise choices. Study hard. Participate. Be open-minded. Most of all, remember the Golden Rule: Do unto others as you would have them do unto you."

Josiah Turner smiled broadly. "Welcome to Turner Academy."

The boys broke out in spontaneous applause.

"I know my wife has been cooking for two days straight now." He raised his hands, palms turned upward. "Please, come and join me and the rest of your instructors in the dining room."

Wyatt nudged Donovan with an elbow. "What do you think?"

"I think we are lucky to be here," he said. "We could have been sent to a much different place. I think . . . I will like it here."

They stood and Miles said, "Those Turners are the original Turner Terrors," he joked.

"I like them," Hart declared. "I dreaded coming here and what I would find. Instead, I believe I will be better educated than at my previous school." He grinned. "And that I will have lifelong friends."

"They want us to like it here," Finch said.

"You don't?" Donovan asked.

"I'll reserve judgment," Finch said. "After all, I'm going to be here a very long while."

Donovan slung an arm around Finch. He felt protective of the boy, who acted tough but seemed to have a streak of vulnerability running through him.

"Come on. Let's go see if Mrs. Josiah's food is as good as her husband bragged."

He marched Finch along and Miles, Hart, and Wyatt followed.

Donovan didn't care what Finch said. Turner Academy was a good place to be.

And he planned to make the most of his experience here.

# CHAPTER THREE

*London—August 1811*

L ADY WYNTER DAY dismissed her maid and picked up a pencil, jotting down a few ideas before she forgot them. The Season was coming to an end and she couldn't wait to return to Chesterfield, her country home, where she could dress as she pleased and not have to think of social affairs and those who attended them. Not that she bothered with the opinions of others. Wynter was known for being charming and impulsive, dressing a bit differently from other women of the *ton*. She also had a reputation for being outspoken and doing exactly what she wanted to do. It attracted a good many single men to her, while most mamas kept their young daughters making their come-outs far away from her.

She didn't give a fig about that. She thought most every young woman making her come-out insipid. They were boring and unimaginative. If there was one thing she couldn't stand, it was someone who was dreadfully dull. Women of Polite Society never showed any emotion. They were prim and restrained. They talked about choosing a new bonnet or what needlework they had recently completed.

Boring.

Wynter had always been attracted to men though never in a romantic sense. Men just were more adventurous. More interesting. More physical. Always in motion, going and doing. Sometimes she thought she should have been born a man. She certainly would be a better man than most men. She had witnessed that the older men got, the more sedate they became, like the ladies of Polite Society. That's why she liked being friendly with single gentlemen in their twenties. They were full of life and fun—especially the rogues.

Thank goodness she had never felt an attraction to any of them. It was only because she hadn't and made it perfectly clear that she would never marry that she had become a darling of the *ton*, functioning as a little sister to so many of the men in society. They sought her as their card partner because she was astute at card play and downright lucky, a deadly mix. They danced with her because she was good at it and they knew she had no designs on them. They took her for drives in Hyde Park, asking for her advice regarding which horses they should purchase.

Even the rogues, when it came time to settle down, asked her opinion of which lady they should offer for. They knew they could trust her opinion, never given rashly. Wynter took her time before making her suggestions for marriage. So far, she had met with success in pairing together over two dozen couples.

Setting her list aside, she ventured downstairs to breakfast. Her father glanced up and gave her a smile.

"Good morning, Wynter."

"Good morning, Papa."

She went to the sideboard and put a few items on her plate. A footman brought her a cup of tea and helped seat her.

"Where is Pickford? He usually drops in about this time."

"I don't know, Father. He may not breakfast with us this morning. He does have his own place to eat," she said.

Just then, Sam entered the breakfast room and greeted them both. He headed to the buffet as if he were at home and filled his plate with rashers of bacon and ham and a mound of scrambled eggs. The footman brought coffee for him.

Wynter loved that Sam started his day with them most mornings. Their London townhouses sat next to one another. Their country estates lay only seven miles apart. Though she hadn't known him growing up since he was six years older than she was and often away at school—and their fathers were sworn mortal enemies—they had become friends once she came to London for her come-out. They saw each other frequently in town and several times a month in the country. Her father adored Sam. Not only because Sam was beloved by everyone but because the earl's friendship with Sam irritated Sam's father, the Duke of Haverhill, to no end.

She couldn't think of a better best friend to have than Sam.

"Father and I are leaving for home today," Sam told them.

"Today?" she asked. "I wouldn't advise it. It's been raining for a good week and doesn't look as if it will let up anytime soon. The roads will be a mess."

Sam shrugged. "You know Father. Once he gets something in his head, there is no persuading him otherwise. Most of his friends left London a week ago. He's bored and restless. Ready to be back at Hillside."

"Haverhill was born restless," the earl observed. "He was like that as a boy and never grew out of it."

"You are right, Lord Cheston. Perhaps you might try and talk some reason into him. I fear with the mud and rain, it will take us three times as long to reach Hillside than it usually does."

"I have no wish to involve myself in an argument with your father, Pickford. We didn't get along as boys and never learned to as men." His eyebrows arched. "You know the reason why."

Wynter had found it hard to believe that anyone couldn't get along with her father, the most reasonable and affable of men.

Until she had met the Duke of Haverhill.

She thought the duke pompous, staid, and mean-spirited. Though Sam was Haverhill's heir, she cringed at times by the way father addressed son. Sam seemed to take it all in stride. He had told her that his father often put him through various tests, wanting him to learn to be what a good duke should. She bit back her retort that a good duke should be the opposite of Haverhill, not wanting to hurt her friend's feelings. Besides, Sam was his father's opposite. He would make for an excellent duke someday.

Sam thought that their fathers merely hadn't gotten along as schoolboys and the animosity continued when they matured. Wynter had once asked her father about it.

*And learned that her father had been in love with Sam's mother.*

The future Duchess of Haverhill had been the most beautiful girl of her come-out group. One look between them and Wynter's father told her that he knew he would wed the girl at Season's end. After all, he was a viscount and future earl. Nice-looking and wealthy. He would make an excellent candidate as a husband.

Unfortunately, the Duke of Haverhill had overheard Lord Cheston tell a few friends at White's of his intentions. That had led to the duke pursuing the girl with a fervor unseen by Polite Society. In the end, she hadn't been given a choice. Her father told her she was to wed the Duke of Haverhill, other suitors be damned. Haverhill was already a duke, wealthy and powerful. She would immediately become a duchess upon her marriage, one of a handful in society.

As any other young girl of her class would have done, she obeyed her papa. Naturally, Haverhill told her she was never to speak to Lord Cheston again. Wynter's father had wed a few Seasons later. His bride was beautiful but a known featherhead. She had given birth to Wynter and died two years later in childbirth, having produced a stillborn son.

"When do you leave?" she asked, missing him already even before he was gone.

"Within the hour. I just wanted to come over and say my goodbyes."

"And eat me out of house and home," Cheston grumbled good-naturedly.

"And that," Sam agreed amiably, winking at Wynter.

The earl rose. "Have a safe journey, Pickford. Wynter and I

will be leaving at week's end. We hope to see you at Chesterfield soon after."

"You can count on it, my lord," Sam replied. Once her father left, he added, "Would you play me one song before I leave, Wynter?"

"Of course."

They went to the drawing room and she sat at the pianoforte. Her father had encouraged her to take up various womanly arts, in addition to being a tomboy and becoming competent at riding, shooting, and hunting. She had learned to play the pianoforte and taken voice lessons, as well as learning to embroider and do other types of needlework. She found sewing boring and had abandoned it. The voice lessons only proved she sounded no better than a croaking frog. She had taken to the pianoforte, though, and played for an hour every day for the sheer enjoyment of it.

Sam joined her on the bench and asked for a lively tune. She obliged him, pounding the keys with skill and enthusiasm. When she finished, he applauded her efforts.

"You are so talented, Wynter. I think you could do whatever you wished if you put your mind to it."

She thanked him but saw something in his eyes. Something she didn't like at all. Inside her mind, she started a mantra.

*Don't say it. Don't say it. Don't say anything. Don't ruin things between us.*

"Before I leave, I must ask something of you." Sam grew serious, something he rarely was. "You know I am past thirty now. It is time I thought of a wife and children."

She glanced down at her hands in her lap as he took one. His other hand slid to the small of her back.

"Wynter, I have never known a more spirited girl than you. You bring sunshine wherever you go. I know we are good friends and that is the basis of any successful marriage."

She met his earnest gaze. "Sam, I—"

He kissed her. Instinct told her he had seen in her eyes what her answer would be and he was doing his best to convince her to change her mind.

She had been kissed before. Several times. No kiss had ever moved her.

Sam's was no exception.

He broke it, his gaze searching her face. "It's a no, isn't it?" he asked, his disappointment obvious.

"You know how I feel about you, Sam," she began. "You are my closest friend. I enjoy every minute we spend together."

"But wouldn't that make for a good marriage? We respect each other, Wynter. We have fun with one another."

She shook her head. "You know I have no desire to wed. Women give up what little identity they have when they become a wife—and brood mare. I am not one of those nurturing creatures who longs for children. I enjoy my life exactly as it is. I am free to come and go as I please. Do what I wish. Answer to no man.

"I am sorry, Sam. I simply cannot marry you. My heart wouldn't be in the marriage. I want you to find a woman you are batty over. One who will bring you joy each day. One who will bear your children and live for your smile."

He looked at her ruefully. "Are you certain you don't want to be that woman, Wynter? I would never try to cage you as other men would. I would let you remain true to yourself."

"If I ever married, it would be to you," she said honestly. "But I have no wish to do so."

He squeezed her hand and rose, a wry smile on his face. "Thank you for hearing me out. I was expecting the answer you gave—but I had to ask all the same."

She rose and took his hands in hers, squeezing them. "You know I think the world of you, Sam. I do believe it is time you wed. I will start considering wives for you at once. You know I have a talent in finding a man the perfect wife. We can see about eligible young ladies in Surrey first. If none proves acceptable, then next Season I guarantee that we will find you the perfect bride."

Sam bent and kissed her cheek. "I do love you, Wynter. You are as a sister to me and the best friend I will ever have." He chuckled. "Be sure whatever wife you find for me won't be jealous of you."

"I would never be a threat to her," she promised. "I will match you with someone who will make you happy, Sam. You can count on it."

She walked him to the foyer. "Take care. The weather is so nasty."

"I will see you soon."

A footman handed Sam an umbrella and opened the door. Sam opened the umbrella as he stepped across the threshold and then turned, a smile on his face.

"Farewell!" he called as he raced away.

Wynter waved and shouted, "Goodbye!"

Returning to the drawing room, she played for an hour, melancholy pieces which matched her mood. She chided herself for not seeing it coming. She had been friends with Sam for so long. They bantered as siblings and spent a great deal of time together. It hurt her to know that she had hurt him, something she would never deliberately do. But she had to stay true to herself. One day, Sam would be the Duke of Haverhill.

Wynter Day simply wasn't duchess material.

WITH THE LAST garden party of the Season rained out, Wynter felt a bit of relief. She enjoyed being around others but this Season had seemed to drag on far too long. She supposed she, too, was ready to leave for Surrey, as Sam and his father had done two days ago.

Escaping to her sitting room, she closed the door. She spent so much of the Season with people surrounding her that she cherished time alone when she could manage it. She had told their butler she wouldn't be at home this afternoon. Not that anyone would come calling in this weather, which threatened to become a monsoon.

She went to the small pianoforte she kept there. This room was hers alone, her sanctuary during their time in London. Here she read, played music, or simply sat and thought. Today, she would play Bach's inventions. She loved how they kept her on her toes, one hand going off in one direction and the other following several beats behind. She decided to start with *Number 8*, a spirited piece that didn't allow her mind to wander.

Halfway through the piece, she heard a knock on the door. Wynter stopped playing, peeved that she was being disturbed. The servants knew she was to be left alone when the door to the sitting room was closed. The butler knew she wasn't receiving any guests today.

"Come!" she called, tamping down her annoyance.

The door opened and their butler said, "My lady, you have a visitor. Not a guest."

He looked a bit perplexed and she asked, "Who is it?"

"It is . . . Haven."

"Haven?" she asked. "The Haverhill butler from next door?"

"Yes, my lady. He said it is most urgent. That he must speak to you at once."

Wynter had no idea why Haven would wish to see her, especially with Sam gone to the country. Curiosity filled her.

"Show him in."

"Very good."

She closed the case which protected the keys of her instrument and stood, moving away from the bench. She took a seat and smoothed her skirts.

The door opened again and Haven appeared. Usually, the butler stood tall and proud, happy for the world to know he served a duke. Today, though, his shoulders slumped. He seemed to have aged several years overnight.

"Lady Wynter, thank you for seeing me," he began.

"You look as if you need to sit, Haven." She indicated a chair near the one she sat in.

"Thank you, my lady. I am grateful."

Haven took a seat and swallowed. "I have news which I must share with you. I did not want you to see it in the newspapers tomorrow morning and have no warning."

The only thing she could think of in the newspapers—especially this time of year—were betrothal announcements.

Had Sam left her merely to go to another woman and ask her for her hand in marriage?

No, that made no sense at all. She and Sam had discussed searching for his bride at home in the country and failing to find one, going about the business next Season of locating the perfect match for him in town. She doubted he would have agreed to all of that only to leave and offer for a woman before he left London.

"Go on," she encouraged.

Pain filled the butler's eyes. "I regret to inform you, my lady, that His Grace and Lord Pickford died in an accident two days ago."

"Died?" she echoed, her mind whirling, her heart beating too fast. "No, you are mistaken, Haven. I saw Lord Pickford two days ago, just before he and His Grace left for Surrey."

Haven shook his head sadly. "It happened on their journey home. The roads were abominable. They reached a bridge, which had washed out, but the driver did not see it in time. Their carriage plummeted into the water. They and their driver drowned. Only the footman survived. He clung to the carriage, trying to get the door open but it was stuck. He was then swept downstream and washed up on the bank."

He paused. "I am sorry, Lady Wynter. I know his lordship and you were very close. I wanted to tell you in person of the tragedy."

She had gone numb as the butler spoke. She could picture the scene in her mind. Her eyes filled with tears, thinking of the moments as the interior of the vehicle filled with water and Sam couldn't get out.

What had been his last thoughts?

Her throat grew thick with unshed tears but she managed to say, "Thank you, Haven. I appreciate you coming to tell me."

The butler rose and she followed suit. "Lord Pickford was a wonderful man. He would have made for a fine duke."

"Yes, he would have," she said faintly.

"Can I summon someone for you, my lady?" Haven asked gently. "I don't wish to leave you alone."

"No, I prefer it," she said, her voice coming from a distance. "Thank you," she said, dismissing him.

Once Haven left, Wynter dropped into the chair again. The numbness receded, followed by a deep anger. If only Haverhill hadn't been so insistent on leaving London with the roads in such a mess. If only the driver had been paying better attention. If only the bridge hadn't washed out.

Change any of those things—and Sam would still be alive.

Regret filled her at their last meeting. How she had turned down his offer of marriage. If she hadn't and instead accepted him, would he have stayed and allowed his father to return to Hillside without him? Would they have gone to the final few events of the Season, happy to receive felicitations from all their friends and Polite Society?

Wynter would never know.

All she did know was that Sam was never coming back.

# CHAPTER FOUR

*Spain—November 1811*

DONOVAN MARTIN POURED a healthy bit of wine into the tin cup and handed it to Hart before doing the same for himself.

"To us!" he said. "Both majors now."

The two men tapped their cups together and downed the wine. Hart held out his cup.

"More!" he cried. "It's not every day captains become majors."

As Donovan refilled Hart's cup, he added, "And majors who are and will always remain lifelong friends."

Satisfaction filled him as he sipped the wine this time since the first cup already warmed his belly.

"So, Major Hartfield, do you have plans this evening?"

Hart grinned. "I suppose a celebration is called for. I assumed you would make your way to the nearest village and find a willing wench to help you celebrate."

Donovan beamed. "You know me well, Aaron."

Hart shuddered. "Don't ever call me that. It was bad enough hearing Wellington use it when he promoted me."

"The last time I recall seeing that was our first day at Turner Academy. Remember how above the beds placards had been placed with our names? So we would know which one was ours?"

Hart took another sip of the wine. "That first day we met was what I thought would be the worst day of my life—yet it turned out to be one of the best. I remember Finch also had his Christian name above his place. William, was it?"

"Yes," he replied. "You two were the only Terrors who went by nicknames. They suited both of you."

"I remember how one of the boys tried to call you Don once. I believe you punched him soundly in the nose and he never uttered that again."

Donovan laughed. "It wasn't my name. I'm rather partial to it."

He liked his name because his mother had named him after her grandfather. She had told Donovan that many times over the years they'd had together. That since he was the second son, the Duke of Haverhill hadn't cared what she called the boy, so she decided to honor her beloved grandfather.

He still missed his mother all these years later. He tried never to think of her and how her life had been cut short.

Thanks to the Duke of Haverhill not wanting half a wife.

It still angered Donovan after all these years. True, the doctor would have had to remove part of her leg but she would have lived. She could have seen him grow to the man he'd become. Sent him off to war. Given him someone to write to, knowing she was home and loved him.

Instead, his mother died because of her husband's selfishness. The duke had sent Donovan away to Turner Academy and had washed his hands of his son. He had forbidden Sam to ever contact Donovan. Sam, ever dutiful, had abided by their father's wishes.

He wondered where Sam was now. Probably at Hillside since it was late autumn. Did Sam go to London often? Had he married? Had children?

Donovan had no clue.

He never asked anyone about Sam, especially the new officers arriving on the Peninsula. Instead, he divorced himself from any thought of his family. Secretly, though, he hoped the day would come when Haverhill would lie six feet beneath the earth's surface and Sam would again be in Donovan's life. He hoped once Sam became the duke that he would do his best to get in touch with his brother. Losing his mother had been gut-wrenching but at least Donovan understood she was dead.

Losing Sam hurt even more because he knew Sam was still alive and not allowed to see or speak of Donovan.

The flap to their tent opened and a fresh-faced private stepped inside.

"Mail for you, Captain Martin. Oh, I mean, Major Martin," he said cheekily.

"Hand it over," Donovan said and accepted the letter.

"Nothing for me?" Hart asked. "And by the way, I am a major, as well."

"Braggart!" Donovan accused.

The private chuckled. "No, Major Hartfield. Nothing for you." He quit the tent.

"There rarely is," Hart sighed. "Unless it's from Miles. At least he's reliable in writing. Unlike Wyatt or Finch."

"Wyatt never liked putting quill to paper," he said. "And Finch has a parish to run."

"Miles is a duke now—and married," Hart pointed out. "And is certainly a father since Emery should have given birth by now."

"Wyatt is also a husband," Donovan pointed out. "Though we barely know that. Three lines and he tells us he's wed. Miles has written us with more information regarding Meadow than Wyatt."

"I am glad Miles and Wyatt have wed," Hart said. "One day, this bloody war will be over and done and you and I will return to England. We'll take a brief leave and head to Kent and meet the remarkable women that have stolen our friends' hearts."

He laughed. "You know you never have to worry about that with me. I love the ladies far too much to ever think of settling down with one. If I were a sailor, I would have a woman in every port."

"No you wouldn't," Hart contradicted. "One in a port wouldn't be enough for you. You would have several and have to juggle them each time you sailed in on shore leave."

"I suppose you are right."

"Read your letter," Hart encouraged. "You know we always share."

They did share. Since it was hard for letters to get through to the front and since they received letters from the same people, oftentimes Miles would alternate sending to either Donovan or Hart. Finch did the same. Wyatt had returned to England back in February but Donovan supposed he would follow the same practice. The Terrors shared everything between themselves.

Glancing down, he didn't recognize the handwriting and paused. It was addressed to Captain Martin. Since he had only recently received his promotion, that wasn't surprising. Donovan couldn't think of a single time a letter had come where he didn't immediately know the hand, though. Occasionally, he received a letter from one of the Turner brothers. The two men had started Turner Academy and, to this day, still wrote the Turner Terrors. Lord Marksby, as well, sent the Terrors letters once or twice a year. The earl had helped give the coin which allowed his friends, the Turners, to start their school, and Lord and Lady Marksby had hosted the Terrors for a few weeks each summer since they had no homes to go to during their holidays.

Frowning, he turned over the letter and broke the seal, which he didn't recognize. An uneasy filling filled him.

"What's wrong?" Hart asked. "Who is it from?"

Donovan glanced to the bottom of the page. Finding the signature, he froze.

"It's from Bagley," he said. "Haverhill's solicitor."

"Then he must be dead," his friend said. "Good riddance to the old sod."

Each of the Turner Terrors, except for Finch, had shared their stories with the group. All had fathers who had banished their second sons for one reason or another, favoring their heir apparents.

He decided to read it to himself because sudden unnamed emotions filled him. He didn't want his voice to break, especially with news of Haverhill's death.

*20 August 1811*

*Captain Martin –*

*I regret to inform you that His Grace, the Duke of Haverhill, has died in a tragic accident, along with his son, the Marquess of Pickford. The pair was returning from London to Hillside when they came upon a bridge which had been washed away by recent, torrential rains. Unfortunately, the driver proved unable to stop the vehicle in time and the carriage plunged into the river below. His Grace and Lord Pickford both drowned. Their bodies were recovered and both have been buried in the family plot at Wickley.*

*As you know, you are the next in line to inherit and are now the Duke of Haverhill. I would strongly advise you to resign your commission and return to England as soon as possible. The estate will be in need of your leadership. I suggest you come to London once you return from abroad so that we can meet and discuss the estate and your financial situation. My office address is listed below.*

*Please accept my condolences on the loss of your father and brother.*

*Yours sincerely,*
*Augustus Bagley*

Donovan reeled as the page fell from his fingertips. He collapsed onto his cot.

"What is it?" demanded Hart, getting no reply.

His friend retrieved the letter from the ground and quickly skimmed it.

"My God. Both dead. I'm sorry, Donovan."

Stunned, he could only shake his head. Finally finding his voice, he said, "Sam wasn't like your brother. Or Miles or Wyatt's. They were all wicked boys. Sam was my best friend even though he was six years older. I worshipped him. I was waiting for the day to hear that Haverhill was dead so that Sam and I could be true brothers once again."

Hart came and sat next to him on the cot, slinging his arm around Donovan. "I know this is a blow to you. I'm sorry."

He cursed. "I am Haverhill now. The one name I never thought would leave my lips again. The one position I would never wish to hold. Me, a duke?"

"You will be a good one," Hart confirmed. "You will need to be the duke your people now need, one far better than the duke they have had for all these years."

"But Sam was meant to be Haverhill," Donovan said, his voice full of anguish. "He had been trained for it from birth. I haven't a clue what being a duke means." Tears filled his eyes. "It's monstrously unfair. Sam was such a good person. To think he perished in a bloody awful accident is so wrong."

"Then you must be the best Haverhill you can be for Sam. Do the things he would have done. Make the changes he would have approved. Be the kind of man he would have been," Hart encouraged. "And," he added, his lips twitching with amusement, "just think that you'll now be able to drink good coffee and eat edible food. No more camp fare."

Suddenly, Donovan felt adrift. The army had been his entire adult life. It had given him purpose.

"I hate to leave you behind," he said. "You'll be the last of us at war."

Hart laughed. "Don't worry, Donovan. Even if there is only one Turner Terror fighting Bonaparte, the Little General will fall. Who knows? I may sell out once the war is over and come live off the largesse of my three ducal friends. Imagine that—Miles, Wyatt, and now you—all dukes. What is the world coming to?"

Donovan only knew his world had just turned upside down.

# CHAPTER FIVE

*London—December 1811*

DONOVAN LEFT THE small inn he had stayed at last night, wearing his uniform and carrying a small satchel with his razor and a few letters to post. Thank goodness Hart had given him some money to tide him over, else he would have slept on the streets last night.

He had never had two farthings to rub together growing up, being dumped at Turner Academy. Though his father regularly paid the tuition and provided him with his military commission and the uniforms required, no spare coin was ever sent. When Donovan began earning a salary as an army officer, he thought he had become rich overnight. He was generous to everyone, buying rounds of drinks when he, the Terrors, and their fellow officers went into the local villages. If he passed a dice or card game and one of his men was running short, he always provided a loan on the spot—which he never bothered to call in and refused it when a soldier tried to repay him. His generosity extended to the camp whores who traveled with the army and orphans they passed along the way.

Hart had teased him, saying he should make good on his word and sell out in order to accompany Donovan to London and then Surrey, just to make certain Donovan actually arrived. Hart joked and said he would travel from ducal estate to ducal estate, keeping his friends in line. A part of Donovan thought Hart might actually be serious. He could tell the war was wearing on his friend. Yet he knew Hart would never abandon his men. He—and Miles—had too great a sense of honor.

It had hurt to leave his men behind but the worst had been parting from Hart. They had spent every day together since they were ten years old, from the academy to university to the army. The Turner Terrors were breaking up. It had started when the four of them had joined the military, leaving Finch behind to minister to his new congregation. Then Miles received word he was the new Duke of Winslow and had sold out, returning to England. Wyatt had been seen sporadically by the three Terrors, as Wellington had called upon Wyatt to be a scout and sometime spy. He always remained with them whenever he returned to camp. Now, though, Wyatt also was back in England, a duke and newly married.

Donovan hadn't been surprised that Miles settled down so quickly. It was in his nature. Miles was reliable, honorable, and mature. He would have taken to his ducal responsibilities quickly. Wyatt's sudden marriage had surprised them all. He had enjoyed quick romantic encounters throughout university, never thinking of settling down. Donovan supposed becoming a duke had changed his carefree friend. Whether or not for the better would remain to be seen.

He had no plans of marrying anytime soon. Of the five Terrors, he was the womanizer, always ready for a quick romp in bed with a variety of women. Being a duke meant he could have his pick of any woman in Polite Society.

He planned to work his way through as many of them as possible.

Marriage was for old men who were ready to give up their wild ways. As far as Donovan was concerned, he would just be starting to live. He would finally never worry about having enough money. He could purchase a horse and a new pair of boots, which he desperately needed. He had Hillside, which he figured would provide him with a decent income.

There also was a townhouse somewhere in London. He had never been to the great city before now, save for a brief visit many summers ago when the Marksbys had brought the Terrors to town. As a boy, Haverhill always left Donovan in the country though he occasionally would take Sam to town with him since Sam was the heir apparent and the duke wanted him familiar with the city. Donovan had hated those times because he idolized Sam and wanted to spend as much time with his older brother as he could when they were home from school.

He would have to find out the location of the Haverhill townhouse. He had arrived too late last night and Bagley's offices were already closed. That had led him to stay at the small inn, which was only a few blocks from the solicitor's office.

Once he posted the letters to his four friends, informing the three of them of his new status and one to Hart to let him know he had arrived safely in London and would head for Hillside, Donovan only had a short walk to Bagley's address. As he arrived, he was still amazed by how large London was and how bustling the streets were even at this early hour. He found the door of his destination locked. A clock chimed seven bells in the distance and he supposed it was too early for men of business to be at work. He decided to walk around a bit and did so for an hour, returning just as a young man was slipping a key into the lock.

Following the man inside, he said, "I am Major Martin. I am expected."

The clerk whirled about, not having heard Donovan come in behind him.

"I beg pardon, Major. I make all of Mr. Bagley's appointments and you aren't one of them."

He frowned. "Let me see Bagley then. He can sort this out."

"Would you care to wait? Mr. Bagley won't arrive for another hour or so."

Donovan snorted. "Half the day will be gone by then," he proclaimed, not bothering to hide his disapproval.

The young man grinned. "I have often thought the same thing. Please, have a seat. Might I bring you some tea?"

"No, thank you. So, you work for Bagley?"

"Yes. I'm Morris, his clerk."

"What is he like? Other than sleeping until noon?"

Morris chuckled. "Mr. Bagley is very good at what he does, Major. He has several important clients, including the Duke of Haverhill. He is a fair man who looks after his clients' interests as if they were his own. Should you wish to hire him to tend to your affairs, I daresay you will be most pleased."

Donovan didn't mention that he was Haverhill. He merely nodded pleasantly.

"If you will excuse me, I must get to work," Morris said, bustling around and getting organized before burying himself in ledgers.

He spent the time waiting for Bagley thinking about Hillside. He hadn't done so in all the years he had been gone. At first, it was because everything was so raw. He had taken his mother's death hard and Hillside meant Mama. The two were linked in his mind. As he got over the first wave of homesickness and grief, he became more involved in his studies at Turner Academy and the new friends he had made in his fellow Terrors. As time passed, he still grieved his mother's death but he only thought of her in abstract terms.

And he never thought of Hillside at all. Doing so would have made him too sad, knowing Sam was there and they couldn't see one another.

Now, though, he would definitely need to think about Hillside. Get to know his tenants. His estate manager. Donovan wondered if it was the same man who had been there when he was a boy. It made him curious how many servants might still be at the house that might remember him. How they would feel about him becoming the duke over Sam. Everyone had always loved Sam.

What if Sam had married? Would there be a wife at Hillside?

If he did and they'd had children, no sons had been born. If they had, Donovan would never have been called away from war to claim the title.

The door opened and a portly gentlemen with graying hair entered. He eyed Donovan with interest and then his jaw dropped.

"Your Grace! I had no idea you had arrived in town."

"Your Grace?" Morris asked. "Oh, dear."

The clerk looked extremely worried. Donovan now regretted not identifying himself properly to the man.

He rose and offered his hand as Bagley nodded deferentially. "Good morning, Mr. Bagley. I came as soon as I received your letter. It took a while to catch up to me since the army has been moving around quite a bit this autumn."

The solicitor took his hand and then tossed an angry look at his clerk. "You should have—"

"Please do not blame Mr. Morris," he said quickly. "I neglected to introduce myself. In fact, this is the first time anyone has called me Your Grace since I haven't begun to use the title yet." He shook his head. "I am having a difficult time seeing myself in the role."

"Get His Grace tea," barked Bagley. "At once." In a more soothing tone, he said, "Come with me, Your Grace. We will get you settled. There is much to look over. When did you arrive in London?"

"Late last night."

"I am surprised Haven did not send word to me."

"Haven?" Donovan frowned.

"Your butler. Haven has always seemed most efficient."

"I did not stay at the townhouse. In fact, I have no idea of its address."

"I see."

Donovan wondered just how much Augustus Bagley knew of the past and how and why Donovan had been banished from Hillside.

Bagley led him back along a corridor and opened a door. They stepped inside and he saw a large table with six chairs. He took one and then the solicitor seated himself.

"It seems we have a lot of ground to cover, Your Grace."

"You don't have to keep saying that. Calling me Your Grace."

The older man's eyes widened. "But . . . that is simply the way of things, Your Grace."

Donovan realized his life was changing. And that he had no power over it. At least not yet.

"Give me an overview of my affairs then. The details can come after I have a better idea what is involved. Frankly, I have no idea what my responsibilities might entail."

"I will return in a moment."

Bagley left and was gone several minutes. During his absence, Morris appeared.

"Tea for you, Your Grace."

"I didn't really want any. I told you that before."

"Yes, but that's before I knew you were a duke," the clerk apologized.

"What does that have to do with anything?" he asked testily.

Morris shook his head. "It has to do with everything, Your Grace. You were not raised to be the duke. Your brother was. This life will seem very strange to you, I would imagine. Especially since you have been at war."

"Normal life would be strange after being at war, Mr. Morris. I cannot fathom what life as a duke will be like."

The clerk sighed. "Be ready for everyone to fawn over you. They will compliment you to the rafters—whether you deserve it or not. They will tell you that you are the wittiest man they have ever met. The most intelligent. The best dressed. You are superlative to everyone in every way."

"Merely because I am a duke?" he asked, only half-believing what the clerk said.

"Exactly because you are a duke. You are the closest thing to royalty in Polite Society *except* royalty itself, Your Grace. Men will want to befriend you—but be wary. Very few of them will do so simply because they desire your friendship. They will want to be known as the good friend of Haverhill. Women will clamor to become your duchess. You will have young ladies pushed upon you by doting mothers who are chasing a title for their daughters."

Morris shook his head sadly. "Watch your back, Your Grace. The friends you had before will still be your friends. Those are the men you should trust. The rest? They will need to prove themselves. Most everyone else will have nefarious reasons for wishing to befriend you."

"Sage advice for a clerk," he pointed out.

"I feel lucky to be a clerk. Hopefully, you will feel fortunate to be the Duke of Haverhill."

"That remains to be seen."

Donovan put a lump of sugar in his tea as Bagley returned. He conferred briefly with his clerk, who scurried from the room.

Setting down several ledgers, Bagley said, "We will look at these in good time, Your Grace. For now, I will give you an overview."

The solicitor began discussing the number of estates Donovan now owned. He had only thought of Hillside being his and learned that it was the country seat of the Duke of Haverhill. Besides it, he owned another estate in Surrey, three more in the east of England, two in the north, and one on the west coast of England. He also owned two warehouses on the London docks which housed goods from ships which traded around the world.

The more Bagley spoke, the more panicked Donovan became. He had thought managing Hillside alongside an estate manager would be difficult. Now, he had a slew of properties and businesses to consider. Though mathematics had been his favorite subject in school, he already knew he would be in over his head. It would take time to be comfortable enough to acknowledge he owned so much, much less do a decent job of running everything.

In that moment, Donovan missed Sam more than he had for the last fifteen years.

"Tell me how they died," he said abruptly.

Bagley looked nonplussed a moment and then regained his composure.

"They were returning from town to Surrey at the end of the Season."

"What is the Season?" he asked, having never heard the term before.

Clearing his throat, Bagley replied, "It is the time of year when Polite Society gathers and attends a whirl of social events. It begins after Easter and finishes up in August. It consists mainly of balls but there are various parties, theater outings, musicales. That sort of thing." He paused. "It is also known as the time in which the Marriage Mart takes place. Young ladies make their come-outs into society and eligible gentlemen court them. By Season's end, a flurry of betrothals are announced and the weddings take place during the following months."

Donovan could only imagine the parade of young girls, straight out of the schoolroom, passing by him each night. Girls who hadn't a thought in their heads other than marrying—and marrying well. As a duke, he would be considered a prime candidate. Thank goodness this Season wouldn't occur for several months. And when it did, he would make it clear that he had no interest in finding a wife. He would seek pleasure with no commitments. That would mean discreet liaisons with widows or the occasional bored wife who had already provided her husband with the requisite heir and spare. He knew enough about society to understand that.

Perhaps he wouldn't even bother to come to London for the Season for the first few years. Already, he realized he would be swamped with work. He wasn't afraid of it. In fact, he thought he would relish having something to do. He wanted to learn as much as he could as fast as he could.

He wanted to make Sam proud of him.

"The rains had come for a good week or more," Bagley continued, returning to the incident. "The roads were in terrible condition but His Grace insisted he and the marquess return to Hillside."

Bagley explained the accident and how it had unfolded, revealing that the only survivor was a footman.

"What is his name?"

"Whose name, Your Grace?"

"The footman who was there."

"I . . . I have no idea."

Donovan would find out. He would ask about Sam. In fact, he wanted to talk to anyone who had known Sam. He wanted to hear about the man his brother had become. It would be the only way he could get to know the man his brother had been.

Bagley passed him the first ledger. "This details your holdings, Your Grace. It also has the current balance of the funds you hold in the Bank of England."

He opened the book and skimmed the first few pages, seeing details about each of the estates that Bagley had mentioned.

"Am I free to take this with me? I wish to study and familiarize myself with it."

"Of course, Your Grace. I had Morris make a copy strictly for your personal use once I sent the letter to you of your elevation to the dukedom."

Turning another page, he stared at the figure, dumbstruck.

Finding his voice, he asked, "And this?" He turned the ledger so Bagley could see what he pointed to.

"That is your account with the Bank of England, Your Grace."

Bloody hell.

Donovan thought he might be richer than the king himself.

# CHAPTER SIX

"HERE WE GO, Your Grace," Morris said, opening the door for Donovan.

They entered the tailor's shop and a man in his late forties hurried over to greet them.

"Ah, Your Grace. It is so good to meet you. I am Mr. Brimley."

"Likewise," Donovan replied.

He had spent the entire morning with Bagley, who had sent Morris off on several errands. The clerk was now accompanying him to the various shops he needed to visit and which Morris had stopped by, making sure each proprietor knew the Duke of Haverhill would soon arrive. Knowing he only had the uniform he wore, he knew clothes were an essential item.

"I am only in London until tomorrow morning," he shared. "I am eager to get to my country seat." He would wait to visit the docks and his warehouses and ships later. Getting to Hillside was what was on his mind now.

"Of course, Your Grace," the tailor said with a smile. "We will get you measured and have your wardrobe delivered to Hillside."

Of course, the man knew the Duke of Haverhill resided at Hillside. It would be his job to know that kind of information. As far as Donovan knew, his own father and brother had their clothes made up here.

Once he had been measured, he asked, "Is there anything you have on hand that I might wear today? My uniform has seen better days. It is all that I now possess."

"I do have a few things," the tailor said, thinking. "Not up to ducal standards, mind you, but something that could tide you over. If you'll come back in two hours' time, I will see that adjustments have been made to them."

"Very well."

Morris accompanied him to the shirt maker and boot maker shops, where he placed orders for what he needed. Actually, Morris spoke with the owners and shop clerks. He seemed far more knowledgeable about the clothes Donovan would need. The clerk requested different kinds of coats and cravats. Hats. Handkerchiefs. A greatcoat. Evening clothes. Morris ordered a banyan, which Donovan had no idea what it might be. He readily agreed to everything, knowing he was wealthy beyond his wildest dreams and could easily afford everything Morris said was necessary.

As they returned to Brimley's shop, he asked, "How does a clerk know so much about a duke's wardrobe and Polite Society in general?"

"My father was a duke's by-blow," Morris said. "Never recognized by his father but brought up on the estate as a servant. Father was intelligent and observed things, cataloging what he saw. He later became his own father's valet so, yes, I do know what is required of a duke."

"Yet you left the duke's estate and became a clerk in town."

Morris nodded. "I won a scholarship to university. My father was so proud. I attended Cambridge, the same as my grandfather."

"That is quite an accomplishment, Morris. Might you take over Bagley's practice one day?"

The clerk looked glum. "I doubt it."

He thought a moment. "Have you ever considered going into estate management?"

Morris nodded. "I would enjoy that but it is a small world. It takes having a position as a steward or assistant steward to gain one."

"Well, I have numerous estates. I am sure one of them could use another hand."

The clerk's eyes lit up. "Are you certain, Your Grace? That would be a dream come true."

"I will have to see what is available and whom I already employ but there will be a position if you wish for one." He paused. "Better yet, what about a secretary? I remember my father having one. He traveled back and forth with him from Surrey to London. Would that be something that might appeal to you?"

Morris now beamed with pleasure. "Most definitely, Your Grace. I would be happy to serve you in whatever capacity you see fit."

"We will work something out. Hand in your notice to Bagley. You can take a mail coach to Wickley. It's the nearest village to Hillside. Come as soon as you can."

"Thank you so much, Your Grace. This means the world to me."

He placed a hand on the clerk's shoulder. "It will be good to have someone I can trust."

As promised, Brimley had a coat, waistcoat, and trousers ready. Donovan used his officer's white shirt underneath. No adjustments were necessary.

"I am sorry for the inferior quality, Your Grace, but it was all that was readily available."

Donovan stroked the worsted wool, thinking it the finest coat he had ever owned.

"Perhaps once the rest of your wardrobe arrives, you might gift this to your valet or a footman," the tailor suggested.

If this was to be given away, he could only imagine the quality of fabrics being used for his wardrobe. Once again, he realized his life was changing rapidly. Like a team of horses out of control, he wasn't sure if he could stop it.

"Thank you, Mr. Brimley."

"I will see that in a week's time that we deliver several items to you. The rest will follow soon after."

"You have been most accommodating, Mr. Brimley. Thank you."

"It is a pleasure to serve you, Your Grace. I look forward to outfitting you every year."

The tailor's words puzzled him and, once they left the shop, he asked Morris about it.

"Oh, you will need to purchase a new wardrobe each year, Your Grace. It would be unseemly for you to be seen in the same clothes year after year."

"This is something I can change," he declared. "I will choose if and when I give up a coat or pair of boots. I don't care if Polite Society judges me harshly or not."

Morris grinned. "Good for you, Your Grace. You will be known as eccentric but I would say please yourself above all. I must return to the office now," he apologized. "Might you do all right going to Tattersall's on your own?"

"I can manage to pick out a horse on my own. That's at least something I am familiar with."

Bagley had taken it upon himself to order a new ducal carriage since the last one had been damaged beyond repair. It would be finished early in the new year. For now, Donovan needed a horse to ride to Hillside. He had asked Morris where to purchase one and the clerk told him Tattersall's was the only place in London to do so.

He now hailed a hackney and ordered the driver to go to The Corner, which is what Morris said a member of the *ton* would call Hyde Park Corner, just outside of London. The clerk warned Donovan that Tattersall's was only open on Mondays this time of year, though, and it would be impossible for the duke to purchase a new horse.

He didn't think it would be a problem.

The driver let Donovan off and he paid him with money

Morris had provided, another of the errands the clerk had run besides making various appointments for Donovan's wardrobe. Bagley had known he was without coin on him and sent the clerk to withdraw banknotes. The solicitor said Donovan only need tell any merchant he was Haverhill and whatever he wanted placed on his account would be listed, to be paid at a later date. He hoped the purchase of the horse would be the same as buying a hat.

As he crossed the yard, he spied a boy who was mostly likely a groom and motioned him over.

"I need to see about purchasing a horse."

The fellow looked him up and down and Donovan supposed his outfit was lacking, after all.

"We ain't open until Monday."

"I am certain you are open for the Duke of Haverhill," he replied curtly.

"When he gets here, let me know. I'm sure Mr. Tattersall will take care of him." He started off and Donovan called him back.

Using his best officer's voice, he said, "He's here. Now." And stared daggers at the groom.

The boy's eyes widened. "Right away, Your Grace."

Soon, he was introduced to Richard Tattersall, grandson of the founder of Tattersall's.

"So, you need a good mount, Your Grace. You actually have a few at your stables in Surrey. Lord Pickford bought all his horses here, with a little advice from his neighbor." A shadow crossed the owner's face. "I suppose you'll need a carriage team, as well. I don't have what you need at the moment but I should soon, as far as the carriage horses go. But if you are eager for a good horse now, I can show you several."

Half an hour and a dozen horses later, Donovan mounted his new horse, Jupiter, a roan of sixteen hands, and turned it toward Mayfair. He had the address of his townhouse and would stay in it tonight before he set out for Hillside tomorrow morning.

He arrived on the square where the townhouse was located

and saw a servant polishing the brass door knocker, with another servant monitoring the process. He assumed it was the butler supervising the footman.

Dismounting, he called out, "Hello. Is there someone who might take my horse?"

Both servants turned and eyed him with curiosity.

"Are you Haven?" he asked the older servant, remembering the name Bagley had mentioned.

"I am, my lord. How might I be of service?"

"I am Haverhill."

Haven studied him a moment. "You have the look of your mother, Your Grace. Her Grace was a fine woman. Kind and generous to a fault." He turned to the footman. "Tend to His Grace's horse."

The footman set down the rag and polish. "Yes, Mr. Haven." He took the reins from Donovan. "Your Grace."

"His name is Jupiter," he called out before turning back to Haven.

"Welcome home, Your Grace," Haven said and opened the door.

Donovan stepped inside, trying not to gawk at the opulence. Polished marble floors. A sweeping staircase. Oil paintings on the walls. A small statue in the corner.

"Come with me to my study, Haven," he instructed.

"This way, Your Grace."

They passed a maid and the butler said, "See that His Grace's bedchamber is readied."

"Yes, Mr. Haven." She bobbed a curtsey to Donovan.

Haven opened the door and Donovan stepped inside. He went to the large desk and took the seat behind it.

Gesturing to the one in front of the desk, he said, "Please sit. I want you to tell me everything you remember about my mother and my brother."

The butler closed the door. "With pleasure, Your Grace."

# CHAPTER SEVEN

W YNTER FINISHED FILLING the basket with the items Cook handed her.

"That should do it," she said. "Thank you for putting this together."

"Not a problem, my lady," Cook said. "The tenants are so fond of you. They appreciate when you bring them things."

"This roasted chicken will come in handy. Mrs. Jernigan's labor yesterday was long."

"It always is with a first babe," Cook said. "Did you get enough rest after the delivery?"

Wynter had delivered the child because the midwife was already at another laboring mother's bedside. She hadn't minded stepping in, something she had done several times over the last few years. Mr. Jernigan had been frantic when the midwife sent word that she couldn't come. He was about to become a first-time father and feared for his wife's life. Wynter had calmed the farmer and returned to his cottage with him after she had gathered her basket of supplies, which she always kept ready for emergencies such as this.

Today, though, would be different. None of the long hours of bending over the mother in labor, reassuring her as she clutched Wynter's hand too tightly. No having to listen to the agonizing screams as the labor pains increased. Thank goodness the birthing process had gone smoothly, with no complications arising. Still, she would check Mrs. Jernigan and remind her of the things she had told the farmer's wife yesterday, knowing the woman might not remember everything that had been said about the care for herself and that of her newborn.

She slipped on her greatcoat, one she'd had created for her by a famous London tailor. She had worn it about Chesterfield the past two winters and found it warm and comfortable. Men's fashions were entirely practical with their fit and materials. It was why she preferred them when she went about the estate.

Wynter walked to the Jernigans' cottage, enjoying the clean, crisp smell of cold in the air. It was two weeks until Christmas and her father would soon be leaving to spend the holiday with his brother's family. While she didn't dislike Uncle Edward, she really didn't like him either. He was bland as a man came and had no conversation whatsoever.

If it had been only Uncle Edward they visited, Wynter would have gladly gone, if only to accompany her father. Instead, her cousin, Edwin, would also be in attendance since he lived with his father. Edwin was an odd mix. He could be quite arrogant and yet he was nothing more than a toady around Wynter's father. She supposed it was because Edwin would one day inherit the title. Naturally, it would go to Uncle Edward first, but his health was fragile. Most likely, Uncle Edward would pass, followed by her father, and then Cousin Edwin would become the new Earl of Cheston. Wynter only hoped that wouldn't happen for many years.

Still, they had entertained their relatives many times over the years during Christmas and she had always been happy to accompany her father when they were invited for Christmas at her uncle's.

Until this year.

After the Season, Edwin had married a harpy named Lydia. While pretty, the girl was unpleasant to be around. She had also gossiped ferociously about Wynter, who had caught her in the act of doing so at a garden party. Lydia had proved to be unapologetic and had even told Wynter that once she was the Countess of Cheston and Edwin was the earl, Wynter would no longer be welcomed in their home.

She hadn't replied to the chit, who had recently become betrothed to Edwin. Instead, Wynter had looked her up and down slowly and then turned to a leading gossip of the *ton*, proclaiming Lydia lacking in everything from manners to intelligence—and walked away.

While she had attended the couple's September wedding, as was expected, she told her father she would not travel with him to Uncle Edward's for Christmas this year. Lord Cheston had said it was up to her. Wynter decided she would give the servants three days off, from Christmas Eve through Boxing Day. She was perfectly capable of taking care of herself for such a short time.

Lydia's words had led her to be thankful that her father had set aside an income for Wynter once he passed. It was separate from the estate and would provide her with the means to purchase a small house in the country and rent something in town for the Season. It would leave her comfortable and independent from any man.

She arrived at the Jernigans' cottage and spent a pleasant hour with Mrs. Jernigan, teaching her more about how to feed her babe and going over with her how often to change his swaddling clothes and how to tend to the cord before it fell off. Mrs. Jernigan was grateful for the basket of food Wynter brought. She removed everything in the basket and put it in the cupboard before making the new mother a cup of tea.

"Once you finish this, try and get a brief nap yourself," she advised. "You will be lacking in sleep for several months so once you are physically able to be up and about, remember to try and nap at least for a little while when your babe does."

"But when am I to clean? Or cook?" Mrs. Jernigan asked, her eyes welling with tears.

"The other mothers will be dropping in. They will help with some tasks and even bring meals to you every now and then. I know you take pride in having a neat cottage, Mrs. Jernigan, but sometimes you have to let things go a bit. What is important is your son. He needs your attention. Your love. If a pot doesn't get scrubbed right away or a floor swept, then it doesn't. Spend your time with your boy. You will blink and he will be walking. Then talking. Cherish the little moments. They pass all too quickly."

"You are very wise for not being a mother yourself, my lady," the young mother told her.

"I have delivered many babes and love to see how women become mothers. It is a role you will grow into and it will change over time. That is something I definitely have seen happen."

"Why have you never wed?" Mrs. Jernigan asked, looking perplexed.

"I simply prefer things the way they are," she said.

What was left unsaid was the one thing which had changed her mind. When she had entered her first Season, she had thought she would wed and have children one day. Then when Wynter had learned how her own father had lost the woman he loved because her father demanded she wed the Duke of Haverhill, Wynter decided she would never want to be in the position of having a man dictate to her. If she wed, her husband would legally have control over her. Wynter never wanted to be helpless and at the mercy of another man.

Thank goodness her father had raised her as a son, teaching her about the estate and helping her learn the things men enjoyed doing. She could bring down a hart as she rode a horse. Play and win at cards. Choose the finest horseflesh. Those things were infinitely more interesting than being an insipid woman who limited herself to a small world of mundane tasks. Wynter was confident and capable of so much. She would never let being a female hold her back from what she wanted to do.

She left Mrs. Jernigan the basket as a gift and returned to the stables, asking a groom to saddle Onyx for her. She had purchased the horse at Tattersall's before she and her father had last left London and took the horse out daily. Onyx was by far the most spirited mount she had ever owned. He kept her on her toes when she was in the saddle.

The same groom brought out the snorting horse and Wynter went to him.

"Stop with the temper," she said quietly as she gently smoothed her hand along his neck over and over. "You are a good boy, Onyx. We are going to have a lovely ride today."

Moving to the horse's side, another groom approached and helped her into the saddle. She sat astride, thanks to the fact she wore trousers, and the greatcoat flared out behind her as she took up the reins and nudged the horse. Onyx took off as fast as lightning and she maneuvered him through the stable yard and around the house. She rode up the lane and then turned into the field next to it, giving the horse his head.

Onyx reacted as she expected and tore across the meadow, running the length of it and then jumping the fence. She allowed him to run another mile before turning him and coming back the same way. As they cleared the fence again and raced across the meadow, she glimpsed a rider to her right, stopped in the road, watching her. She whizzed by too fast to see if she recognized him and only noted he sat tall in the saddle.

Slowing Onyx, she turned from the meadow back onto the lane and rode to where it joined the road. The man had turned his horse and now cantered toward her. Wynter brought her mount to a stop and watched him approach.

The first thing that caught her attention was his sheer size. He was a large man, tall and broad of shoulders, with a head of thick, curling, black hair. She knew because he wore no hat. His face was tanned, as if he spent a majority of his days in the sun, even during this time of year. As he reached her and reined in his roan, she was drawn to his piercing, blue eyes.

If the Devil became incarnate, he would look exactly like this man. No man should be this sinfully handsome.

"Good afternoon," he said, his voice deep, his tone as rich as honey.

Wynter felt a chill ripple down her spine.

"Good afternoon," she replied. "What brings you this way?"

She kept her tone pleasant yet she was cautious. The man was a stranger to these parts. If he made a sudden move toward her, she would take off. While his horse looked to be prime horseflesh, Onyx would outrun any horse in a race.

He smiled. It almost knocked the breath from her.

Confusion filled her. She had never had a physical reaction to any man before. Never. She wasn't happy about it and tensed. Onyx stirred beneath her, sensing her discomfort.

"I am new to these parts. Or I suppose I shouldn't say new. I grew up near here but left many years ago."

"Oh, where?" she asked, her heart beating quickly. Too quickly.

He focused on her as no one else ever had. It was as if she were the only person in the world and the most important one to him.

Wynter blinked rapidly several times, trying to break the spell that he seemed to cast over her.

"Do you have something in your eye?" he asked.

"No. Yes. I mean, I did but it is gone now."

Damnation. She sounded like some foolish schoolgirl. His smile widened. Her pulse quickened.

As did where she sat. The place between her legs. A place she had never paid an iota of attention to, other than washing it perfunctorily whenever she bathed. It throbbed. She wondered why since it never had before.

She decided she didn't like this man. He was confusing her. Wynter was all about control. She was afraid to open her mouth, afraid she would sound like a giddy girl at her first come-out ball. She decided he was a rogue. He certainly looked like one, with his handsome face and muscular body. And his smile. That smile should be outlawed. It was one which had probably drawn dozens of women into his bed.

Her cheeks heated at that thought and she cleared her throat, trying to distract herself.

And him.

But he was gazing at her steadily. Interested.

"Where is your home?" she asked, trying to understand and rein in her body's response to merely looking at this stranger.

"Hillside. I believe I only have a few more miles until I reach it," he replied.

"Hillside?" she echoed. "You . . . are the new Duke of Haverhill?"

Something flickered in his eyes. It was gone in a flash. Wynter wondered what it meant.

"I am. Haverhill," he said, disgust crossing his face.

Now, that was interesting.

Wynter hadn't known who the heir might be. In her mind, it had always been Sam. She hadn't thought to ask beyond that who might be next in the family to assume the title. Even all these months later, she forced herself not to think of Sam and his awful death.

"Are you not happy to become a duke?" she challenged. "If so, you would be the first man in England to react in such a manner."

"I was never meant for the dukedom," he said, sorrow tinging his words. "Sam, my brother, should be here in my place." He swallowed. "He died. So, I am it."

*Sam's brother?*

"Why didn't I know this?" she asked, shocked.

"That I am Haverhill? Well, this is the first time we are meeting, my lady. And who might you be?"

She shook her head. "Sam had no brother," she declared. "I would have known."

His eyes widened. "You knew Sam?" He paused. "Wait. You called him Sam?"

"Of course. We were friends for years. I live here at Chesterfield. Hillside is but seven miles down the road, the other side of Wickley. Our fathers' London townhouses sit side-by-side."

Wynter frowned. "Sam was my closest friend. I would know if he had a brother. You may have considered him as a brother because of your familial connection but whatever you are—however you are related—you were no brother to my Sam."

With that, Wynter whirled her horse and charged up the lane toward home.

# CHAPTER EIGHT

*MY SAM.*

    The woman had called him *my Sam.*

In his experience, women never addressed men by their given names. Only their titles. In the ten years he had lived at Hillside, Donovan had never heard his mother call her husband by name. He was always, always Haverhill. In fact, Donovan didn't even know what his father's Christian name had been.

The fact this woman referred to Sam as she did set bells off inside him. He wondered if they were sweethearts. Even lovers. She wasn't fresh out of the schoolroom though she was fresh of face. He would be hard pressed to think of a more beautiful woman.

Donovan took off after her. Though Jupiter was a superb horse, the woman's mount, a huge black, was a magnificent creature. It was why he had paused to watch horse and rider as he traveled the road to Hillside. At first, he hadn't realized it was a female on the horse's back. The pair moved as one across the meadow, jumping a fence with ease. It was only afterward when she rode toward him and he came closer that he realized a woman held the reins.

She wore masculine clothes and sat astride the great beast but the tailored clothes only accentuated her femininity. The heart-shaped face. The high cheekbones. The ice-blue eyes. If Sam had been involved with her, it wouldn't have surprised him. But why wasn't she wed at her age? She had to be in her early to mid-twenties. Women of the *ton*, especially women of great beauty, wed quickly. Could she have wed and already be a widow, returned to her father's house before she sought another marriage?

Would Sam have been her next husband?

A house loomed before him, one very similar to Hillside. He took a chance, guessing the stables would be to the right. As he rode up to the yard, he saw her toss her reins to a groom and head toward the house. He shouted to the groom who held her horse.

"Take mine!"

Donovan leaped off Jupiter's back and hurried to the woman, who had turned to face him, arms akimbo.

"What?" she demanded as he approached.

Without thinking of the impropriety of his actions, he caught her wrist. An electric shock struck him. She must have experienced it, as well, because her eyes widened.

As if singed, Donovan let go of her wrist and begged, "Please. I am eager to hear about Sam. I didn't see him for the last fifteen years. I want to know him. Even if he is dead and I can never laugh with him again."

"Fifteen years?" she asked. "Why, that is when his mother would have passed."

"You knew my mother?"

"No," she said quickly. "I never met Her Grace. Sam spoke of her often, though. I remember him mentioning this past summer how long she had been gone." She paused. "So, the duchess was truly your mother? You are Sam's brother?"

"I am," he told her, a wave of sadness passing over him.

"Come along then," she said and began briskly moving toward the house, her greatcoat swirling behind her as the wind caught it.

It gave him a glimpse of a perfectly rounded bottom in the tight breeches she wore.

Donovan fell into step behind her, his long strides catching up to her as she opened a door. He found they were in the kitchens.

"Cook, would you please send tea to the drawing room? We have a guest."

"Right away, my lady."

"Thank you."

He liked that she thanked the servant. It was a small gesture that most of the *ton* would never think to do. But it was something his mother always did, grateful for small kindnesses from those she employed.

It made him like this woman, being reminded of his mother.

She continued through the house, greeting servants they passed, leading him upstairs to the drawing room. Just before they reached it, she stopped as the butler hurried past them and opened the door for her.

"Is Lord Cheston still in Wickley?"

"Yes, my lady."

"Would you please have him join us once he returns?"

"I shall, my lady."

She entered the drawing room and Donovan followed, crossing the room and taking the seat she indicated.

"Tell me about Sam," he urged.

"No. I must hear about you first, Your Grace."

He flinched, the title still wearing upon him. "Why?"

"If my best friend had a brother I never knew existed, there must be a reason he never spoke of you. I'd have that first."

He steeled himself. "You certainly are forthright for a woman."

She smiled. "Yes, I believe I've been told that on more than one occasion."

"And to have a best friend who is not a female is most unusual, isn't it?" he pressed.

"I am not like other women in the *ton*, Your Grace." Her hand swept along her body. "As you can see, I am not dressed as most women. My father tells me it is called being a tomboy. At least in my youth that is what he called me. Now, I am simply my own woman. I have opinions. I do as I please. And I never plan to wed."

Her words took him aback. Though Donovan had never moved in Polite Society, he couldn't imagine any woman announcing she would never wed.

"So there were no romantic feelings between you and Sam?" he asked.

A blush tinged her cheeks as she said, "Absolutely not. I looked upon Sam as a brother and friend."

The blush belied her words, however. Perhaps she hadn't had feelings toward him—but had Sam wanted her? Donovan could understand why. She was beautiful, spirited, and unlike any woman he had ever met. He could see Sam being intrigued by her. Challenged by her. Desiring her.

"Tell me about him."

"Tell me about you," she countered, not cowering under his gaze.

He sighed. "Haverhill blamed me for my mother's accident. When she passed, he wanted nothing to do with me. He never really had before the incident. Sam was his heir and the focus of his interests. I was no one to him. After Mama's death, I was sent away."

Sympathy filled her face. "That must have been very difficult. Losing your mother and having to leave your home. Did you go to stay with relatives?"

"No. I was sent to Turner Academy, a school known for sheltering troubled youth. I remained there until university. Afterward, I joined the His Majesty's army. I would still be on the Peninsula fighting with Wellington had I not received Bagley's letter informing me I was now the duke."

He watched as she mulled over his words.

"Haverhill told me that I would never return to Hillside. That Sam was not allowed to ever contact me. I suppose after I was sent away he ordered Sam never to speak of me."

Anger sparked in her eyes. "That sounds exactly like Haverhill. He was a hard man, always putting Sam through his paces, testing him continually." She paused. "I don't know how he did it but Sam never let his father dampen his sunny nature. He was friendly to all. Polite Society adored him. Sam was the kindest, sweetest man I have ever known."

For the first time since entering the house, Donovan relaxed. "Yes, Sam was always kind and cheerful despite Haverhill browbeating him constantly. I am sorry to hear that it extended beyond childhood, though."

"Sam spent little time in His Grace's presence," she revealed. "Going to university helped. They rarely attended the same social events. For the most part, I would say Sam was happy. I spent a great deal of time with him, especially during the Season. We lived next door to one another and Sam came to breakfast with us most every morning. He was great friends with my father."

The tea cart arrived and she took the time to pour out for them both. Despite labeling herself a tomboy, she did the womanly chore with grace.

"Sam taught me how to play chess and we did so often. He was generous, helping me learn how to strategize instead of beating me soundly each time."

"He did the same for me when I was eight years old. I would start to make a move and he would say, 'Now, Donovan, I would think about that.' If I didn't know why it was a poor move, he would walk me through it, showing how two, three, even five moves down the line it could hurt me."

"Yes," she cried, her eyes lighting up. "He did the same with me. He would test me sometimes, making a move and asking me if he should or shouldn't have done so."

"I liked that about him," Donovan admitted. "That he took the time to help me not only learn the rules but to truly understand the game. Playing chess with Sam was my favorite activity. I still enjoy the game to this day."

"Perhaps we might set up the board and play sometime, Your

Grace," she suggested.

"I would like that. Very much."

The door opened and Donovan turned to see a man coming toward them.

"Now, who might this visitor . . ." His voice trailed off.

He rose. "Lord Cheston, may I introduce myself to you? I am—"

"Donovan. You are Donovan," the man said, apparently shaken.

"How in the blazes do you know my name?" he demanded.

"Because you are the image of your mother."

⇉⇉✕⇇⇇

WYNTER WATCHED HER father's eyes search their visitor. Where she had been reluctant to believe he was Sam's brother, her father had known immediately. Sam had been tall and rangy, very blond and fair, closely resembling his father—and the opposite of the new duke who stood before her.

She should have known who he was when he told her he was Sam's brother.

Because she had seen the miniature.

Years ago, Wynter had gone to her father's study, hoping to find him there. When she discovered the room was empty, she had sat in his chair behind the massive oak desk, savoring the smell of his tobacco which hung faintly in the air. Ever curious, she had examined the papers strewn across his desk and then began exploring the desk's drawers.

To her surprise, the bottom drawer contained a miniature of a woman, one who was not her mother. She had seen her mother's portrait hanging in the picture gallery. The woman in the miniature looked nothing like her. She was a great beauty with hair as black as midnight and mesmerizing blue eyes. Wynter had studied the woman for a long time before returning the miniature to the drawer and closing it.

She had probably been eight or nine at the time of the incident and had never asked her father why the miniature was hidden away in his desk. When she met and became friendly with Sam and her father revealed the enmity between him and the Duke of Haverhill, her thoughts had immediately gone to the woman in the miniature. She realized it was of the Duchess of Haverhill, the woman her father had loved and lost.

Wynter saw the duke struggling to make sense of the situation. She rose and touched his arm.

"Your Grace, this is my father, the Earl of Cheston. Papa, this is the Duke of Haverhill. Your Grace, my father knew your mother from when she made her come-out."

She knew that wouldn't explain everything to this man, a man who had come crashing into their lives. One who was making her feel all kinds of unusual things that she couldn't put a name to.

"Shall we be seated?" she suggested. "Papa, would you care for a cup of tea? I am sure it is still cold outside. It will warm you."

Her father, who had been staring at the duke, glanced away. "Yes, of course. Thank you, my dear."

He sat and the duke followed. An awkward silence followed. She knew she must fill it and smooth things over.

"His Grace was on his way to Hillside when he saw me out riding and stopped to make my acquaintance." She looked at the duke and nodded.

He took the hint and said, "Yes, I was coming from London. I met with the family solicitor there."

Papa nodded, his mouth tightening. "I offer you condolences on the loss of your father and brother, Your Grace."

"I will accept them for my brother. Haverhill can rot in Hell for all I care."

Wynter nearly spewed her tea. Instead, she swallowed awkwardly and began coughing.

The duke leaned over and patted her on the back. It only made it worse.

Because of his touch.

She jerked away, waving her hands before her.

"Take another drink," the duke suggested.

She brought her teacup to her lips and sipped at it. While her throat still felt tight, the coughing ceased.

"Thank you," she managed.

"You seem to be frank in your opinions, my lady," Haverhill said. "I hope you don't mind that I was free in giving mine, as well."

Papa snorted. "It's not every day someone expresses such a . . . strong opinion about a parent." One corner of his mouth turned up. "Then again, I daresay your brother would have been of the same opinion."

"Your daughter told me you were close with Sam."

"Pickford was as a son to me, Your Grace. We were close. Probably to the chagrin of your father." He hesitated. "Haverhill and I were not on speaking terms."

The duke smiled. "I am sure it was his fault. That—and the fact that you were so friendly with Sam—encourages me to also seek your friendship, my lord."

Her father's eyes misted with tears. "You are very like your mother. She was always forthright yet kind."

"You seem to have known her well," the duke remarked.

"We ran in the same circles," Papa said. "Knew many of the same people. She was a wonderful girl."

"She was an excellent mother."

"It doesn't surprise me hearing so," Papa said. "Sam turned out so well. It seems you, too, have done well for yourself, Your Grace. I do hope we can see one another upon occasion."

"I would like that," Haverhill said. He turned to Wynter. "The tea was lovely, my lady, but I must make my way to Hillside. I fear I have much to do once I arrive."

"I will walk you out," she volunteered, surprising herself.

Wynter led him down the stairs and out the front door before they headed toward the stables. She called for his horse.

As they waited, he asked, "Where did you purchase your mount? He is one of the finest I have ever seen."

"At Tattersall's. Sam and I went two summers ago and picked him out. We always helped one another when it came to horseflesh."

"Hmm. Mr. Tattersall mentioned that Sam's neighbor had helped him select a few horses. I suppose that was you, my lady?"

"Yes. Don't mention it in polite company, though. Tattersall's is strictly for men. I am the only woman who is allowed in as a customer. Mr. Tattersall likes to keep that fact under his hat."

She glanced up and saw the groom returning with his horse. "You have also chosen a fine mount."

"His name is Jupiter. He's been a pleasure to ride from London to Surrey. I do look forward to seeing the other horses in the stables."

"Your stables. They are yours, Your Grace. It seems you are having difficulty accepting the fact that you now hold the title."

"I suppose it will take time."

He took her hand and she felt her heart quicken. "It has been a pleasure meeting a neighbor today. Even if the village of Wickley stands between us. The previous Haverhill may have ignored you but I am happy to make your acquaintance, as well as that of Lord Cheston. I only have one more question for you."

"What?" she asked, her insides fluttering madly.

"What is your name?"

# CHAPTER NINE

DONOVAN AWOKE AND groaned.

"Bloody hell," he murmured.

He had dreamed of her again. Lady Wynter. It was bad enough that his thoughts had been constantly muddled by her during the past ten days when he was awake. No, she had to go and invade his dreams every night, leaving him decidedly unsatisfied when he opened his eyes each morning.

Closing his eyes again, he tried to remember the dream before it dissipated. All he could conjure was her pert nose. The curve of her breasts and hips. The faint scent of lemon that wafted from her skin. Skin that his fingers longed to skim.

He had seen her twice since that first encounter. Lord Cheston had sent an invitation to dinner three days after Donovan arrived at Hillside and he had been happy to go to Chesterfield. He told himself it was to get to know the earl and possibly make a friend in the older man but he knew he lied to himself.

Wynter had worn a gown, surprising him a bit. It was of midnight blue, making her ice-blue eyes stand out and contrasting with her silver-blond hair. Donovan had never seen hair that shade before and thought it would suit no one but her. She had been friendly but not overly so and he thought she relegated him to being a possible future friend, as Sam had been before him.

In return, Donovan had invited the pair to tea two days ago.

While they were there, he learned that Lord Cheston would be leaving to spend Christmas with his brother's family.

Lady Wynter was staying home.

It puzzled him why she wouldn't travel with her father to visit with her uncle. Perhaps they were estranged for some reason though he couldn't see why. Lady Wynter was most affable and easy to converse with. Donovan kept quiet, deciding it wasn't his business to ask about something so personal. But ever since he knew she would be alone at Chesterfield, he had thought about asking her to come to Hillside. At least for Christmas dinner.

Donovan decided he would ride over and ask her to do so this morning. It wouldn't be as if it were the two of them alone. Wyatt had written—a small miracle in itself—and informed Donovan that he and Meadow would be coming to Hillside for the holiday. Wyatt was eager to see Donovan and also show off his new wife. The following day, another letter, much longer, had arrived from Miles. He, too, expressed an interest in coming to Hillside with Emery and the baby for Christmas. Donovan had laughed. Wyatt had told him they were coming. Miles had asked if he and his family might be invited. It was exactly like the two of them.

His guests were expected sometime early tomorrow after-noon, which was the day before Christmas Eve. Preparations had been made, none of which he had a part of. Cook was preparing a veritable feast. His housekeeper had all the guest bedchambers ready. All Donovan had to do was play host to his friends—and Lady Wynter.

If she agreed to come.

He thought she would get along well with Miles and Wyatt. Though he didn't know Emery and Meadow, from what his friends' letters had told him, they were very amiable, intelligent women. He thought the six of them would have a splendid time.

If she would accept his invitation.

He could have Morris write it out and deliver it but his gut told him it would be easier for her to turn him down. If he came in person, she would have to look him in the eyes and say no.

Donovan hoped she wouldn't do that.

He raked a hand through his hair as he sat up. This was insane. He had never been taken with any woman before—and there had been many of them. Too many to recall their names. He coupled with a woman and easily forgot her after leaving her bed. He never thought he would wed until the dukedom was thrust upon him. Even then, he had planned to enjoy himself for several years, sampling the sweets of the ladies in Polite Society before he ever settled down with one. He believed he would get an heir off his wife and then they would both go their own way, as seemed to be the accepted practice in the *ton*.

Meeting Lady Wynter had changed that. Physically, he was attracted to her but it went beyond that. He felt an overwhelming need to possess her. To brand her as his. The thought of wedding and bedding her and then allowing her to have countless affairs after she provided him with an heir caused a sour taste in his mouth.

What was it about her?

He couldn't say.

And what worried him—if he decided to pursue her—was not only knowing she had such a control over him but being aware she had no plans to marry. Ever.

He chuckled. Perhaps this was a case of forbidden fruit, as in the Garden of Eden. Adam and Eve were told never to partake of the fruit of the Tree of Knowledge yet both had been tempted to. It caused them a world of grief and pain. Donovan thought he would be better off not pursuing Lady Wynter and sticking to his original plan.

Still, he should ask her to Christmas dinner. It wasn't right allowing her to be alone on such a day.

When had he started lying to himself so much?

Not wishing to answer that question, he rang for his valet. He had inherited Hall from Sam. Haverhill's valet hadn't waited around, not knowing when Donovan would be located, much less when he might make his way to England. Though he didn't like the idea of having a valet, Morris assured Donovan he needed one. The former clerk had arrived at Hillside a week ago and had taken Donovan under his wing instead of the other way around. Morris told him how he should dress and behave. What was expected and what to avoid. They breakfasted with one another every morning and went over what their day would be like.

Within the year, Donovan had decided he would make Morris Hillside's steward. The current one had been ready to be pensioned off just before Haverhill died. Donovan had begged him to stay on for a few months, in order for both the new duke and Morris to be adequately prepared. For now, Morris was learning as much as he could from the estate manager while also serving as Donovan's secretary and tutor.

Hall arrived and shaved and dressed Donovan for the day. More of his new clothes had arrived from London, with others promised to be there shortly after the new year began. Already, his wardrobe seemed stuffed to the gills but Morris explained how a duke needed a large number of every piece of clothing for a variety of social situations. It was amusing how the son of a duke's by-blow knew more about being a duke than a duke himself. If Donovan had remained at Hillside while growing up, he would have had at least an inkling of what would be required by having watched everything Sam learned and how his brother prepared to one day wear the mantle of Duke of Haverhill.

He had yet to visit Sam's grave. He wanted to but couldn't bring himself to go just yet. It was as if he did, he would have to acknowledge the fact that Sam was truly gone and would never return.

Donovan joined Morris at breakfast, reminding him that visitors would be arriving at Hillside the next day.

"I remember, Your Grace. I will make sure to leave you with them."

"What?"

"You will be entertaining. I will take my meals in the servants' hall while your friends are here."

"I won't hear of it."

Morris frowned. "It's another thing you need to get used to, Your Grace. It is one thing for me to breakfast with you each morning and us to discuss estate affairs. It is quite another to have guests. You will want to spend your time with them. We can pick up once they depart Hillside."

"How will I know how to behave if you aren't around telling me what to do?" Donovan asked, only half-teasingly.

"You have told me your friends are also dukes, ones who were not the original heir apparents. I'm certain they have figured out how to act accordingly, especially since you mentioned both have wed. Let them—and their wives—guide you over the next few days."

"All right," he conceded grumpily. "Have you need of me today? I thought I might go to the village and pick up a few presents for my friends."

And Lady Wynter. If she accepted his invitation.

When Morris said he could manage without Donovan's presence, they finished the meal and he headed to the stables, asking for Jupiter to be saddled. He had ridden the horse a few times as he'd gone out on the property, as well as testing some of the other mounts in his stables. Jupiter proved to be his favorite, though, and he set out on the horse with a feeling of optimism.

He rode the four miles to Wickley, the nearest village, and stopped at the shop that had seemed to hold everything imaginable when he was a child. Entering, he saw Mrs. Penny, who had been kind to him when he was a boy.

"Good morning, Mrs. Penny. It is the Duke of Haverhill who comes calling."

Her eyes widened. "Your Grace! It is so good to see you again after all these years." She paused, looking him over. "I see a bit of the boy in the man. May I say how sorry I am, hearing of the loss of your father and brother?"

"Thank you. What brings me here is the need for a few gifts.

Christmas gifts. I am spending the holiday with old friends and their wives, whom I have never met. I thought it would be nice to have some token to give them."

"Do you have anything specific in mind?" she asked.

"Frankly, I have never purchased a gift of any kind, Mrs. Penny. I have been at war for many years. The fact that I am able to celebrate the Christmas season at all is a miracle in and of itself."

"Hmm." She thought a moment and came out from behind the counter. "Let me see."

He watched her wander the store, stopping and starting again, fingering a few things, before turning to him.

"Come look at these shawls, Your Grace."

Donovan followed her and looked at the display.

"These are of a good quality wool and come in several colors."

He brushed his fingers across one. "Yes, indeed, they are very nice. Let me think a moment."

He knew Emery had raven hair and brown eyes and thought the hunter green would suit her. Meadow was a brunette and the tan shawl would be a good color for her. Then he stroked one of deep blue. This would be perfect for Wynter. Lady Wynter.

"I'll have these three," he declared and Mrs. Penny took them to the counter and set them down.

"Gifts for your gentlemen friends, as well? Three, I suppose?"

Donovan realized since he had picked out three shawls that Mrs. Penny assumed three friends and their wives would be coming to Hillside.

"Yes, let's take care of my friends now."

Once again, she moved about the store, asking him a few questions. He thought about something Morris had said, about men staying after dinner and drinking port and smoking cigars or pipes while the ladies went to the parlor. That hadn't occurred during his dinner at Chesterfield, probably because it would have left Lady Wynter alone. Neither Miles nor Wyatt smoked as far as he knew but he did like the pipes they had passed.

He returned to them. "What about a pipe and smoking tobacco?" he asked.

Mrs. Penny smiled. "An excellent idea, Your Grace."

She told him about a few of the different types of tobacco and he chose the mildest form, as well as three pipes. One would be for him.

"Could you keep my purchases for me? I have a few errands and hate to carry them about. I can return for them when I am done."

"That won't be necessary, Your Grace. I will wrap them and have my son deliver them to Hillside."

"That is kind of you, Mrs. Penny. You were always so nice to me."

She smiled gently. "We were all sorry to hear you were gone, Your Grace. Your brother would come in to browse but it wasn't the same without you. All of Wickley was sorry to see the marquess pass but we are delighted you have returned and taken up the title."

A lump formed in his throat. "Thank you," he said and took his leave.

Donovan mounted Jupiter again and crossed the length of Wickley. Leaving the village behind, he headed for Chesterfield.

Hoping Lady Wynter would accept his invitation.

Hoping it would be a start. Of what, he was reluctant to say.

# CHAPTER TEN

WYNTER WALKED WITH her father out to the waiting carriage.

"You could always change your mind, you know," he said, a hopeful look in his eyes.

"No, I am happy with the decision I have made, Papa."

"Edward will miss you."

"He might. But Edwin and Lydia certainly won't," she replied.

"Are you certain you will be all right here? Alone?"

Her father hadn't liked the idea of Wynter being at Chesterfield by herself. She had stuck firmly to her decision to release the servants tomorrow morning. In fact, she might do so today once he was gone, giving them even more time than she had promised.

"Go," she urged him. "Give Uncle Edward my love."

"But not Edwin or Lydia," he retorted, a cheeky grin on his face.

She snorted. "Say whatever you will to those two. I am still put out that Lydia said such nasty things about me."

"At least she has given you ample warning that when I am gone, you will not be welcome at Chesterfield." His tone was light but Wynter knew he was upset with what Lydia had shared with Wynter.

That was why she was grateful Papa had provided for her. She would be able to maintain her independence, without having to be subservient to any man.

Her thoughts turned to Haverhill. Just as quickly, she slammed the door upon them.

"Give me a kiss," Papa said and she brushed her lips against his cheek.

"Take care," she told him, watching him climb into the carriage. He gave her a jaunty wave and shouted, "Goodbye!" as the carriage pulled away.

As Wynter watched it go down the lane, a sudden fear seized her.

What if Papa's carriage met with an accident as Sam's had?

"No," she said under her breath, refusing to believe tragedy could strike twice in the same manner in so short a time.

She entered the house and rang for the butler and maid, telling them that she had changed her mind and that all the servants might also have today off, as well. The two were surprised but grateful, thanking her and saying they would spread the word.

Next, Wynter went to the kitchens, where Cook waved her over.

"I've just finished a nice ham for you, my lady. You can eat off it for several days. Two loaves of bread will come out of the oven soon, along with a mincemeat pie."

Cook named other items that Wynter could dine upon the next few days and then asked, "Are you sure you don't want me to stay, my lady? I don't mind a bit."

She shook her head. "You yourself have told me how you are looking forward to seeing your sister. No, I want you to go and enjoy yourself. In fact, once everything is out of the oven, douse the fires and let the scullery maids go. I've given permission for everyone to leave Chesterfield today."

"Not even a maid is staying? Who will light your fire or empty your chamber pot?" Cook asked.

"I am perfectly capable of doing both of those tasks and you know that, Cook." She hugged the old woman. "Go and have a happy Christmas with your sister and her family."

"Thank you, my lady. You are a generous soul."

Wynter returned to the foyer and slipped into her greatcoat hanging nearby. She headed for the stables and asked for Onyx to be saddled before all the grooms left. Fortunately, she knew everything about horses, from different breeds to what they ate and how to saddle and unsaddle a horse.

The head groom told her, "Young Will is staying, my lady. He has nowhere else to go to. It will save you from having to feed and exercise the horses."

The boy led Onyx toward her. "I hear you will be spending Christmas with me, Will."

His eyes grew round. "No, my lady. I mean . . . I suppose so."

"If you will feed the horses, then I will help you exercise them. Is that all right with you?"

"Yes, my lady," he said with enthusiasm.

"Cook is leaving us things to eat in the kitchen. She's done up a big ham for us. We can eat from it while everyone is gone and even make sandwiches, I suppose. Feel free to enter the kitchens whenever you wish and take what you like."

"Thank you, my lady." He hesitated. "May I help you mount?"

"That isn't necessary, Will. I can put my foot in a stirrup the same as any man." She did so, swinging her leg over. "See. A woman can do the same as a man."

He nodded, his eyes full of worship.

Wynter cantered from the yard. She had today—and the next three—to herself. Yesterday, she had taken a wagon and delivered baskets of food to all their tenants, along with mittens for the children in the various families. She had knitted them herself over the past year. Though she wasn't fond of sewing, knitting was a mindless activity to her. She could think as she did so, allowing her mind to wander far and wide.

As she rode, she did her best to focus since Onyx was a handful, too challenging for her to be distracted as she rode. That was a good thing because she had been distracted plenty as of late.

Thanks to the Duke of Haverhill.

She had seen him three times now, each one making her more aware of him as a man. She had never even thought about the difference between males and females, only whether she liked someone or not. Usually, those she liked were men because they spoke frankly about many different topics. Some of them flirted with her. All of them were infinitely more interesting than any female of her acquaintance.

But there was something vastly different about Haverhill. His wicked good looks were a part of it. He was better looking, taller, and broader than other men in Polite Society. He had a way of looking at her as if he saw straight to her heart. No, to her very soul. He was amusing, recalling stories of his time at war, though she doubted it to be the lighthearted time he made it seem to be. He had asked good questions of Papa and her, explaining he was trying to learn everything he could about managing an estate and figuring out the responsibilities he had to his tenants. He was sincere, intelligent, and friendly.

All she wanted to do, however, was run her fingers through his thick, curly hair. And kiss him.

Did he know how to kiss well? None of the men who had kissed her in the past seemed to do a good job of it. With Haverhill's looks, however, Wynter expected he had a great deal of experience with the opposite sex.

And not just in kissing.

His lips, full and sensual, had become something she watched whether he spoke or not. She tried to look at him when he spoke to Papa so she could study him better. When she was speaking to him, his penetrating gaze seemed to rattle her. She refused to appear nervous around him. She was no green schoolgirl. She was a mature woman of four and twenty, soon to be five and twenty in a month.

Wynter suddenly realized her mind had wandered and she rushed back to reality, looking about her, trying to recognize where she was. Onyx pushed off his powerful back legs, jumping the fence that appeared. Unfortunately, she was unprepared to make the jump. She bounced from the saddle and fell on her left side, hitting her hip and ankle the hardest against the unforgiving, cold earth.

Onyx raced on without her.

"Ungrateful horse!" she called after him.

Then she spotted another rider approaching. She knew who it was before he came close enough simply by the way he sat his horse.

The Duke of Haverhill galloped toward her, leaping from the saddle and kneeling beside her as she pushed from her side to an upright position.

"Are you injured?"

"Probably," she muttered, embarrassed to have been thinking about this man.

"What happened? You are such a superb rider."

"I think Onyx might have stepped in a hole. He shifted oddly and threw me off-balance before he took the fence," she claimed, knowing she would be mortified if the duke ever learned the true reason for her spill.

"Let's see if you have broken any bones," he said.

Haverhill stripped off his riding gloves and pitched them to the side. He took her hands in his, sending pleasant shivers along her spine. Slowly, he rotated them one way and then in the opposite direction.

"Your wrists seem fine."

He released her hands and eased her greatcoat from her shoulders. His fingers gently traveled up her left arm before doing the same to her right. Butterflies exploded in her belly, causing her to suck in a quick breath.

"Does that hurt?" he asked.

"No," she told him. "It is merely chilly without my coat."

He leaned toward her, giving her a chance to inhale the scent of leather, horse, and man. He lifted her greatcoat and placed it about her shoulders.

"That should be better," he told her before continuing his examination.

She frowned when he touched her left hip.

"It will be bruised. Severely," she said. "This isn't the first time I have taken a spill."

The duke nodded and placed his hands about her thigh, encased in the tight breeches she preferred wearing when in the country. Dressing as a man was the only reason she had been able to dismiss her maid for the holiday. With no corsets to lace or gowns to button up the back, Wynter had been certain she wouldn't need any help. Now, she worried about how she would get out of bed tomorrow. If she could even mount the stairs to make it to her chamber. Already, her hip ached and her ankle throbbed mightily. She might be sleeping on a settee tonight on the ground floor.

As Haverhill's fingers moved down the rest of her leg, she grew restless. Something began stirring in her, something foreign and exciting and a bit frightening. Wynter had never been one to be afraid of anything and she was eager to find out why she was reacting in such a manner. Her pulse quickened. Her breathing seemed shallow. At the apex of her legs, a throbbing had begun which was almost as painful as her ankle.

Almost.

He reached her ankle and she flinched, a whimper escaping her lips.

Haverhill took it firmly but gently, one hand about her foot and the other holding her ankle. He said, "I am going to rotate it very slowly. Tell me if there is any pain."

She sucked in a breath as he rotated it.

"It's not broken but it certainly is sprained. We need to get your boot off immediately, else it will swell so badly that we'll need to cut it off."

"Not that!" she cried. "I paid a fortune for these boots. I won't see them wasted because of my carelessness."

His gaze met hers, his hands still on her ankle. "Were you

careless?" he asked, his voice deep and tempting.

She licked her lips. "I suppose I was because I didn't see the hole," she replied, her insides flip-flopping now.

"I see."

Haverhill released her ankle and examined her right leg. She shuddered.

"Cold?" he asked, a knowing look in his eyes.

"Yes. Very cold."

In fact, she wasn't cold at all. She was burning hot, almost as if she had a fever. But she only had a swollen, sprained ankle. No wound. And even if she had been wounded, it was far too soon for infection to set in and having her shivering with a high fever.

No, whatever this heat running through her was, *he* was causing it. It was his fault she had been tossed from the saddle and his fault that she was coming undone.

Gently, he removed her boot. Already, Wynter could see how her ankle swelled. The duke touched it lightly again before untying his cravat and pulling it from his neck. He bent close and wrapped it firmly about her ankle, once more allowing her to inhale that marvelous, masculine scent that came from him.

He sat back on his haunches. "I was coming to see you."

"You were?"

She grimaced, not in pain but because she sounded like an eager debutante, happy for the attention from him.

"Yes. I remembered Lord Cheston mentioning he would be leaving to visit with his brother and that you were staying behind. I hated the thought of you alone."

"You were thinking of me?"

He nodded, his eyes never leaving hers. "I was. I thought to ride over and ask you to come to Christmas dinner."

"That . . . would be lovely. I have given our servants several days off. It was probably going to be ham sandwiches and cold cider for Christmas dinner."

The duke frowned. "You dismissed all your servants?"

She nodded. "All except one groom. Will. He is probably

eleven or twelve years old."

"That won't do."

"What won't do?"

"I was going to see you home but with no one but a stable boy to care for you, I cannot have that."

Confusion filled her. "I don't understand, Your Grace."

Haverhill's gaze met hers. "You will be coming home with me, Lady Wynter."

# CHAPTER ELEVEN

"ARE YOU JOKING?"

Donovan shook his head. "Not about this. You cannot return to Chesterfield and be left in the care of a boy. Don't worry. I have friends coming for Christmas so you will be appropriately chaperoned."

"That was the least of my concerns," she muttered.

"You should think of your reputation, my lady."

"Why?" she challenged. "I have no plans to wed so if I were considered ruined, it wouldn't make a bit of difference to me."

"It should," he said, his blue eyes darkening. "Your reputation is everything."

His emphatic tone gave her pause. It led her to wonder how much he had been affected by being sent away by his father and having no contact with his brother for so many years.

"Who are these friends coming to Hillside?" she asked.

"Fellow Terrors," he replied.

"Terrors?" Wynter smiled. "Oh, there is a story for sure behind that nickname."

"There is—and you won't hear it unless you agree to come home with me."

She pretended to consider it and then said, "Well, I have always been of a most curious nature. I suppose if I am to hear the tale I should do as you ask."

He smiled, causing her heart to leap. "A wise decision,

Wynter."

*Wynter.*

He had called her Wynter.

Before she could call him out on using her Christian name without permission, he handed her boot to her and then swept her into his arms. All of a sudden, she was enveloped with his heavenly scent, his strong arms about her as he strode toward Jupiter.

He reached his horse and said, "I am setting you down. Don't put any weight on your ankle. Hold on to the saddle horn for support."

She did as he instructed, reaching a hand to clutch the saddle horn as he swung up into the saddle. Then he leaned down and lifted her with no problem, turning her so her back rested against his firm, muscular chest. An arm went about her, drawing her near.

Wynter thought she had died and gone to heaven.

Which was the most ridiculous thing in the world. She had never been physically affected by any man. Why this one? Why now?

"Should we go after Onyx?" she asked, her voice sounding unsteady.

"No. Your well-being is far more important than a horse that's taken off."

She sniffed. "Onyx is a very expensive horse. The most expensive in our stables."

"And you are far more precious than any horse, Wynter."

Again, he had used her name. Hearing it pass from his sensual lips seemed . . . right.

"Besides," he continued, "if he is that valuable a mount, he has to be smart. He will head back to Chesterfield."

"That will frighten poor Will to no end," she declared. "For Onyx to arrive without his rider?"

"I will send a groom to Chesterfield to inform the boy of your mishap. My groom can stay and help Will care for the horses in your father's stables. Of course, they will return to Hillside on Christmas Day so that they might celebrate the holiday in the servants' hall."

It amazed Wynter—and warmed her heart—to think this powerful duke would even consider a small servant boy unknown to him and make certain that boy was not left alone at Christmastime. She had underestimated this man.

"That is most kind of you, Your Grace. Will is a delightful boy and will be so pleased to be included in your servants' celebration."

His features softened. "No boy should have to spend Christmas alone."

His words and tone made her wonder if he had actually endured a Christmas alone during his own childhood.

"I find it hard to believe only a child was left to feed Lord Cheston's horses," he continued. "That is quite a bit of responsibility, for a boy to handle such a large number of horses."

"First of all, several horses went with Papa to Uncle Edward's. The carriage horses and Papa's own mount. Besides, I was going to help Will."

"You were going to feed horses." He sounded doubtful.

"I was," she said. "I can also curry a horse better than any groom. I was going to do that and help Will exercise the remaining horses."

"You are a woman of many talents," he observed.

Wynter laughed. "Feeding and grooming a horse isn't what I would call a talent."

"It is more than any lady of my acquaintance knows how to do."

She looked over her shoulder. "And how many ladies are you acquainted with, Your Grace?" She turned back around before hearing his answer.

He leaned close, his lips grazing her ear. "Donovan. Call me Donovan."

The name suited him. Strong. Independent. Commanding.

"Your Grace, I think—"

"I think that we are neighbors. That you were close friends with my brother. And that we, too, might become friends. Besides, you will be my guest for the next several days. If I have to put up with you Your Gracing me, I might go mad."

She felt they had crossed some invisible line in their relationship but she said, "All right, Donovan. Now, could you explain why you are walking Jupiter?"

"Because I don't want to jar your ankle."

"That is thoughtful of you but as much as it is starting to pain me, I believe returning quickly to Hillside would be more advisable."

"Very well."

His arm tightened about her, drawing her closer to him, sending delicious tingles along her spine. He nudged the horse and Jupiter increased his pace until they seemed to be flying.

Riding up to his stables, a groom rushed out, surprise on his face to see her in his master's arms.

Donovan swung down and then lifted Wynter from the saddle, shifting her in his arms until he could again have her in a position to carry her.

"Have a cart readied to go to Chesterfield," the duke told his groom. "Once you've done so, ride to Chesterfield on a different mount. You will be staying for several days, helping to care for the horses there. You may return to Hillside on Christmas Day for the celebration held in the servants' hall. Bring the boy from the Chesterfield stables with you when you do."

"Yes, Your Grace," the groom replied without question. He led Jupiter away.

"You don't have to carry me," she said as Donovan started toward the house.

"On the contrary, I will be carrying you wherever you wish to go for the foreseeable future."

She felt the blush heat her cheeks. "That really isn't necessary."

"It is. Too many times a person with a sprained ankle puts their weight on it too soon. It continues to pain them. It doesn't heal properly. I will make certain you recover in record time. Get used to being pampered." He smiled, his even, white teeth dazzling her.

Her belly felt as if she had been turned upside down and right side up several times in a row.

Donovan cut through the kitchens, causing a flurry among the servants there. He stopped in front of a stout woman with graying hair.

"Cook, Lady Wynter has injured her ankle. I need a large bucket filled with the coldest water to be found. And whatever food an invalid needs. Some kind of light fare."

"I am not an invalid," Wynter insisted. "I have no fever or cough. In fact, after my ride, I am extremely hungry."

The cook looked to her employer.

"Very well. Fix Lady Wynter whatever she wishes to have."

The cook turned to her. "Whatever you have on hand and is convenient will be fine, Cook. I eat anything put in front of me other than Brussels sprouts. I find them most offensive."

"Ah. We have something in common," Donovan said and left the kitchens.

A butler and housekeeper appeared magically and the duke said, "Send for the doctor, Preston. Lady Wynter has taken a spill from her horse and has injured her ankle and hip."

"Do no such thing, Preston," she quickly said. "I know what to do. No doctor is needed."

The butler faced the duke, who nodded.

"Mrs. Preston, Lady Wynter will be staying with us for a few days. Please have a room made up for her."

"There is already one ready, Your Grace," the housekeeper said. "I prepared an extra one in case you had another guest who might drop by. Better to be prepared, I always say."

"Excellent. Show me which one."

Mrs. Preston went to the stairs and Donovan carried Wynter

up them to a lovely bedchamber done in soft rose with small tea roses on the wallpaper. He placed her in a chair as a maid entered with the bucket of water. With great care, he unwrapped the cravat from her ankle and tossed it aside.

"Place your foot inside, my lady. Careful. It will be dreadfully cold but you need to tolerate it for a quarter-hour or so. It will make all the difference in the swelling and prevent some of the subsequent pain."

Donovan took the bucket from the maid and placed it before Wynter. Gently, he lifted her leg and submerged her foot and ankle into the water.

"Brrrr!" she exclaimed.

"Get a blanket," he ordered and the maid quickly returned with one, which he placed about Wynter's shoulders.

He continued kneeling beside her and told the housekeeper, "Find Richards and have him go with you to Chesterfield. A cart is already readied for you. Lady Wynter needs to tell you what to pack for her. She will be with us at least through Boxing Day, if not longer." To Wynter, he said, "I will fetch my banyan for you."

She explained where her bedchamber was and the two women discussed what should be brought back. Since she would be around Donovan's guests, she didn't ask for her usual breeches and shirts. Mrs. Preston assured her she would be able to locate everything Wynter might need.

The duke returned, carrying a dark brown silk banyan. He handed it to the housekeeper.

"Help Lady Wynter from her clothes and into my banyan then you may leave for Chesterfield. I will wait outside."

He left the room and it seemed somehow smaller. His vitality filled a room. Overwhelmed a room.

Overwhelmed her.

Mrs. Preston and the maid helped her out of the greatcoat, shirt, and the breeches and into the banyan. The robe smelled of the man, causing her insides to flutter wildly. The maid rolled the sleeves up since they drooped far beyond Wynter's hands. Mrs. Preston helped tie the belt firmly and then Wynter sat again.

"I will be back soon, my lady," the housekeeper promised.

She and the servant left. Immediately, Donovan entered the room again. His eyes swept quickly over her, causing her cheeks to sting with heat again. She recalled his words regarding her reputation, realizing they were now alone. In her bedchamber.

"Servants talk, Donovan. You know that. You warned me regarding my reputation. I intend to heed your words." She glanced to the door. "The door should be kept open while you are tending to me. I suggest stationing a maid outside it so, if asked, she can report that nothing untoward occurred in this room between us."

He nodded. "You are right, Wynter. I will see to it now. I apologize for not heeding my own advice. I want your stay at Hillside to be pleasant and free from gossip."

A maid arrived with a tray of food at that moment, a towel draped over her arm.

"Place the tray beside the bed," the duke commanded. "Give Lady Wynter the towel to rest in her lap."

"Yes, Your Grace."

The servant did as requested and turned to go but Donovan told her, "Leave the door open if you would and remain just outside it. Lady Wynter might have need of you."

The maid nodded, understanding the situation. "Yes, Your Grace."

"How does your ankle feel now?" he asked once the maid exited the room, concern written on his handsome face.

"It doesn't feel like anything. It is so numb you could chop it off and I doubt I would feel a thing."

Donovan tossed back his head and laughed. The rich laughter struck a chord within her. She had always enjoyed being with quick-witted men who could make her laugh. The fact she had made him laugh pleased her a great deal.

"Then it's done the trick. What we need now is a poultice for it. And something for your hip."

A new maid entered the room, saying Cook had sent her to see if His Grace needed anything else from the kitchens. Donovan told the servant what he needed next. She repeated the items before leaving to make sure she remembered everything he requested.

"I thought I knew a bit about folk medicine," she said. "Where did you learn all this?"

"In the army. Men are forever being injured and not just from bullets or bayonet wounds. I learned about how to care for various injuries from the doctors. I would visit my men in the surgical and medical tents and learned to ask the right questions."

She studied him a moment. "You cared for your men."

"A great deal. You have to depend upon the man to your left and to your right when you are in battle. Trust is tremendously important in fighting a war. You become family with them. An officer is like the head of a family. He must care for and be responsible for the men under his command but he cannot care too much. A certain distance is required. Else, you would never survive emotionally."

His words revealed a great deal about him. She kept silent, though, as he lifted her foot from the bucket and gently dried it. Donovan went to the bed and turned the covers back, as well as fluffed the pillows. He returned and lifted her in his arms.

This time when he lifted her, there was only the thin layer of silk between them. Her pulse quickened. Her belly tightened. Her core pulsed.

Setting her onto the bed, he took two of the pillows which he had set aside and placed both under her ankle so that it was elevated. Then he bent and touched it gently, his fingers sending a frisson of tingles through her.

"It will be more sensitive due to the sprain. The joint will hurt. Even throb some. That is why you don't need to move your foot or try to stand on it for a day or two." His fingers gently probed more and he said, "It may bruise but for now, it will most like turn red. The area will flood with warmth. That is due to more blood flowing there."

Wynter didn't know about her ankle but she knew the rest of her flooded with warmth.

Because of this man.

He rose to his full height. "It will take five to seven days before it seems back to normal. Even then, you need to make sure you don't test it too much. No stomping. No sudden turns or pivots. Resting it is important. Once the poultice has sat on it for a while, I will wrap it again with bandages to help take pressure off the joint. The compression also keeps down the swelling."

She smiled. "See, I told you that we didn't need a doctor. You have more than enough knowledge."

"Just be glad it isn't broken."

Wynter sighed. "I would go mad if it had been. I am not used to sitting much, other than when I play my pianoforte."

"You play? I would like to hear you sometime."

"I will do so for you—if you tell me about these Terrors who are coming to call at Hillside."

Donovan chuckled. "Perhaps later," he said, his eyes on the door.

She saw it swing open and the same maid returned, along with two footmen carrying the supplies the duke had requested.

"There was no stale beer, Your Grace," the maid said. "I brought the vinegar with the oatmeal and rags for you to use in the ankle poultice." She indicated one bowl a footman carried.

"Bring it here," he ordered. He looked to the other footman. "Is that the warm vinegar?"

"Yes, Your Grace."

"I'll take it and the pitcher, as well."

The maid came closer. "And here is the brandy," she said, handing a crystal decanter to him. "I took this from your study. I hope that was all right."

"You did well. Place the bandages on the bed. Thank you. That is all."

The three servants vacated the room and Wynter watched Donovan go to work, mixing vinegar, oatmeal, and a bit of brandy in one bowl and then placing it inside one of the bandages. He brought it to her ankle and made sure the concoction covered the injured part before winding the bandage around several times and tucking it in.

"Does it feel too tight?"

"No," she assured him. "It is snug but it isn't cutting off the blood in any way."

"Good."

Next, Donovan poured water from the pitcher into the bowl of warmed vinegar. Since he had already concocted the poultice, she had no idea what this was for.

He dipped more bandages into it and squeezed the excess water out.

"Wynter, I need to bathe your hip now."

Fire swept through her. She sensed her face begin to flame. "What?"

"You fell hard on it. A bruise shouldn't be neglected."

"But . . . I don't have anything on under this banyan."

"I know."

"You can't . . . I mean . . . well, you shouldn't . . . it isn't . . ." Her voice trailed off.

He grinned. "I didn't know the loquacious Lady Wynter could be silenced."

She felt the blush from her roots to her toes.

"I will think of you as one of my soldiers, Wynter. I promise nothing untoward will occur. After all, I am a gentleman. Albeit a very recent one."

She swallowed. "Very well."

Wynter may have responded bravely—but her insides shook like jelly.

# CHAPTER TWELVE

DONOVAN HAD NEVER wanted a woman more than he did Wynter.

And because of that, he had to rein himself in. Practicing self-control was not something he ever exercised. Especially around beautiful women.

But he would do it or be damned forever. Because for some ungodly, crazy, wonderful, incredible, impossible reason—he saw a future with this woman.

It scared him but he had never been one to let fear manipulate him. He dictated to it, not the other way around.

Whatever it took. However long it took. Someway, somehow, someday.

He was going to wed and bed this woman.

Despite her declaration of never planning to marry.

In fact, he looked upon it as the greatest challenge of his life, one which would bring the sweetest reward. Wynter was an amazing woman. She would keep him on his toes. She would never bore him. And suddenly, though he had never given children a moment of thought, he wanted to plant his seed deep within her. Donovan wanted to see Wynter's belly swell with his child. No other man's. He wanted to mate with her. Build a life with her.

And possibly become the duke Sam would have been.

"I am going to help roll you gently onto your right side," he said, already trying to control his breathing, the blood thundering in his ears. "Keep your ankle and foot propped up on the pillows as best you can."

"All right."

Damn, but she sounded calm.

He eased her toward him until she rested on her right side. The banyan had shifted, revealing a creamy expanse of flesh. His fingers itched to trace the curve of her breast but he stepped away, picking up bandages and the bowl and retreating to the other side of the bed. He decided it was best that she faced away from him.

Else she might be frightened away by what his face revealed.

"I know this is awkward but I am going to lift the banyan. I need to examine your hip and then bathe it in the solution."

She nodded, a strangled noise escaping from her.

Donovan smiled. So she wasn't as blasé as she appeared.

*Good.*

Slowly, he pushed the banyan up her leg. Higher and higher over an expanse of smooth, porcelain flesh that called out to be touched. Licked. Worshipped. He sensed her stiffening.

"Try and relax," he urged.

"You try being half-naked with a strange man running a hand up your bare thigh!" she snapped.

He chuckled. "I am not a strange man. I am your neighbor. And your friend."

She snorted. "You haven't even told me yet why you are a Terror."

"In good time, my lady. As for any man running a hand up my bare thigh, I can assure you that would never happen. Now, a strange lady—especially if she were beautiful? I can try to imagine that possibility if you'd like."

"You are impossible," she proclaimed, gripping the bed-clothes.

He chuckled. "I have been called far worse."

Donovan had moved the banyan far enough to see her injured hip. "It is severely bruised," he told her, doing his best not to salivate at the curve of her naked derriere.

"Well, I did slam to the ground from a horse going who knows how fast. I should be grateful that I didn't break my hip."

He ran the cloth across the bruised surface. She sucked in a breath.

"I don't mean to hurt you," he said softly.

"You aren't. I am merely humiliated that you are doing this. Mrs. Preston could have done so. Or the maid."

"Ah, but would they take as great a care as I am?" he asked, not bothering to hide his amusement.

"You are enjoying this," she accused.

"Seeing you in pain? No."

But he certainly was delighting in the beautiful curve of her bare hip. He longed to capture her waist and then run his hands from it to her hips and hold them steady as he thrust into her, over and over.

Donovan told himself to focus as he dipped the cloth into the bowl again and smeared the warm liquid across the bruising.

"I'm afraid it's going to take more than a combination of vinegar and water," he told her. "Don't be offended but I believe I should use—"

"Liniment!" she cried. "Of course. I should have thought of that."

She had moved slightly and the banyan had, as well, revealing the full curve of her buttocks. His mouth grew dry. He forced his eyes away as he drew the material lower, covering her hip and leg again.

"Time to sit back up," he said unsteadily, helping her to turn over.

Wynter pushed herself up and he fixed the pillows behind her back and then adjusted the ones under her ankle.

Her face was flushed, the color making her even more appealing. Her single braid fell over her left shoulder and he longed to undo it and run his fingers through the cool, silky locks.

"Shall we see what Cook sent up?" he asked, coming around to the other side of the bed and lifting the silver cover from the plate. "Hmm. Cold chicken. Sliced apples and cheese. Bread and butter."

"I am starving, Donovan. Hand it over."

He liked how she had taken to using his name with ease. When he heard his name coming from her, for a moment, he could forget he was a duke.

"Shall I keep you company?" he asked, moving the tray from the bedside to her lap.

"You better. You are to tell me about your coming guests— and the nickname you share with them."

"Ah, yes."

He reached for the chair he originally had placed her in and brought it beside the bed. Sitting in it, he leaned over and snatched a slice of the cheddar.

"Are you stealing food from an invalid?" she accused.

"I thought you said you weren't an invalid," he retorted.

"Perhaps I would gain more sympathy from you if I were," she said, a teasing light in her eyes.

God, he wanted to kiss her.

She buttered a piece of the bread. "So, tell me. Who is coming? How long have you been friends? Are these friends from the army or your school days?"

"Both. Once Haverhill sent me away, I found myself at Turner Academy. It was a place for boys who had supposedly done some tremendous wrong. In my dormitory room were four other boys, all the same age as I was."

"How old?"

"Ten. We spent every day together. The school was small but the five of us bonded that very first day and have been the best of friends ever since. It's a good thing we got along so well because none of us ever had the opportunity to return to our homes again. Our families had written us off for imagined wrongdoings."

Wynter almost said something but he saw that she didn't

94

want to interrupt his story, afraid he wouldn't continue to be so open with her.

"We all went to university together, again sharing rooms. Then four of us went off to war and the fifth became a vicar."

"That is a long time to be friends," she said wistfully. "I envy you. I never went away to school. I had a governess instead. At least for a while. Then I surpassed her in knowledge. She was a timid creature. Very unsure of herself. One of those impoverished gentlewomen forced to earn her own living. Papa helped me make sure to help find her a good position. She left Chesterfield when I was twelve, going to a family of two little girls. She still writes to me occasionally. She remained with the youngest girl, who recently had her come-out and wed. The girl wants her to serve as governess to her own children."

"That was kind of you to help find her a position when you no longer had a need for her."

Wynter shrugged. "She was a sweet woman. But back to the Terrors, please."

"Miles named us that on the very first day. It was a moniker that stuck. We always refer to ourselves as the Turner Terrors. Terrors, for short."

"Is Miles one of the friends coming to visit Hillside?"

"He is. Miles inherited his dukedom about a year and a half ago, totally unexpected. He wed Emery, the estate's manager."

"A woman managed a ducal estate?" she asked, her eyes lighting with intrigue. "Oh, I already like this Emery a great deal."

"From what I gather, her father was the steward of Wildwood but he was in ill health and Emery took over completely. She had been assisting him for years. Anyway, she taught Miles how to run an estate and now they are wed and have a baby."

"A baby? I hope they are not coming from too far away."

"From Kent. Miles wrote and said that Emery believes it will be easier traveling with an infant who sleeps in her lap versus a rambunctious toddler who would bounce about their carriage."

"I suppose that makes sense. I have no experience with children so this will be interesting."

"They are bringing a nursery governess with them."

"Who else?"

"Also from Kent will be our fellow Terror, Wyatt. Wyatt was in the army with us, though oftentimes he was relieved of his officer duties and sent out as a scout or spy for Wellington."

"How exciting!" she proclaimed.

"I wouldn't mention it to him," Donovan warned. "Wyatt saw some dreadful things. I believe he is glad to have put that part of his life behind him."

"Why did he leave the king's army? I am assuming he did from your remarks."

"He, too, became a duke with the death of his brother. Miles is the Duke of Winslow and Wyatt is the Duke of Amesbury. Wyatt married a few months ago."

"Another steward's daughter?" she asked, pushing the tray aside.

He laughed. "No. Meadow was a widow who enchanted him. I'll be frank. I never thought of Wyatt as the marrying kind. Meadow must be incredibly special to have caused Wyatt to want to settle down so quickly."

"Perhaps the weight of his dukedom weighed upon him," she suggested. "After all, a duke needs an heir."

Donovan poured her some of the brandy left over from the poultice. "Enough talk for now. Drink up," he told her.

She did, downing the entire brandy in one, long swallow. It surprised him. He didn't know of any women who drank brandy, much less like a man.

"That will make you a bit sleepy, I venture, along with the stress of your accident."

He drew the bedclothes over her, taking care not to jar her ankle.

"Get some rest, Wynter. I will be back in a few hours. I will send a maid in to sit with you."

"Please don't. Having someone hover over me isn't something I like."

"Very well."

Donovan bent and brushed his lips against her brow. He wanted to do far more but knew it was too soon. He would nurture their friendship first—and then hope she found him so indispensable that she wanted more of him.

All of him.

Because he certainly wanted all of her.

# CHAPTER THIRTEEN

WYNTER AWOKE FROM her nap feeling unsettled. Restless. She had dreamed of Donovan. In her dream, he had seemed so lifelike. So real. He had touched her cheek with his long fingers. Trailed them down her throat. Brushed his lips against hers. Always fleeting. Teasing.

She supposed she had awakened out of frustration. If he had been at her bedside, she would have grabbed hold of his lapels and pulled him toward her for a kiss. Disappointment filled her, not finding him here.

At least he had listened to her. He had wanted to call in a doctor. She refused. He wished to leave a maid with her. She didn't want one and he agreed. Donovan was the rare man who not only listened to a female but took her feelings into consideration and did as she asked.

It made him all the more attractive to her.

She determined to kiss him—at least once—during her time at Hillside. He was right. Going back to Chesterfield would have been disastrous with only Will to tend to her. She never would have made it up the stairs to her bedchamber, much less back and forth to feed herself and help the young groom with all the horses. Wynter decided it was very thoughtful of Donovan to have brought her home with him, as well as sent a groom of his own to help young Will look after the horses.

Deciding to test her ankle, she moved it slightly. It hurt only a bit. Perhaps it wasn't as badly sprained as Donovan had believed. Funny how easily she now thought of him as Donovan and not Haverhill or Your Grace. Of course, in her mind, Haverhill was the cold, cruel man who made Sam's life miserable. Sam had closely resembled his father in height and build, not to mention his facial features. Donovan, on the other hand, looked nothing like his sire or brother. From what she could remember of the miniature her father kept, the new duke most definitely was his mother's son in looks.

She wondered if she should tell Donovan of what had been between her father and his mother. She never had shared this with Sam but, somehow, that had seemed different. Wynter knew Donovan was very close to his mother. It was probably that closeness and his resemblance to her that had made the old duke wish to send him away. But forever? Her eyes misted with tears as she thought of what he had told her. To never be allowed to come home again at such a young age. To be cut off from his beloved brother. To be alone, with only other boys in the same circumstances, to cling to and forge a new family with. She knew Donovan had done nothing wrong and wondered if the friends who came to visit him soon also had been accused of misdeeds which were imagined.

A soft knock occurred at the door.

"Come," she called, her heart thudding inside her chest.

Mrs. Preston entered, followed by a footman carrying a trunk.

"Set it over there," the housekeeper told the servant. Once he left, she said, "I was able to find everything you asked for, my lady. May I unpack for you?"

"Please do so, Mrs. Preston."

The two chatted as the housekeeper put up what had been brought from Chesterfield.

"I added a few extra gowns, knowing that His Grace would be entertaining during your stay with us. A lady can never have enough choices of gowns," Mrs. Preston joked.

"When do His Grace's guests arrive?" she asked, not recalling what Donovan had told her.

"Most likely early tomorrow afternoon, if not a bit sooner. His Grace is quite excited to have them here. He has said these are men who mean a great deal to him and he wants everything to be perfect for their visit."

"He will probably want to show off Hillside to them. It is a beautiful property."

"I suppose so. There will be two wives who accompany His Grace's friends. I'm certain the three of you will get along well." Mrs. Preston smiled sadly. "You were always such a good friend to the marquess, my lady. We miss him very much."

Wynter nodded. "I miss him every day, Mrs. Preston."

"Shall I bring you some tea?"

"That won't be necessary, Mrs. Preston," a voice from the door said.

Donovan stepped inside, carrying a chessboard. "I asked Cook to send up a hearty tea, knowing Lady Wynter has a voracious appetite."

The housekeeper chuckled. "You shouldn't say such things, Your Grace. Most ladies would have their feelings hurt with you calling attention to the size of their appetites."

"But not Lady Wynter," he said with confidence and grinned. "Though she might box my ears."

Mrs. Preston picked up the luncheon tray from earlier and excused herself as Donovan came closer.

"I hope you don't mind. I found the chessboard and thought perhaps we might play a game. It would help you to pass the time. I know you enjoy being active so sitting in bed can't be much fun."

She thought if he crawled into bed with her, there would definitely be fun to be had.

*Where did such an idea come from?*

Wynter swallowed, nervously picking at the banyan's tie, but said, "I would be delighted to play a game with you, Your Grace."

He rested the chess set on the bedside table. "I will go find a small table."

The thought of him leaving, even for a few minutes, upset her. "Perhaps we could merely place it on the bed. It is rather large."

His blue eyes twinkled at her. "You are inviting me into your bed, Lady Wynter?"

She fought the smile that threatened to show itself and lost. "In a way, Your Grace."

Donovan lifted the board and leaned over her, placing it next to her. He went around to the other side and perched at the bottom half of the bed, facing her.

"I suppose this might do."

Wynter grinned. "When you lose, do not claim you were at a disadvantage because of your seat."

"*When* I lose? Oh, Wynter, Wynter. Your false confidence will soon turn to sorrow." He paused. "What is your surname, by the way?"

She had dreaded this moment but supposed it was better now than him hearing it for the first time when she introduced herself to his friends.

"Day. I am Wynter Day."

He stared at her a moment and then his head fell back. Uproarious laughter spilled from him.

"Day. Wynter Day. You are Wynter Day." He burst into laughter again then tried to calm himself. "I apologize, Wynter Day. Truly, I do. Might I ask about how you came about your name?"

"You may. *If* you stop laughing, that is."

He tried to turn sober, fighting a smile. "All right."

"I was born in mid-January, during an especially cold bout with a heavy snowstorm the day of my arrival. Thus, I became Wynter." She sighed. "I suppose I should be glad Papa was the one naming me. He was the rare man who delighted in having a daughter and told my mother that I would be his ray of sunshine."

Donovan grinned mischievously. "So, you could have been Lady Sunshine Day."

She shuddered. "Yes. Wynter sounds infinitely more appealing compared to that."

"Sunshine," he mused. "I rather like it. I think I will call you Sunshine."

"You will not!" she protested.

He arched an eyebrow. "I am a duke. Dukes do as they please. If I wish to call you Sunshine, you must simply suffer through it."

"Donovan," she warned, "You wouldn't."

His lips twitched in amusement. "Perhaps it will merely be my nickname for you and I will only use it when we are alone."

"Thank goodness that won't happen very often."

His intense gaze caused her to grow warm.

"I shall have to come up with a moniker for you, as well," she said.

He shrugged. "I am already a Terror. I need nothing else."

"Your Grace, tea is here," Mrs. Preston said, sweeping into the room, a maid pushing a teacart following in her wake. She placed an empty tray upon Wynter's lap.

Donovan rose from the bed, eyeing what had been brought. "Thank Cook for me, Mrs. Preston. This looks wonderful."

"It looks as if it could feed everyone at Hillside," Wynter said. "I fear you have exaggerated my appetite to your cook, Your Grace."

His eyes gleamed at her. "Oh, I think you would be surprised how hungry you might be, Lady Wynter."

She knew he wasn't talking about food.

A footman appeared with an amber jug and cloths. "Your Grace, the liniment you called for."

"Yes, leave it over there."

"Shall I stay and pour out for you, Your Grace?" the housekeeper asked.

"No, I believe I will do so for our guest. Thank you." His tone dismissed the three servants.

Donovan asked her how she liked her tea and he added the two lumps of sugar she enjoyed. Handing her the saucer, he poured a cup of tea for himself and then filled a plate for her.

"Ham sandwiches," she noted. "My cook had left a ham for me to eat from while she was gone. I hope Will and your groom will make good use of it. Oh, there are tarts! I love a tart more than most."

"My cook makes excellent tarts," he praised. "Better than any I have ever had."

Wynter bit into one, still warm from the oven. "Mmm, apple. My favorite."

She didn't tell him that she had eaten tarts many times with Sam at Hillside. She had been a frequent visitor, as had Sam at Chesterfield. She kept quiet about it, though, because she didn't want Sam to stand between them. She wanted Donovan to like her for herself, not because his brother had. What she meant by like, however, wasn't something she wished to explore at this time.

He asked about the neighborhood and she told him about the various neighbors near Hillside and Chesterfield.

"Viscount Amos has given a ball on Twelfth Night for as long as I can remember. I am certain you have been invited to it."

"I may have. Morris, who is acting as my secretary, told me about a few invitations that I have received. Frankly, I wasn't interested in any of them."

"But you must become part of the neighborhood," she told him. "You are a duke. The leading peer."

"I've already led men into battle. I don't see how being a duke means I need to lead any lords anywhere."

"That is where you are wrong. It is because you are a duke that others will look to you. They will be interested in your opinions regarding politics and the economy. You will set the fashion, too."

A look of horror crossed his face. "Egads, not that."

"Don't worry. What I see you wearing lets me know you are in good hands with your tailor."

"I hadn't a clue what I should order," he admitted. "I'd been at war and worn a uniform after my university days. Morris, the man I mentioned, had a father who was valet to a duke. It was Morris who helped me select fabrics and told me what to order, including the banyan you are now wearing."

"It is very nice," she said, thinking how marvelous the silk felt against her bare skin and how his scent enveloped her as she wore it.

"You should definitely come to Lord Amos' ball," she continued. "It will be a perfect way to meet your neighbors and others from Wickley. You see, it is a country ball so all the village's inhabitants have been invited. Lord Amos' servants and tenants will also be in attendance."

"Do you always go?"

"Why, I wouldn't miss it. I love to dance."

He frowned. "It might be too soon to do so with your ankle healing."

"Pish-posh. The ball is two weeks away. I will be fine by then."

"I'll be the judge of that."

She frowned, rankled by not only his words but his tone. "While I appreciate you coming to my aid when I injured my ankle, Your Grace, and I certainly am grateful of the care I am receiving at Hillside, I believe I will determine whether or not I can dance."

This was the reason she never wanted to wed. Wynter refused to have a man telling her what she could and could not do.

"What happened to Donovan?" he asked.

"What happened to being friends?" she countered. "Friends don't order one another about. Friends might give advice but they never demand a certain behavior from one another."

His blue eyes darkened to the shade of midnight. "I'm not

sure if I want to be friends, Wynter."

He set down his saucer and rose, going to the bedchamber's door and closing it. Her heart slammed against her ribs as he turned and faced her.

Her mouth dry, she managed to say, "Then if not friends, what?"

Donovan strode toward her. He lifted the tray from her lap and placed it on the ground. Then he sat next to her on the bed.

One hand went to her waist. The other cupped her cheek, his thumb softly stroking it. The tingles returned, firing through her.

"This," he said, his mouth coming to rest on hers.

His lips brushed slowly against hers, agonizingly slow, causing her breath to hitch. She had kissed probably a dozen or so men over the years and none had taken this approach. Most had perfunctorily pushed their lips against hers for a moment and then broken the contact. A few had mashed theirs against hers hard, which had been most uncomfortable. One had jammed his tongue inside her mouth when she had pushed on his chest, trying to gently move him away. The action had shocked her.

Donovan, though, was taking his time. His hand still cradled her cheek. The one on her waist held her in place. Not that Wynter was going anywhere. She was, in effect, stranded, thanks to her swollen ankle.

And she decided that was definitely a good thing. He wasn't going anywhere. Neither was she. She was curious where this kiss might lead.

His lips moved to her cheek, his breath warm. They slid down her cheek to her jaw. He pressed soft kisses along it, making the tingles riot within her. Her breasts grew heavy. She felt hot all over. Then his mouth went lower, kissing her neck. Donovan found where her pulse leaped out of control and nipped there, causing a frisson of pleasure to ripple through her. He licked it soothingly and then nipped her again.

Oh, dear. The place between her legs tightened. And tingled. And pulsed.

His mouth returned to hers and he kissed her with a bit more pressure. She welcomed it. Her hands moved to his chest and clutched his waistcoat. She needed something to anchor her because she was spinning out of control.

His tongue touched her bottom lip, gliding back and forth along it, stealing her breath. Then it slid along the seam of her mouth and she parted for him.

That's when the magic occurred.

Wynter never knew this is how people could kiss. Donovan certainly knew, though. A man of his looks and age had to be incredibly experienced—and she was reaping the bounty of that experience. He leisurely explored her mouth with his tongue. She heard sounds and realized they were coming from her. Little whimpers. Of pleasure. Of desire.

He deepened the kiss, his tongue sweeping everywhere, leaving nothing untouched. Timidly, she joined in the fun. Once she heard his groan and felt his fingers tighten on her waist, she grew bolder. Soon, she matched him, stroke for stroke, their tongues colliding and mating and dancing. Her hands slid up his chest and pushed into those thick, black curls. He made a noise that sounded like satisfaction and she tightened her hold.

His hands both now held her waist, the thumbs moving back and forth, grazing her breasts. Her core pounded fiercely, a physical feeling she had never experienced. Instinct told her she wanted him to touch her there. Just the thought of it made her grow hot all over.

Donovan broke the kiss, both of them breathless. He gazed for a long moment into her eyes and then seized her mouth again, ravishing it. She thought her heart might explode from her chest as they kissed for what seemed like an eternity. Once more, he broke the kiss, his lips traveling down her neck and to the top curve of one breast. Lazily, he ran a tongue across the curve, his effort pushing the banyan aside until her breast was revealed.

Wynter knew she should stop this madness.

She didn't.

His tongue traveled her breast, exploring it as thoroughly as he had her mouth. Her breathing now came in rapid spurts. Then his teeth grazed the nipple and she almost flew off the bed. Her fingers clutched his hair, keeping him at her breast, afraid he would leave. He laved the nipple and then sucked on her breast so hard, she whimpered and writhed against him.

Donovan moved to her other breast, giving it his undivided attention. Wynter hadn't known such feelings were possible. She gasped as he sucked, wanting it to go on and on.

His lips journeyed back to their original destination and covered hers. Once more, long, drugging kisses occurred, building her up and then weakening her.

Finally, Donovan broke the kiss and smiled.

"I don't think this is what friends do."

# CHAPTER FOURTEEN

DONOVAN LEFT BEFORE Wynter could say a word. Already, her face wore a dazed expression, as if she didn't quite comprehend what had just occurred between them.

What had happened had changed him—and there was no going back.

Not that he wanted to. No, some fundamental shift had occurred within him. He had always been a lover of women.

Now, he only wanted to love one woman.

He cursed under his breath as he continued down the corridor. He didn't mean it the way it sounded. What he meant, he told himself, was that he had found the one woman who would continually satisfy him. The one he was eager to pleasure. The one he could tolerate having in his life because she was bright, articulate, and beautiful beyond any woman he had ever known. He was eager to make love to her. Make her scream his name. Fill her with such rich pleasure that she would not only bear him an heir but that she would remain in his bed beyond that obligation.

He wanted Wynter Day. He did not love her. That would be ridiculous, to love a woman after such a short acquaintance. But he certainly desired her. To the point where all other women ceased to exist for him.

Chuckling, he entered his study and closed the door. Yes, her father had had a sense of humor, naming his daughter in such a manner. But she was far from being as cold as winter. She was fire encased in winter's ice. Donovan could tell that she had limited experience in kissing. Part of him secretly celebrated that fact. It meant he would be the one to introduce her to the pleasures of the flesh. He assumed she had been kissed before but not by anyone with any skill. Gradually, Wynter had blossomed beneath his touch, growing bolder and kissing him back.

He had stopped far too soon to satisfy himself but he knew she must be reeled in slowly. She had already declared she had no interest in marriage. She was incredibly independent. He would have to finesse his way into her heart. By his kiss. By his touch. By showing her that she needed him as much as he did her.

That's why he wouldn't go to her room the remainder of the day. Though he wanted to play chess with her and sup with her, he wanted her to think about what had occurred between them. He didn't want to be too readily available to her. It was important that she realize how good they could be together. If that meant not spending a few hours in her company for the rest of the day, so be it.

Donovan wondered if this was how Wyatt had been struck. Had he found an overwhelming need to make Meadow his? His friend was always full of fun and flirtation. It would be interesting to meet Meadow and see how she had felled a giant such as Wyatt. As far as Miles went, he was the most loyal and steadfast of the Turner Terrors. Donovan could easily see Miles wanting to do right by his title and find a bride. From what Miles' letters revealed, though, Emery was an extraordinary woman. He was eager to meet her, as well.

He worked in his study until he was interrupted by a knock.

Preston entered and asked, "Will you be dining with Lady Wynter this evening?"

"No, I think not. It would be difficult for her to come downstairs. It would be best if she took a tray in her room and then got a good night's sleep."

*Something he hoped she wouldn't get if she were thinking of him.*

"Very good, Your Grace." The butler turned to leave.

ALEXA ASTON

"Preston, do we have a reclining chair? I seem to remember one. It would be nice for Lady Wynter to use during her stay with us."

The butler contemplated the question. "If we do, it would be in the attics, Your Grace. I will go myself now and search for it."

"Thank you."

Preston returned half an hour later. "I located the reclining chair, Your Grace. Dinner is also ready."

"Thank you. Wait on taking the chair to Lady Wynter. In fact, place it in the drawing room if you would."

"Certainly, Your Grace."

Donovan closed the ledger he was examining and went to the small dining room, which only seated a dozen. Even so, he felt dwarfed by the eleven empty chairs. At least by this time tomorrow, he would be dining with his friends.

And Wynter.

He wondered what they would think of her. What she would think of them.

What she thought of him.

He hoped she was doing nothing but thinking of him. He certainly had been distracted by thoughts of her ever since he'd left her. Donovan doubted he would get much sleep tonight. His body was tense after their kissing session and eager for release. Up until today, he would have ridden to the village and sought out company in the local tavern. There was always a willing wench among the inhabitants there.

Yet for the first time in his life, coupling with a stranger had no appeal to him. It startled him how much Wynter had already changed him.

Once he finished with his dinner, he went to the library. Skimming the shelves, nothing appealed to him. He roamed the room, restless, not knowing what to do. Then he found himself angry.

Why should he avoid Wynter's company? It would be one of the few times they could be alone. There was no need to punish himself. No need to deny himself of her company.

Eagerly, he went up the stairs two at a time, giddy as a schoolboy. As he moved along the corridor, he tried to calm himself. He didn't know what he would walk into. Hadn't a clue how she might receive him. Donovan promised himself that whatever he did, he wouldn't kiss her.

But promises were made to be broken.

He rapped lightly on her door and paused, listening. No sound came from within. Disappointment filled him. She must have already fallen asleep.

Then the door opened, surprising him, and a maid said, "You may come inside, Your Grace."

"Thank you." He watched the maid go down the hall and then entered Wynter's chamber, leaving the door open to keep him from temptation.

She sat in the bed, no longer wearing his banyan. It was laid out across the chair. Instead, she had on a dressing gown, belted at her waist. Beneath it, the ruffle of her night rail peeped out.

"I see the maid helped you ready yourself for sleep," he said lightly, moving toward her and taking a seat in the vacant chair.

"Yes, she did, though I forgot to have her bring my brush. Would you fetch it for me?"

"Certainly." He rose and found it on the dressing table and brought it to her.

As he sat again, she untied the ribbon at the bottom of her braid and began loosening the sections of her silver-blond hair.

"You have lovely hair," he said. "I have never seen such a unique shade before."

"Papa says his mother had the same color of hair. She died before I was born but I have often gone to the picture gallery and viewed her portrait there."

"Do you favor her?"

"Not really. Except for my hair. My eye and skin color come from my mother. I don't remember her at all. She died in childbirth when I was two."

"I am surprised your father did not remarry."

She looked so sad for a moment and then it passed. "Papa wasn't happy in his marriage. He says I am the only good thing that came from it. I don't think he was eager to try it again." She hesitated and then said, "You see, he was in love with another woman. She was made to wed someone else. It broke Papa's heart. He never really recovered from it."

Donovan could only imagine what he would feel if Wynter chose to wed another man. It would kill him.

"I am sorry to hear that."

"Don't be. He says he has had a happy life. He is perfectly willing to hand Chesterfield over to his brother or nephew when the time comes."

"The uncle and cousin you chose not to visit?" he asked.

"The very ones. I am not fond of them either." She paused. "I am happy I remained behind this year."

"Even if you did injure your ankle?"

"Because I injured my ankle. Else I wouldn't have spent time with you."

He warmed at her words.

"I am very happy to have you here, Sunshine."

She blushed at the nickname. "That's a silly name."

"No, I believe it suits you quite well," he replied. "What will happen when your father passes?"

"You mean will I stay at Chesterfield? Absolutely not. My cousin's wife has already told me in no uncertain terms that I will not be welcomed there. She is a flighty girl, full of venom and gossip. We never hit it off. Even if Cousin Edwin urged me to stay, I would leave simply so I wouldn't have to be under the same roof as Lydia."

"Where will you live then?" he asked, curious as to her plan. Knowing Wynter as he already did, there certainly would be a plan.

"Papa has settled an income on me, independent of the estate. His will also give me several horses and jewelry. I know enough about investing to take this nest egg and allow it to grow. It will enable me to rent something small in London so I can be there to enjoy the Season each year and then I will choose a place in the country to live. Though I love Surrey, I don't want to be near Lydia. Perhaps Kent or Hampshire. I prefer a warmer clime." She brightened. "Maybe even Sussex. I have never lived near the water. That would certainly be enjoyable."

Donovan didn't like this one bit. She sounded so sure of herself, as if leaving Surrey and him behind would be the easiest thing in the world.

"Hopefully, that won't happen for many years, though," she finished. "Papa is in excellent health. I hope he will stay that way for another two decades." She chuckled. "By then, I will be an old woman in my forties. The men who dance with me now will be old themselves—and married. They will have graying hair and paunches and gout and children. I may skip the Season altogether and only go to London upon occasion, to visit the museum or attend a few lectures."

"You will still be beautiful then, Sunshine. Your beauty is one which will grow with time." He meant every word he uttered.

"It doesn't really matter to me. I know I am more than the sum of my looks. Sam knew that about me."

The mention of his brother gave Donovan pause. He envied the years Sam had spent in this beautiful creature's company.

She grinned. "Besides, in twenty years' time, you will be graying at your temples. I think it will make you look distinguished, though. Men seem to age much better than women do. I am sure you will still cut a fine figure yourself in society."

Donovan planned to cut that figure with Wynter by his side. Even then, he knew he would be the envy of most men, having her as his duchess.

"I came for the liniment," he said. "And to check your poultice."

"Mrs. Preston actually brought a new poultice to me less than an hour ago."

"How did the swelling appear?"

"It had gone down remarkably. The ankle isn't hurting much though I wish she had wrapped the bandage a bit tighter."

"Let me."

He went and unwound it, checking her ankle for himself.

"It does look remarkably better," he agreed, "because you have been the ideal patient. You have kept it elevated and the poultice on it. You have gotten the appropriate amount of rest. You have stayed off it."

"I may have today but tomorrow I don't know if I can exercise as much patience. I fear I will grow restless lying in this bed."

"You won't have to stay here. My friends are arriving. I wouldn't want you isolated and alone when you can be with the group. I will make sure you join us in the drawing room."

"Thank you, Donovan," she said, her face lighting up, her smile radiant, causing his heart to skip a beat. "I am never still for very long."

"Except when you play your pianoforte," he reminded her.

"You remembered that?"

"I remember everything we have talked about, Sunshine."

Wynter lowered her gaze, her cheeks pink.

He moved to the liniment bottle and brought it and a few cloths back to the bed.

"Before you go to sleep, we need to brush this against the bruises along your hip. It will smell to high heaven and sting like the dickens, but it will make a difference."

She bit her lip, her eyes meeting his. "I would prefer to apply it myself, Donovan. It wasn't proper before with you doing so. I am not quite certain what overcame me. Perhaps my brain was addled a bit from my fall from Onyx."

"At least you cannot blame our kiss for rattling you, Wynter, since that occurred after I ministered to you."

Her face flamed at the mention of the kiss. She reached out her hands. "Hand it over, Your Grace. I will make sure I coat my bruises myself."

"Everything comes at a price, Wynter."

She frowned. "What will it cost me?" she asked, her voice unsteady.

"One kiss."

She nibbled on her full, bottom lip. Donovan did his best to restrain himself and keep from leaping onto the bed and doing the same. He had the taste of her now and she was like an addiction he never wanted laid to rest.

"You know that's something a rogue would do. Demand a kiss. Are you a rogue, Donovan Martin?"

"I am a former soldier. Now, a duke. I have never thought myself a rogue but I suppose I might have been a bit of a scoundrel at times." He paused, his gaze penetrating her. "Are you willing to pay the price, Sunshine?"

"Yes." The word came out almost as a sigh.

Donovan perched on the bed next to her and thrust the liniment and cloths into her hands. He framed her face with his hands and gave her a sweet, tender kiss.

"Thank you," he said as he rose. "I will see you tomorrow. Sweet dreams."

He left—hoping he had given Wynter Day something to think about.

# CHAPTER FIFTEEN

WYNTER PUSHED ASIDE the confusion that had turned her mind to mush. Or perhaps it was mushy thanks to the lack of sleep. Either way, she wasn't going to let Donovan discombobulate her further.

Her dreams had confounded her. She awoke multiple times throughout the night with a deep yearning for something unknown. All she knew was that it had to do with Donovan. Whatever he had awakened within her yesterday had snowballed into something of monstrous proportions, invading her sleep and now her waking thoughts. He was far too handsome for his own good. Much too confident. He was a man who seemed to do everything with ease.

And she wanted to kiss the life out of him.

Who knew kissing could be so pleasurable? That it could go on for minutes. Hours. That it brought about the most delicious feelings and longings—as well as wicked thoughts.

Wynter certainly had had her share of those since parting ways with Donovan last night. She had even dreamed of some of the things she wanted him to do to her. Places she wanted him to touch. With his lips. With his hands.

She shook her head back and forth violently, trying to clear those thoughts away.

Which only made her think of their last kiss. He had demanded one in exchange for giving her the liniment. Typical behavior for a scoundrel. Yet the kiss was unlike the many they had exchanged earlier in the day. It was brief. Tender. With only a hint of desire lingering behind when he left her, all muddled and frustrated. She supposed he did so deliberately. To make her think of him even more than she would have.

Oh, the Duke of Haverhill was one clever man.

She would need to prove even more clever.

Mrs. Preston arrived and helped her from the bed to relieve herself. With the housekeeper's help, Wynter washed, trying to rid herself of the strong scent of the liniment she had rubbed into her hip after Donovan had left. The housekeeper also helped her dress for the day. Wynter chose a gown in pale blue with silver trim in which to meet his guests. Something told her Donovan's friends would be just as impressive as he was—and that their wives would be even more so. She wanted to look her best for them.

She actually knew who the two couples were from the previous Season. Though she had never been formally introduced to them, Polite Society had raged with gossip about the two new dukes making their appearance for the first time. Winslow brought his wife, a woman taller than any Wynter had ever seen. She was a definite beauty with the darkest of hair and beautiful skin. She also was with child and Wynter had heard the duke and duchess would only be in London for a short while.

Amesbury had set his sights on Lady Selfridge from the moment the Season began and pursued her with a passion. He had wed the widow shortly into the Season and then both couples had vanished. Wynter hadn't given them any thought since she didn't travel in the same circles but now she was quite curious to see what these two new dukes—and their wives—would be like. She hoped her reputation for gaiety did not color their view of her. She truly wanted them to like her.

Afterward, a maid had come and changed the sheets since the liniment had spread across them. Wynter apologized for the smell and stains but the maid had laughed it off.

"Not a problem, my lady. Everyone hopes you will heal quickly. If the liniment helps, so be it."

Her breakfast tray arrived, carried none other than by the duke himself. He looked fabulous in fawn breeches, with a tan waistcoat and coat of hunter green setting off his dark looks.

"How is the patient this morning?" he asked cheerily, setting the tray over her lap. "I see you are wearing a gown today and looking quite lovely in it, I might add."

"I do wear gowns, you know. I thought it would be easier on my ankle rather than wearing trousers and trying to slide my foot inside my boot. Besides, I do know something about manners. Though Papa raised me to be independent and think like a man—"

"You do dress as one."

"Quit interrupting," she admonished. "I have my clothes which Mrs. Preston packed and I'll have you know that she brought back nothing but ladylike clothing. I can easily put a slipper on my foot when I need to."

"Or leave it off," he suggested. "I think one of my cravats would serve better to hold your ankle in place than a bandage. Might I examine it?"

The thought of his long, lean fingers touching her ankle caused her pulse to leap.

"Go ahead. Tell me what you think."

She hadn't put stockings on yet because she had known he would want to see her ankle. She hadn't thought she could stand him slowly pulling them down and removing them so she had merely informed Mrs. Preston that she would put on the stockings later when she went downstairs and had the housekeeper prop up the ankle on pillows.

Wynter now inched her gown up slightly, revealing her ankle. Donovan bent over it, his fingers gently prodding as he nodded.

"Much better," he agreed. "I am going to try and turn it some. Tell me if you experience any kind of pain."

She held her breath as he rotated it slightly to the right and then the left.

"No, just a slight twinge."

"Good. It's healing nicely." He took the hem of her gown and moved it to where it covered her ankle again. "You don't have to put on slippers for my friends. They will understand your ankle is swollen."

"I will decide when it is closer to their arrival," she told him. "For now, I am starving."

She lifted the cover and saw ham, eggs, and potatoes on the plate, with a cup of sliced fruit and two pieces of toast. Donovan settled into the chair.

"Have you already eaten?" she asked, buttering one of the toast points.

"I did earlier. I still rise well before dawn. It's the army in me, I suppose. Old habits are hard to break."

He sat with her as she ate, telling her a little bit more about Miles and Wyatt.

"You should refer to them by their titles. That is how I will know them."

"Miles is Winslow and Wyatt is Amesbury," he reminded her, laughing. "You will easily keep them straight. They are as different as night and day but both as loyal as they come."

Wynter finished her breakfast and he lifted the tray, placing it beside the door before returning to her bedside.

"I like your hair arranged that way," he said. "It is simple yet elegant."

She laughed. "It is easy to style this way. That comes in handy when a lady is stranded without a lady's maid though Mrs. Preston has been most helpful."

"Would you care to play a game of chess?"

"Now?"

He shrugged. "Why not? My guests won't arrive for several more hours. I suppose I am curious as to how well Sam taught you."

She sniffed. "You think you can beat me."

Donovan grinned, his eyes twinkling mischievously. "I know I can beat you."

"You are full of yourself, Your Grace. I believe it is time to take you down a peg or two."

"Go ahead and try, Sunshine."

The chessboard had been moved to the far corner of the room. He retrieved it and placed it between them as he had done yesterday. Instead of playing chess, though, they had spent the afternoon kissing. She sensed her cheeks heating and coughed to distract herself as he arranged the pieces on the chessboard.

"Ladies first," he said.

"That isn't necessary. When you lose, you will say it is because of that."

"Guests first?" he countered.

Wynter grinned. "I'll accept that."

She moved the first piece, a strategy already forming in her mind. Sam had taught both of them so she believed they would have a similar style of play.

She was wrong.

Donovan was much more aggressive so she adjusted quickly. That was one thing that Sam had stressed. Observe your competitor and make your moves accordingly. They played for almost half an hour before she moved her queen. Before she could release her fingers from it, his fingers covered hers, sending a sizzle down her spine. Sam had done the same thing numerous times over the years.

Her body had never reacted in this way to Sam's touch. Only Donovan brought about such a reaction.

"Are you certain that is the move you wish to make, Sunshine?" His voice was low and husky.

"It is exactly the move I planned to make several moves ago, Your Grace," she retorted.

He removed his fingers and she returned her hand to her lap—and kept her face placid when he made the move she predicted he would.

Seven moves later, she called out, "Checkmate!"

"You sacrificed your queen," he said, incredulous. "At entirely the wrong time."

"Yet somehow, I won," she said, trying not to puff up too much. "I knew what I was doing, Donovan, when you tried to stop me. I think ahead."

"You always seem to know what you are doing. A confident air is very attractive," he stated, his eyes burning into her.

Wynter felt herself grow warm.

"Would you like to go downstairs?"

"And leave this room and bed? With pleasure," she told him. "But first, I must put on my stockings. Even if I go without my slippers, I simply cannot meet people for the first time in bare feet."

"Very well. Where are they?"

She told him and he brought them to the bed. She took one and gathered it, leaning down and finding it rather awkward.

"That will never do. Allow me."

Donovan took the stocking on the bed and bunched it up. He sat on the bed next to her and slid the silk over her foot. His touch sent waves of heat rolling through her. They only continued as he pulled it slowly up her leg.

By the time both stockings were in place, Wynter felt the need for a fan. In December.

Donovan leaned over and scooped her up without warning. She gasped and then brought her arms about his neck to anchor herself. Being so close to him made her senses go wild. She could smell the spice from his shaving soap. Her cheek brushed against his chin and she felt the faint wisp of whiskers. His body radiated heat, warming her.

He carried her all the way to the drawing room, where she saw something odd. As he brought her to it and then placed her in it, he said, "This is a reclining chair. It is usually used when someone has a broken leg, but I thought it would work well in this case."

He raised her leg and she heard something click into place.

"This way, your leg will stay elevated. Here, let me get a cushion for you."

From the nearby settee, he took a cushion and gently lifted her leg, slipping the pillow under her ankle as a buffer.

"See? You can sit up with ease. I can push you around wherever you wish to go. It will even allow you to dine with us."

"I have never seen something like this before. It is perfect. Thank you, Donovan."

His eyes glowed at her. "You are welcome, Sunshine. Would you like to test it out?"

"Certainly."

Donovan rolled Wynter all around the floor, to various wings of the house. She saw rooms she had never seen in her many visits to Hillside. He asked her advice about some things, especially the décor, which he thought seriously needed updating. She agreed since it looked as if many of the rooms hadn't been touched since the last century.

Finally, he returned her to the drawing room after a brief stop in the library, where each of them chose a book. They read until his butler entered the drawing room.

"Your Grace, the carriages have been spotted."

"Thank you, Preston." Turning to Wynter, Donovan said, "I want to go and greet my friends. Will you be all right here alone?"

"Of course," she assured him.

"I want to give them time to freshen up but then I will bring them here to meet you."

"I look forward to it."

Wynter watched him leave—and made a decision.

A part of her knew that she might live to regret such a decision, one made seemingly in haste, regarding a man she had not known for very long. The rational side of her told her choosing this path was utterly foolish. It could affect her not for a short time—but for a lifetime. It might change her perspective on everything. It involved not only her.

*It involved Donovan.*

If she carried through with her plan, she would come out of the situation a different person. One she might not even recognize. And yet even as her mind battled with her heart, Wynter knew in this instance that her heart would win. She quieted the warring factions in her head and told herself to stay focused on the conclusion she had come to. It was a decision she did not take lightly, despite how quickly she had come to it.

She wanted to ask Donovan to her bed.

# CHAPTER SIXTEEN

DONOVAN RACED DOWN the stairs, eager to finally see Miles and Wyatt after so much time had passed. He joined Preston and several footmen in front of the house and saw three carriages making their way up the drive. Morris had tutored him enough for him to know that the *ton* always brought more than one carriage. One vehicle would convey his friends, while the others would include servants who would tend to their needs and their various trunks of clothing. He wondered if one had even been reserved for the baby and his nursery governess.

The first carriage pulled up and the others followed suit. Donovan's footmen sprang into action under Preston's watchful eye. He looked to the first vehicle, though, and moments later, Wyatt appeared, waving jovially at him. He came down the stairs and held out a hand. A woman with an hourglass figure appeared, her glossy, brown hair shining in the sun. Wyatt escorted her to him.

The two men hugged one another, Wyatt slapping him on the back.

"It is ever so good to see you, Donovan. And to introduce you to my duchess."

Donovan took her hand and kissed it.

"I am happy to make your acquaintance, Your Grace," she said.

"None of that," he proclaimed. "Wyatt and I are like brothers.

I am Donovan to you."

She smiled. "Then I am Meadow. Thank you for inviting us to spend Christmas with you."

He burst out laughing. "I am afraid it is the other way around. Your husband invited himself—and the others."

She turned to Wyatt and gave him a brilliant smile. "Why doesn't that surprise me?"

Electricity seemed to crackle between them and Donovan took a step back. "I must greet the others," he said and hurried over to where Miles stood outside the carriage.

His friend reached up and took a bundle, which had to be the baby. Casually, he cradled the infant in one arm and helped his wife down from the carriage with the other. Turning, he beamed.

"Donovan!"

He went to Miles and threw an arm gently about him, not wanting to crush the baby.

"It is so good to see you, Miles. It has been a while."

"This is Emery, my better half."

He took the hand of the tall, beautiful woman, her brown eyes rimmed with amber, and kissed it. "It is good to finally meet you in person. Miles' letters speak of nothing but you."

"Not anymore," her husband protested. "Future missives will be about nothing but Ben." He smiled down at his sleeping son. "Ben is the light of our lives now." Miles cooed at the baby and then looked at his wife.

Once again, Donovan saw something powerful between the pair. It was obvious both his friends had the good fortune of making a love match.

Clearing his throat, he said to the duchess, "We are going to be on a first-name basis this holiday. I hope you don't mind."

"Not at all," Emery said. "I prefer it. I have been lucky to get to know Wyatt since his return from war. I look forward to knowing more about you, as well, Donovan."

"And I look forward to seeking your advice about a few matters regarding my estates," he replied. "Miles brags that you have run Wildwood with efficiency. I am an infant, much as Ben is, when it comes to understanding an estate. I hope you might spend some time with my steward and me and give us your opinion on a variety of matters."

"Oh, Emery will do that freely," Miles said good-naturedly.

"I can vouch for Emery's deft hand," Wyatt said, as he and Meadow joined them. "I hadn't a clue what to do or how to handle anything at Amberwood. Emery stepped in and guided me with a firm hand. She isn't merely beautiful. She is as clever as any man I have met."

"Thank you, Wyatt," Emery said.

Donovan saw that most of the luggage had been removed and servants were being taken into the house.

"Would you care to go inside? Your bedchambers adjoin one another and there is a sitting room between them where you may relax. The room next to yours, Emery, will be occupied by your nursery governess. I hope that is convenient. I had a cradle brought down from the nursery for Ben."

"That is very thoughtful of you, Donovan," Miles said.

"It was actually my housekeeper's idea to have mother and babe close together," he shared. "I will take credit for going to the nursery and seeing that the cradle and a rocking chair was removed."

"You are already a good host," Meadow praised.

"If you would like to change from your traveling clothes and freshen up, we can meet in the drawing room in half an hour," he suggested. "I have one other guest who will be spending Christmas with us. A neighbor of mine who had a riding mishap and sprained her ankle."

Surprising himself, he added, "I plan to make her my duchess."

WYNTER WAITED FOR the arrivals to come to the drawing room. Normally, she would have perused the room but was unable to since she was confined to the reclining chair. It was a thoughtful gesture for Donovan to have it brought for her use. He was proving to be kind as well as attractive.

She admitted to herself that she had felt an attraction to him from their first meeting. She had ignored it then, still being upset about Sam's death. Yet the following encounters had proved more than pleasant. Now, being in his house and spending so much time alone with him had led to a growing admiration for him. Donovan was intelligent, articulate, and had a good sense of humor.

And Lord, how the man could kiss.

He was the first man that had actually done a good job of kissing her. All those who tried before had failed miserably. Of course, with his looks and charm, Wynter was certain Donovan had bedded his fair share of women, both in England and abroad while he served in the army. In a way, that was part of her fascination. He was very experienced in an area which she had absolutely no expertise.

Moreover, she was a very curious person. What he had stirred within her made her realize she needed to explore this sensual side of her. Who better to do it with than a man of Donovan's charisma? He would certainly know how to introduce her to the art of lovemaking. Not that she had any yearning to marry. No, that was still something which held no interest for her. She liked who she was and the freedom she had. If she wed, her husband would tell her what to think, say, and do. She would no longer have any opinions of her own but merely be a reflection of him.

Still, she longed to know what went beyond a kiss. Donovan had given her a glimmer of it when he had fondled her breasts and used tongue and teeth to play with them. Just the thought of that caused the place between her legs to tighten and a pleasant shudder to rumble through her. What else might he touch—and how? Where else would he kiss? Her thoughts made her blush, thinking back on some of the dreams she'd had the previous night. Wynter wanted to feel those tingles he brought again. She wanted to explore what lovemaking was.

Now was the perfect time to do so.

It would be impossible once her father and their servants returned to Chesterfield. It was too cold to meet him outdoors and try to couple in nature. With her being under Donovan's roof, she was only a few doors away from his ducal bedchamber. It would be so much easier to invite him to her bed during the next few days and satisfy her curiosity for good.

The only thing left to do was to decide how, exactly, to ask him. Usually, she brimmed with confidence. Asking Donovan to bed her, though, would take some thinking on her part as to how to approach him. With him being more experienced than she was, Wynter worried that he would find their encounter unfulfilling. Worse, he might actually think merely because he deflowered her that he would have to offer for her. That could possibly lead to him turning down her request. She must let him know that she had no kind of expectation in that regard—but that would be a very delicate conversation.

Once he agreed to her proposal, though, she was eager to learn as much as she could from him. Already, the world of kissing had been opened to her and occupied her waking hours. Perhaps when she returned to town for the Season next spring, she would be able to find a man who knew how to kiss as well as Donovan.

Wynter even thought if she enjoyed lovemaking that she might begin to take a few lovers. Discreetly, of course. She knew of women who did it all the time in the *ton*. Debutantes making their come-outs who wanted to sample a man's goods before committing to him. Wives who had provided the required heirs and spares and looked for personal fulfillment. Widows who celebrated their freedom, no longer being under a husband's thumb. Why shouldn't she join in on the fun?

As long as no babies were made. She knew there were ways to prevent that from occurring. She had heard talk in retiring rooms of French letters and had even had one of their maids purchase one for her, just so she could see what it looked like. It had been rather strange, in her opinion, and she had slipped it in the bin after she had taken her time to examine it. Who knew the day had arrived when she would have need of one herself?

Donovan, being a man, certainly would know of other ways. She would be perfectly clear when she spoke to him so that he understood she wasn't interested in having a child. She had never been around children, being an only child. Most of her friends were male and unwed so they didn't have any children running around them. The few women she liked and conversed with were older ones who had already had their children many years ago. Wynter didn't really want a child and didn't believe she was missing anything by not having one.

The door opened and Donovan came in, followed by two rolling teacarts.

"My friends are getting settled but will join us shortly," he told her. "I thought we would have a heavy tea now since we are between luncheon and teatime."

"Did they have a safe journey?"

"They did and all are in good spirits, even if little Ben was sleeping. He is Miles' and Emery's baby. I also told them of your riding mishap and how you came to spend Christmas with us. We have agreed to not stand on ceremony and throw titles out the window."

Before Wynter could reply, the two couples came in and crossed the drawing room to where she sat. She recognized them from last Season and tried to calm the sudden nerves that sprang up within her.

"Forgive me for not rising," she apologized.

The taller woman with dark hair said, "I have taken a few spills from horses myself and also had a sprained ankle once. I am Emery, Miles' wife." She took Wynter's hand. "I am so glad to meet you."

"Likewise," the other woman said, stepping up. She had a kind smile. "I am Meadow and very happy to make your acquaintance."

"I am Wynter—and ready to guess which husband is which. I do admit that I saw you both from a distance at a few *ton* events this past Season." She looked at the two incredibly handsome men, her eyes flicking back and forth between them, wondering if all Turner Terrors were required to be incredibly attractive. "I would say that you are Miles," she said, pointing at the man to her left. "Which makes you Wyatt."

"How did you guess?" Wyatt asked, coming and taking her hand.

"Because of the two—based upon not only physical descriptions from Donovan but from the stories he told—you are the one full of mischief. I can see it in your eyes."

Meadow laughed. "Oh, she has you there, Husband. Yes, Wyatt is full of devilry, even as an adult. I have no doubt our child will take after him and forever stay in trouble."

"Your child?" she asked, glancing down at Meadow's belly and not seeing anything amiss.

Wyatt slipped an arm about his wife's waist. "I suppose the cat is out of the bag. Yes, Meadow is almost two months with child now." He pressed a kiss to her temple. "She hopes for a boy. I long for a girl."

Everyone began congratulating them, with Emery asking how Meadow felt.

"I am still very queasy in the mornings when I rise. The midwife told me that would continue for another few weeks or longer. But once I have hovered over a bowl when I rise and lose whatever is in my belly, I feel fine for the rest of the day."

"I am surprised the carriage ride here did not bother you more," Miles remarked. "Emery couldn't even look at a carriage during those first few months when she carried Ben."

"Why don't we all sit and have something to eat?" Donovan

suggested. "I fear Wynter will strain her neck looking up at all of us if we don't come down to her level."

Emery poured out for them and Donovan made up a plate for Wynter since she couldn't reach anything.

Handing it to her, he said, "If there's anything I've missed or something you want more of, just let me know."

"Thank you," she replied.

They spent a delightful hour together. Although these were strangers to her, Wynter warmed to both couples immediately. She had never truly had female friends close to her age but found she liked Emery and Meadow quite a bit. Miles and Wyatt were as different as night and day but she could see the good in both of them. From the stories the three men shared, she also knew how fiercely loyal the three were to each other.

Donovan cleared his throat, getting their attention. He raised his teacup.

"Though I only have tea now, I wanted to make a toast. To my good friends and brothers who have come to share in my first Christmas at home in many years—and to the ladies who will celebrate with us."

"Hear, hear!" Wyatt proclaimed and they all tapped teacups and sipped their brew. Then he said, "All right, Donovan. You know me well enough that I have sat still for an entire hour—and that doesn't count the carriage ride here. I am ready to see some of your estate."

"I second that," Miles declared. "What we could see of it driving to the house looked lovely."

"I am happy to show it to you." He glanced to Wynter and then the wives. "Would that be acceptable to you ladies?"

Wynter spoke for the three of them. "We are more than happy to excuse you. That way, we can talk about you all we wish." She grinned. "That is, if we wish. Most likely, we will think of a myriad of topics to cover besides you Turner Terrors."

Everyone laughed and the men excused themselves.

The moment the door closed behind them, Meadow asked, "What is going on between you and Donovan?"

# CHAPTER SEVENTEEN

FLUSTERED, WYNTER ASKED, "Why would you ask that? Nothing is going on."

Meadow studied her. "I may have only met Donovan but he paid you quite a bit of attention during tea."

"He didn't speak to me anymore than he did to either of you," she protested.

"But he did look at you a majority of the time," Emery pointed out. "No matter who was speaking."

She felt color flood her cheeks. "We are neighbors. That is all. We have dined together and Donovan had Papa and me for tea one afternoon. Yes, I have gotten to know him better since he brought me to Hillside after I sprained my ankle but . . ." Her voice trailed off.

She couldn't lie to these women.

"Let me say this. Already, I feel very comfortable in your company. I haven't any female friends my age. The ladies of the *ton* bore me to tears with their silliness and games. You two seem very different."

"I know from having attended the recent Season that you enjoy the company of men," Emery said. "You were in constant demand as someone to dance with or to partner at cards."

"Yes, I have always gotten along well with men," Wynter admitted. "Papa raised me to think like a man. I am more comfortable in their company. Meeting you two gives me hope that not every woman in Polite Society is a complete feather-brain." She took a deep breath. "Because of that, I will share something with you in friendship.

"Donovan kissed me."

Emery and Meadow exchanged a triumphant look.

"I knew it!" Meadow said. "He is besotted with you, Wynter. It is very obvious."

"I wouldn't say that," she demurred.

"How was his kiss?" demanded Emery.

"Enjoyable."

"Enjoyable?" Emery scoffed.

"Oh, it was marvelous," Wynter amended. "I have never been kissed by any man like that. I broke out in tingles from my scalp to my toes. I had no idea kissing could be so . . . so . . ."

"Fun?" Meadow supplied.

Wynter hesitated.

"Earth-shattering?" Emery ventured.

She nodded. "Both."

"That's wonderful," Emery said. "You look quite good to-gether."

"Oh, we are not a couple. Just because we have kissed, I do not expect anything from him."

"Do you have an understanding with someone else?" Mead-ow asked.

"No, nothing like that. In fact, I don't plan on marrying any-one."

Both women looked nonplussed for a moment.

Emery recovered first. "You just haven't found the right man before now."

Meadow nodded in agreement. "Yes, that's it. Wyatt has told me that he and Donovan were quite the womanizers over the years. Yet once we met, Wyatt knew exactly what he wanted. Me. He gave up his roguish ways and is a perfect husband in every way."

"No, you both misunderstand me. I am not waiting for the

right man to come along. I never planned to wed at all."

Again, the two women looked as if she had gone mad.

"Why not?" Emery asked.

"As I said, my father raised me with a good deal of freedom. He has even settled an income upon me so that I do not have to worry about having to seek a husband to support me after Papa is gone. I like my life the way it is. I like not having to answer to anyone but myself."

"But what about children?" Emery asked. "Don't you want them?"

She shrugged. "Not particularly. I have never been around children, being an only child. My few female friends are far older than I am and their children are all grown. I don't think I would miss anything by not having a husband or a child. I am free to come and go as I please. Do what I want and say what I think without being censored by a husband. No, ladies, I am happy to remain unwed."

"When you meet the right man, you may change your mind," Emery said. "You will know inside. Something will stir you. A look. A kiss. You will want to share your life with him and no other. Let me say this about marriage, Wynter. I was probably more independent than most women of your acquaintance since I was not a member of Polite Society. My father earned his living, as did my mother's father. I was given a great deal of responsibility at an early age and helped Mama run Wildwood's household and Papa manage the estate."

Emery paused. "I saw myself doing something like that for the rest of my life. Then I met Miles. He was different from any man I knew. I longed to be in his company. Yearned for his kiss. And I made it perfectly clear that I would not shed my independence merely because I became a duchess. He understood that. In fact, he embraced it. He gives me all the freedom I need—and yet he also supports me even as he loves me."

"It is the same with me," Meadow shared. "My first husband was years old than I was. He was a collector of the finest things he could buy. I was something he collected and placed upon a shelf. When I became a widow, I was determined never to be under a man's thumb again. Then I met Wyatt and fell hopelessly in love with him. He knew I refused to compromise myself ever again. He encourages me to be me. I am a better woman for having such a man love and support me."

It had been obvious to Wynter during tea that both Terrors had made love matches. The way Miles and Wyatt looked at their wives in an adoring manner, which was returned by Emery and Meadow, let her know exactly how the two couples felt about one another. She didn't love Donovan, though.

"I am happy the two of you found such wonderful spouses but I am not you. Any stranger could see that both of you love your husbands very much and that they return that love. But I don't love Donovan. I have only known him for a few weeks. Yes, he is a fabulous kisser and has opened a new world to me because of it. That is not enough to base a marriage upon, especially to someone who is adverse to marrying at all."

"Enjoying his kiss is certainly a good beginning, though," Meadow pointed out. "You are beautiful and well-spoken. It is no wonder Donovan is attracted to you."

Emery gazed at Wynter steadily. "If you reach a point where you cannot even think because you yearn for Donovan's kiss, you may change your mind. If he crowds into your mind during your every waking moment and even while you are asleep, you might consider the possibility of marriage. From everything I know about Donovan from Miles and Wyatt, he is a very good man. He will make for an excellent duke—but he will need the right woman by his side to bring out the best in him. I hope you will give him a chance."

Wynter nodded, worried that what Emery said might be true.

Should she reconsider her stance on marriage? Even if she did, there was no certainty that Donovan would even ask her to wed him.

"I will keep your words in mind," she promised.

"Then let's change the subject," Meadow suggested. "We have talked about the men long enough."

They spent another hour getting to know one another. At the end of it, Emery said, "Whether you believe Donovan is for you or not, I hope that you will know that Meadow and I are certainly your friends and plan to remain so."

She smiled. "I do feel that way, Emery. I think sharing Christmas with you two will be very special. For now, I want to lie down for a nap. I have sat in this reclining chair long enough."

"Let me ring for someone to help you upstairs," Meadow said.

When a footman arrived, he lifted Wynter from the chair and took her to her bedchamber. She felt absolutely nothing in his arms though he was quite good-looking.

He simply wasn't Donovan.

The footman placed her on the bed and even solicitously put a cushion under her ankle before leaving.

She fell asleep, wondering how Donovan felt about her.

And how she truly felt about him.

>>><<<

DONOVAN LED HIS two friends from the drawing room, knowing they would pepper him with questions.

Which they did.

"I like Wynter a great deal," Miles said. "How long have you known her? How far is her father's estate from Hillside?"

"Why didn't you take her to her home when you came upon her injured?" Wyatt asked. "Surely, her father must want her with him, especially at Christmastime." He grinned. "Though I do like her, Donovan. She is very spirited and well-informed."

"That's true," Miles agreed. "She knew quite a bit about politics. She and Emery also had an interesting discussion regarding tenants."

"As to your myriad of questions, Chesterfield is about seven miles from Hillside. Her father, Lord Cheston, left to visit his brother for the holidays. Wynter is indifferent to her uncle, dislikes her cousin, and abhors the woman her cousin wed this past September. She had dismissed their servants for several days as a Christmas gift, which is why I brought her home with me. I couldn't see her trying to lumber about an empty house with a sprained ankle."

They left the house and headed toward the stables.

"As to meeting her, I saw her riding Onyx, her incredibly feisty horse, when I was on my way to Hillside from London. I stopped and visited with her. She invited me inside for tea and I met the earl. They had me over for dinner on another occasion. To reciprocate, I asked them for tea. Then, Wynter turned up with her ankle injured and I brought her home with me."

"And you want her as your duchess," Miles reminded him.

"Why I told the two of you—no, the four of you—that, I haven't a clue."

"Perhaps because you are taken with her?" Miles suggested.

"Taken with her?" Wyatt snorted. "He was like a dog in heat looking at her during tea."

"I was not!" he protested.

"You were and you know it," Wyatt said. "It's all right, Donovan. I understand. We have both been libertines and have pursued a good number of women over the years. However, I know exactly what it is like to be thunderstruck by a woman. That is what Meadow did to me. I wanted to breathe her. Sleep with her. Make love to her night and day. All thoughts of other women simply vanished. I have been loyal to her both before and during our marriage and will be to my grave and beyond. She is my light and my life."

"Emery is the same for me," Miles said. "I simply knew she was the one." As they approached the stables, he stopped. "Is that how it is for you, Donovan?"

He raked a hand through his hair in frustration. "I suppose so.

I am not sure. I have never felt about a woman like I do about Wynter. She confounds me. She challenges me. If I could do whatever I wanted for the next week, it would be to have her in my bed and the door locked, keeping the world at bay."

His friends grinned at one another. "He has it bad," Miles said.

"I agree. Maybe worse than I did," Wyatt replied. "All right, enough talk about our wives and your future one. Let's get horses saddled and see some of Hillside."

They rode the property for over two hours, with Donovan pointing out things he wanted to share with them.

As they returned to the stables, Miles said, "Emery will certain wish to ride out and see the estate. Knowing her, she will find things you have missed that need to be addressed."

"That is what I was hoping for," he said. "I want Hillside in good working order before I visit any other of my ducal estates."

"For a honeymoon?" suggested Wyatt with a smile.

"No. Wynter doesn't wish to marry."

Donovan dismounted and gave Jupiter's reins to a groom and his friends followed suit.

On the way back to the house, he said, "She hasn't quite explained it to me but, for some reason, she is damned independent and doesn't wish to have a husband. I think Lord Cheston may have spoiled her a bit. He's settled an amount upon her and she has no need of a husband's protection."

"Income or not, that won't keep her warm in bed at night," Wyatt said.

"I know. I simply have to make her understand that."

"Have you kissed her?" Wyatt asked.

"Wyatt!" Miles chided.

"It's a perfectly reasonable question under the circumstances," Wyatt said. "So, have you?"

He nodded. "I have. And yes, it was heavenly. We would be well suited in the bedroom."

"Then take her to bed," Wyatt proposed.

"He can't do that," Miles protested.

"No, I can't," Donovan agreed. "Somehow, I have to somehow make her change her mind."

"We will help you in any way we can," Miles assured him. "Emery and Meadow can help, too. In fact, knowing them, they have already started chipping away at the armor Wynter wears."

"I will see you at dinner. Meet in the drawing room beforehand for a drink," he told them.

Reaching his rooms, Donovan called for a bath. As he soaked, he thought about Wynter. How well she had fit in with his friends, utterly at ease with perfect strangers. He relived their many kisses and his lips teasing her perfect breasts. There wasn't anything he didn't like about her, other than she was entirely too self-sufficient. He wanted her to depend upon him.

He liked carrying her in his arms and it bothered him that a servant had done so while Donovan had been out riding. Wynter would never be any man's possession and yet he wanted to possess her. Let the world know she was his. His feelings had grown so quickly that they frightened him. In no way did he want her to know how much she consumed his thoughts. No woman had ever held power over him.

Until now.

He couldn't let her know how he craved her attention. Her kiss.

Should he do as Wyatt suggested and take her to his bed? She would have to wed him then. Yet Donovan had never been a man who forced himself upon a woman. He wouldn't start now with Wynter.

After his bath, he had Hall shave him again and then he dressed for the evening meal before going to Wynter's bedchamber to help her downstairs. The door stood open and he looked inside, seeing her sitting on the bed in a gown of pale blue trimmed in dark blue, a sash of the darker color tied under her breasts. She had a cushion supporting her ankle and one on her belly, propping up the book she read.

"Good evening," he said, entering the room.

"Hello." She closed the book and set it on the bedside table.

"You look beautiful tonight."

She smiled. "You also look very handsome," she replied.

"I've come to take you down to dinner. Is your reclining chair still in the drawing room?"

"Yes. I thought it best to leave it there since I assumed we would return there this evening."

"If you are ready, I can take you now."

Wynter nodded and Donovan slipped his arms under her, lifting her from the bed and to his chest. Her arms went about his neck. He caught a whiff of lemon.

"You shaved again," she said as he carried her from the room. "I can smell your shaving soap."

"My beard has a tendency to grow quickly," he told her and then ventured further. "I did not want it to scratch your face if we did anymore kissing tonight."

She blushed prettily. "Oh, you think we will kiss? Will that be the price for you to convey me downstairs?"

"Yes, I believe it is," he said, playing along.

Donovan stepped inside the next bedchamber they passed. Though he longed to set her down so he could kiss her properly, he didn't want her to put any weight on her injured ankle.

Wynter's hand touched his face, her thumb stroking him. "Mmm. So smooth. Not a hint of whiskers."

She lifted her face to his as he bent and their lips touched. Her hand slid from his face into his hair. Donovan kissed her slowly, enjoying the hitch in her breath as he did. After a few minutes, he reluctantly broke the kiss.

"You have paid for a trip downstairs and the one back up."

Her brows knitted together in disappointment.

He liked that. She enjoyed kissing him. He would devise some way to do some more of it tonight after dinner.

"Shall we?"

Once more, Wynter slipped her hands about his neck and

they made it to the drawing room without any further stops. Donovan was proud of the self-discipline he exercised. If it were left up to him, he would have stopped in each room along the way and kissed her senseless before moving on to the next.

They entered the drawing room, where his friends already had gathered. He took her to the reclining chair and set her in it. The lever had already been raised that would keep her leg elevated.

"That is a clever device," Meadow said. "It's a good thing it has kept the weight off your ankle."

"Yes, it is barely swollen now," Wynter said. "I am thinking only one more day in the chair and then I might try to test my ankle."

Donovan thought of a cane his father had used upon occasion and would have Preston search for it. It would help her move about.

Preston brought in drinks to them and Donovan told him what he wanted the butler to look for.

"I will do so after dinner, Your Grace."

They were left alone for a few minutes and then Preston returned again. "Dinner is served, Your Grace."

He pushed Wynter in the chair to the dining room, where a chair had already been removed from the table. Rolling her up to the empty spot, she was able to move close to the table and still keep her leg extended.

Dinner consisted of excellent conversation and food and ended almost too quickly.

"Would you ladies care to go to the drawing room for a bit while we men indulge in our port?" he asked.

"No, I believe we will stay with you, Your Grace," Wynter said. "Women don't need to be put away in a box. I daresay these two duchesses would enjoy a glass of port as much as their husbands would." She smiled at him.

"Port for everyone," Donovan told Preston. "Lady Wynter is right. We will be better served spending time in the ladies' company."

He liked how spirited Wynter was. It made her even more attractive to him. Donovan would have to be careful when he took her upstairs.

And not bring her to his bed.

# CHAPTER EIGHTEEN

THEY RETIRED TO the drawing room after dinner, still finding things to talk about. Donovan made a point to spend time with Meadow and Emery, sitting off to the side with them, since he had spent time earlier with Wyatt and Miles. Both women impressed him and he found he was pleased for his friends to have found women of worth to be their duchesses.

The two regaled him with tales about Polite Society and the Season they had recently undergone. He thought social affairs a waste, unless they were small ones such as this gathering tonight. To think that hundreds of the *ton* came together night after night, crowding into ballrooms, gave him even less reason to want to go to London. He would need to soon, however, because he wanted to check on his warehouses along the London docks.

"You haven't made the Season very appealing to me," he told Emery and Meadow. "Seeing the same people each night? Hearing the same stories and rehashing the same gossip? I can think of at least a thousand other ways to pass my time more pleasantly and productively."

"Part of the Season is dedicated to bachelors hunting for a bride," Meadow said. "From your earlier remarks, it seems you have no further need to look."

Panic struck him. "You didn't pass along my comments to Wynter, did you?"

"Of course not," Emery assured him. "We did, however, talk

about how much you stared at her during tea."

Mentally, Donovan kicked himself. He thought he had done an excellent job of not looking at Wynter too much.

"What did she say when you brought it up to her?"

Emery arched an eyebrow. "Women don't reveal private conversations. What Wynter shared with us was under the guise of friendship. Being very new friends, neither Meadow nor I would think of betraying any confidences shared with us."

"Did she mention not wanting to marry?" he asked.

"She did," Meadow shared. "So, you are aware of that?"

"I am. It is a challenge I am willing to face." He glanced to Wynter, who laughed at something Wyatt said. "I want her. More than I should."

"I, for one, think you will make a handsome couple," Emery said. "I am guessing that you both have a stubborn streak running through you, though. It will make for an interesting courtship."

He frowned. "I never thought of having to woo a woman."

Meadow chuckled. "Everything has always come too easily to you, Donovan. Especially beautiful women. If you believe Wynter is worth it, you will pursue her with a passion."

"I intend to do just that," he stated. "If either of you has a chance to put in a good word for me, though, I would appreciate it."

"We will," they chimed in unison and then burst out laughing.

"You are having far too much fun," Wyatt admonished. He stood and came to Meadow's side. "My lovely wife looks tired."

A teasing light came into her eyes. "I don't believe I am tired at all, Your Grace."

Wyatt grinned. "You will be by the time I am through with you." He took her hand and pulled her to her feet. "It was a pleasure to meet you, Wynter. I hope we can continue our conversation tomorrow."

"We are off to the nursery," Miles said, going to Emery and taking her arm.

"Miles' favorite thing is to hold Ben. His second favorite is to watch his son sleep. We spent over an hour before dinner playing with Ben this evening. I suppose now it is time to gaze upon him as he slumbers."

"Then I bid you all goodnight," Donovan said. "Are you ready to go upstairs, Wynter?"

"I am."

He lingered a bit, waiting for the other two couples to clear the room, and then asked, "What do you think of my friends?"

She smiled. "I like them a great deal. I will admit I am a bit envious, though."

"Why so?"

"You have such a history with Miles and Wyatt. You were young boys who literally grew up together, a day at a time, until you became men. You are fortunate that you live fairly close to one another now and can visit frequently."

"I only wish Hart was home from war," he said, missing his good friend, the only Turner Terror still on the front.

"What is he like?"

"Hart has very high standards. He sees the world in black and white. No shades of gray. He is focused on bringing justice to those around him. Like all Terrors, Hart is loyal to a fault."

"And the last Terror? You said there were five of you."

"Ah, that is William Finchley, perhaps the Terror I was closest to." Donovan smiled, shaking his head. "Finch is a remarkable man."

"What made you closest to him?" she asked. "I can see how strong the bonds of friendship are between you, Wyatt, and Miles. It is hard to imagine you could be even closer to this Finch than you are to them."

He thought back to the first time he met his friend. "I was an easygoing lad and made friends quickly. Finch was much more guarded. Our first day at Turner Academy, we went to an all-school assembly." He chuckled. "Of course, there weren't that many pupils present. I had just met the other four boys in my dormitory room. Funny how being placed with those four led to lifelong friendships.

"Anyway, one boy tried to stare me down. I had never been bullied in any way before and, suddenly, there was this boy intimidating me. I quickly glanced away—and Finch noticed. He told me in no uncertain terms to continue to look at that bully until *he* was the one who looked away."

"Did you?" she asked.

"I most certainly did. With success. It was the first of many lessons Finch taught me. I could be brash and had a tendency not to follow rules. Finch would rein me in before I could get into too much trouble. When rage seethed within me, he had a way of calming me unlike any other. Though I had never considered myself to be selfish or self-centered, I truly had never thought of the feelings of servants."

"And Finch did?"

"Very much so. He continually thought of others and re-minded all the Terrors to do the same. I have never seen anyone more considerate of servants. It left a lasting impression upon me."

"He sounds like a very moral man," Wynter observed.

"It is funny you should say that. Donovan paused. "Finch did not go off to war. Instead, he became a vicar."

"A vicar?" Wynter laughed. "Somehow, I find it hard to be-lieve that any Turner Terror became a vicar."

"I felt the same way. Finch is perhaps the smartest of us all—and the most unhappy. In all the years we have known him, he has never revealed why he was sent to Turner Academy. The rest of us spilled our guts that very first day, each of us wrongly accused of some injustice. Yet Finch never has spoken about why he landed at Turner Academy. Frankly, it surprised the hell out of me when he told us he would become a man of the cloth. Finch has the living at Marbury now in Surrey, near the Earl of Marksby, who took us Terrors under his wing."

"Why do you think he chose a path toward God when the

rest of you went to war?" she asked.

It was a good question. One which Donovan had asked over and over through the years. Finch was a born leader and would have made for an excellent officer. He was a great judge of character and the most intelligent of all the Terrors. His keen mind would have made him a natural at military strategies. Yet he had chosen to serve God and a small flock at a country parish.

"I wish I knew," he declared.

"Do you think it has something to do with the secrets he keeps?"

Donovan believed it did. He hadn't a clue why Finch had been dumped at Turner Academy as the rest of them, abandoned by his family. Perhaps one day his friend would share with his fellow Terrors just what had occurred to cause him to be sent away.

"Possibly. Until Finch reveals his past, however, it is all speculation."

"I hope I can meet these other Terrors one day."

He smiled at her. "I will make certain it happens."

Leaning down, Donovan lifted Wynter from the chair, holding her snuggly against him. He carried her up the stairs. Neither of them said a word.

When he reached her bedchamber door, he leaned down to open it. She placed a hand over his.

"Wait."

"Ah, perhaps Lady Wynter is interested in a goodnight kiss?" he asked lightly, his heart pounding faster at the thought.

Her eyes darkened. "No, I am interested in much more." She licked her lips. "I would like to go to your bed, Donovan. Not mine."

His heart slammed hard against his ribs. He tightened his hold on her so as not to drop her.

"What?" he asked hoarsely.

She swallowed. "You heard me. I invited myself to your chamber."

"Why?"

"Take me there and I will tell you."

He hesitated a moment, not sure if this was a wise move. His feet suddenly had a mind of their own and began to propel him down the corridor.

They reached his door and Wynter was the one who leaned down and turned the handle. She pushed open the door and Donovan stepped inside.

He watched as she looked about. "Oh, you have a sitting room. That's nice."

"I don't use it very often."

He took her to a settee and placed her upon it, making sure her leg was stretched out before her. Kneeling next to her, he took her hands.

"Talk to me. Tell me why you asked this of me."

She bit her lip, worrying it. He tamped down the desire running through him.

"You know I have no wish to wed," she began. "I have also told you I am most curious. While I have kissed other men, none of their kisses have proven as pleasurable as the ones we have shared."

He smiled. "Is that so?"

"Don't turn arrogant on me," she warned and swallowed again. "I feel . . . that is . . . I would like to explore a different side of myself."

"Your sensual side?" he suggested.

"Yes," she said, her cheeks filling with color. "Since you seem to be an expert in kissing, I believe you would definitely be able to satisfy my curiosity about lovemaking."

"I see." Donovan's heart beat so wildly now he was afraid his chest might burst open.

"I don't have any French letters—"

"What?" he gasped.

"Oh, I did at one time. I was curious as to what they looked like. I don't have one anymore. But I thought with you being a man of experience, you would certainly know how not to make a baby while you . . . taught me a few things."

"Taught you," he sputtered.

"Yes. Even though I won't ever have a husband, I would like to see what lovemaking is like. I know you might not wish to do this with me, though."

"Why do you say that?" he asked, curious as to what she would say next.

She pulled her hands from his, twisting them nervously in her lap. "Partially because you are so experienced. I suppose you are used to making love to women with a vast amount of experience. Since I am a novice, I fear I would leave you unsatisfied."

His blood heated. "I seriously doubt that, Wynter."

"I also fear that you will feel obligated to do something silly afterward and offer for me. I don't want that from you." She hesitated. "You know I have no wish to marry. I simply want to see what I might miss. If I am going to learn about this, I want to do so with you."

Donovan took possession of her hands again. "I am honored that you wish me to introduce you into the ways of love."

"You are? You don't think this is a ridiculous idea?"

"No. Not at all." He released her hands and cupped her cheeks. "I am touched that you would ask."

"If I do bore you, you will tell me, won't you?"

He grinned. "You won't bore me, Wynter. I guarantee it."

"Promise me you won't offer for me immediately afterward. I want us both to go into this without a guilty conscience and without worrying of what comes later."

"I won't offer for you while you are still in my bed," he stated, knowing that he would definitely ask her to be his duchess before the new year arrived.

"All right then." She brightened. "How do we begin?"

"With a kiss."

# CHAPTER NINETEEN

WYNTER KNEW SHE wasn't the expert Donovan was at kissing but she had picked up a few things from him previously. She relaxed, knowing this is how they would begin, and wondered for a moment if all couples started this way.

Donovan gently lifted her and sat on the settee, settling her upon his lap. It still allowed her leg to be supported. He even leaned over and removed a cushion from where it sat and placed it under her ankle.

"Is that all right?" he asked, his voice husky, sending a chill along her spine.

His eyes had also darkened. She wondered if that was a sign of desire.

"I want you, Wynter," he said, confirming her guess.

"I want you, too," she replied, not really certain what that meant but knowing she did want to kiss him. Badly. Very badly.

He cupped her nape with his large hand and brought his lips to hers. His other hand rested against her waist. Both held her in place as he gently kissed her. He started slowly, as he had that first time. This time, Wynter knew what was coming and her body tightened in anticipation.

"Relax," he murmured against her lips.

She raised her mouth until it was almost touching his. "Well, it's a little hard since I have no idea what is coming," she retorted.

"You know nothing?"

"Not a thing," she said blithely.

"Perhaps that is an advantage," he replied, his mouth touching hers again.

With her mother dying when Wynter was so young, she had no one to tell her about the things that passed between a man and a woman. She had been warned not to kiss men because she would be ruined if caught at it. Plenty of women in the *ton* kissed men, though, and she had learned a little about kissing during walks on a dark terrace or stops on a bench while others in a garden moved forward.

None of those times she had been kissed, however, compared to what Donovan's kiss did to her now. It caused her body to come alive, almost as if it vibrated. Her breasts seemed to swell larger. Her breathing grew shallow. Blood pounded in her ears. Those marvelous tingles that he alone seemed to bring about began running through her.

He took his time, leisurely exploring her mouth, teasing her with his tongue, as if he asked her to come out and play with him. She readily followed, enjoying the ensuing battle for domination. His kisses went deeper. Longer. Her head began to spin. And still, he kissed her, so much that she wondered if her lips could bruise as her hip had done. She clung to his shoulders, her nails digging into his coat.

Little noises came from her. Him, as well. Satisfied ones that let the other know they were on the right track. Once more, Wynter hoped she wouldn't disappoint him.

She felt him rise from the settee and knew he was taking her into his bedchamber. He broke the kiss and closed and locked the door behind them.

"In case Hall decides to show up," he explained. "He only comes when I ring for him. Oftentimes, I ready myself for bed without his help. But there could always be a first time." His eyes glowed. "And I want no interruptions."

"Neither do I," she said, her breathing erratic.

Gently, Donovan placed her upon the bed, which had already

been turned back by a servant, and took his time undressing her, layer after layer, until he finally pulled her chemise over her head and she sat there naked. Wynter felt as if she were blushing from her roots to her feet, sitting with not a stitch on as he admired her.

"You are so beautiful."

He kissed her again, his hands framing her face. She longed for the kiss to go on forever. Perhaps that was what heaven was like, kissing someone you loved for eternity.

She started. Oh, no. She hadn't thought that. She didn't believe it. Thank God she hadn't said it aloud.

"Is something wrong?" he asked.

"Not at all." She smiled. "I was merely wondering when I might see you as you do me."

Donovan grinned. "Your wish is my command, my lady."

His clothing came off much more quickly than hers had but she had ample time to admire his broad shoulders. The muscular chest with a light furring upon it. The flat belly. And oh, goodness.

His manhood.

It was in a thick nest of curls, similar to the ones covering her sex, but it came to life and stood at attention. As if it wanted her attention. Curious, she reached out and encased it in her fingers.

He sucked in a breath, holding perfectly still. Wynter supposed she had permission to explore since he didn't stop her. She moved her fingers along the rod, slick as satin and yet as firm as steel. A bead formed at the tip and she bent to look at it. It seemed to call her name.

She licked it.

Donovan gasped, grabbing her shoulders and pushing her back.

"Why did you do that?"

"I haven't the faintest idea," she admitted.

"You can't do that. At least not now. If so, I will explode and that's not what you want."

"It isn't?" She smiled at him lazily. "Then what do I want?"

"This."

He moved her head to the pillows and then lay beside her. As they faced one another, he kissed her. This time, though, one hand roamed her bare back, sliding sensually up and down. Immediately, her core tightened and the throbbing began.

He better do something about that. If he didn't, she would ask him to . . . do . . . whatever. Wicked thoughts of what he could do began to fill her.

Wynter stroked his chest, feeling the muscles bunch beneath her fingertips. She touched his nipple, flat as a disc, and rubbed the pad of her thumb over it. He growled. She raked her nail over it. He growled again.

"Do you like that?" she asked, already knowing he did.

"Are you certain you haven't done this before?" he asked.

"No. But you did something similar to mine. I thought if I liked it as much as I did that you might be the same."

"I do like it. I like you."

He pushed her hands away and then cupped her breasts, fondling them. Then using his mouth, he worshipped them. Soon, Wynter writhed on the bed, raking her nails along his arms. His back.

He sat up and pushed his back against the pillows and pulled her into his lap, her back against his chest. His left arm came around and pinned her to him. She glanced down at his forearm, dark against her belly. He pushed her right leg away from her body and his free hand slid up and down her inner thigh, going a little higher each time. Then it went to the place that had begged for attention. His attention.

Donovan's finger moved lazily up the seam of her sex, causing shivers to ripple through her. As his lips nibbled on her neck, his finger pushed into her. Wynter gasped. He began stroking her, the sensual move causing her hips to rise. A second finger joined the first and moved inside her. She should be appalled. Horrified.

Instead, she was thrilled.

He increased the pressure and something shifted in her. Something unknown began to build. His fingers responded to the call within her.

"You are wet for me, love," he murmured.

Wynter could only nod. Words were beyond her at this point. She didn't know what was happening to her body as it moved toward a crescendo.

"More!" she cried. "More."

His fingers responded and, suddenly, it was as if an eruption occurred. Something exploded within her. She saw stars as she moved her hips against his hand and moaned. Wave after wave undulated through her, pushing her higher, harder, faster than ever before.

Finally, she collapsed. Not that she had anywhere to collapse. She merely went limp against him.

His hand slid up her body until he brought it to his lips. Donovan licked his fingers and sighed.

"You taste marvelous. Sweet, like honey."

His actions didn't shock her. They only made her want more.

Turning, she scooted down to his manhood, which was huge and throbbing.

"Now can I?" she asked and without waiting for his response, Wynter licked the tip of it.

Donovan groaned.

She did it again. And again. Oh, the noises he made. It made her feel powerful, to have so much control over a man like this. Encouraged by them, she opened her mouth and took him in. She had no idea what she was doing but instinct seemed to take over as she moved up and down, listening to him.

"Stop," he begged, pulling her from him. "Else I won't be able to satisfy you."

"You already have," she informed him. "I want you to feel as glorious as I did."

With a quick spin, she found herself under him, her back flat to the mattress as he hovered over her. He kissed her hungrily, as if he might never be satisfied. His fingers found her again, toying with her, teasing her, until she once more felt that sensation growing.

He broke the kiss. "This will hurt. Sting. I cannot help it. It always does the first time."

"I don't care," she said, knowing she needed something from him.

He parted her folds and pressed his rod against her. It slid inside her and she did feel some mild discomfort. He stopped.

"Are you all right?"

"Yes. I feel very full. It didn't hurt much."

"Good."

Slowly, he rocked against her. Wynter caught her breath.

"Oh!"

He grinned. "Oh, is right."

Donovan began moving and she moved against him. It was as if they were learning a new dance, starting slowly and then beginning to speed up as he pumped into her. She met every thrust, reveling in the new, wonderful feelings.

The fire inside her built again. He continued moving and kissing her and then she screamed into his mouth. He quickly pulled out from her and Wynter thought she had frightened him. Suddenly, something warm touched her belly and she looked down, seeing he spilled his seed there.

"So, that is how not to make a baby," she said.

"Yes."

He rose and came back with a basin of water and a cloth, gently bathing and then drying her.

Once he put it away, he returned and climbed into bed, gathering her into his arms.

"Has your curiosity been satisfied?" he asked.

"Most definitely," she purred. "What about you? Did I make it pleasant enough for you? It seemed—"

"You were perfect, Sunshine," he told her, kissing the top of her head. "Go to sleep. You need some rest."

Wynter didn't bother to argue with him. A lethargy enfolded her as much as his arms being around her. She closed her eyes, breathing in his masculine scent.

And slept.

⋙✕⋘

DONOVAN DETERMINED NOT to fall asleep. He was enjoying this moment too much. He pressed his cheek into Wynter's soft hair, which had come undone during their love play. That faint lemony scent that seemed to cling to her surrounded him. He relished her warm body against his.

And knew without a doubt that he had fallen hopelessly in love with her.

It wasn't merely because he had made love to her. He suspected it had happened before then. When, he couldn't say. Only that he wanted to go to bed every night with this woman in his arms and awaken every morning and still find her there. He understood what Miles and Wyatt had found with Emery and Meadow. Donovan knew he wanted to be a better man simply to make this woman proud of him.

When should he tell her?

It worried him to think she held such power over him. That he had been reduced to nothingness by her. He wondered if the act of making love had changed her mind about marriage in general—and to him in particular. He prayed it had. She had to want to be together after what they had just experienced.

Donovan smiled, thinking how Wynter had been worried that she would disappoint him due to her inexperience. If anything, it heightened his own. He looked forward to introducing her to so many ways to love and be loved.

If she would let him. If she would marry him.

Here, he had worried just a few days ago if she would accept his invitation to dine at Hillside for Christmas dinner. Now, he worried that she would reject his suit and leave him in abject misery.

He tried to push all negative thoughts aside and simply enjoy the moment. Wynter's nearness. How she had pleased him beyond measure.

Two hours later, she stirred and turned in his arms so she could face him.

"Could we try it again?" she asked hesitantly.

He shook his head. "No, you will be too sore."

She sniffed. "I have been more sore riding Onyx, especially when I was breaking him in."

Donovan grinned. "You think to compare what we did to riding your wild horse?"

She thought a moment. "It was, in a way, like riding. Free. Liberating. I had thought it more like a sensual dance but you may be right."

His grin widened into a smile. "I am always right. Remember, I am the one more experienced in these matters."

"You are," she agreed. "I might like to catch up to you a bit. Shall we try again?"

"Only because you are so insistent."

After another bout of lovemaking, even more fulfilling than the first time, he pressed a kiss to her brow.

"I must return you to your bed. If you fell asleep in mine, the gossip would never end."

He threw on his banyan and placed her chemise over her head before gathering up her clothes and folding them, placing them in her lap. Then he picked her up from the bed and padded down the hallway, returning her to her room, even helping her into her night rail and tucking her into bed, a pillow under her ankle.

"Thank you, Donovan," she said softly.

"For what?"

"For making me feel like a woman."

"You most certainly are and will always be a woman," he

assured her. "You are the most beautiful one I have ever seen, Sunshine."

"And I didn't do half-bad, did I?"

He kissed her mouth softly. "You were perfect, Wynter. Goodnight."

Donovan returned to his own chambers. It was a long time until sleep finally came.

# CHAPTER TWENTY

DONOVAN KNOCKED ON Wynter's door and she bid him come in. She had wondered what she would feel like when she next saw him. Her answer was a fluttering in her belly that threatened to explode at any moment. Her palms grew damp. Her mouth went dry. All she wanted to do was throw her arms around him and kiss him.

That wouldn't be happening, thanks to the maid in the room. She had come in Mrs. Preston's place to assist Wynter this morning and had just finished arranging her hair.

"Good morning, my lady," Donovan said cheerfully, his eyes sweeping over her appreciatively.

She turned her gaze downward, not wishing the maid to see the furious blush spilling across her cheeks.

"You may go," she told the servant.

"Oh, that's all right, my lady," the maid said. "I will stay and tidy up things for you while you are at breakfast."

"Thank you," she said, finally glancing up at Donovan.

"Are you ready to go downstairs?" he asked, his gaze warm.

"Yes, please."

He came to the dressing table where she sat and picked her up, carrying her from the room and down the hallway. The house was busy today. They passed two more servants so she knew there would be no ducking into an empty bedchamber on their way to breakfast.

"Did you sleep well?" she asked as he started down the stairs with her.

"Did you?"

She finally looked him in the eyes. "Actually, I did. I suppose I was rather weary after all the activity from yesterday."

"I hope you found all that activity enjoyable."

She bit her lip and then nodded. "Yes. Very much so."

They arrived at the breakfast room and greeted the two couples who were already there. Wynter saw the reclining chair had already been brought to the room for her. Next to it rested a cane.

"What is this?" she asked as Donovan set her down.

"I thought we had one and had Preston look for it. Perhaps by tomorrow, you might be able to put a bit of weight on your ankle. The cane would help you balance so you don't take another spill."

"What a marvelous idea," Meadow said. "Especially if you try and go to church tomorrow morning."

"No, you don't need to attempt to go to church," Donovan admonished. "I will stay home with you while the others go."

"Of course, I will attend church on Christmas morning," she corrected. "And you will go, as well. It is expected."

"Why?"

"You are the new duke," she said. "Everyone will want to meet you or at least get a glimpse of you. Besides, it is the Christmas season."

"I am not big on church," he said flatly.

"Don't let Finch hear you say that," Miles said, slathering jam on a toast point.

"You do need to go, Donovan," Wyatt agreed. "It's what a duke does."

Wynter saw the grimace on Donovan's face. She longed to reach for his hand and comfort him, knowing that he was still finding it hard to have replaced Sam.

"How is the weather this morning?" Emery asked.

Donovan looked relieved at the change of topic and said, "Though it is cold outside, no breeze is evident. The sun makes the morning seem warmer than it is. Are you ready to see the estate?"

"Today would be ideal," Emery said. "We plan to return home on Boxing Day so that only leaves today and Christmas to tour it."

"I am game if you are. I hope you don't mind if my steward and secretary join us," Donovan said. "Morris, my secretary, is set to replace the current steward so I am certain he will have a multitude of questions for you."

"That means we will be in charge of decorating Hillside," Meadow told Wynter and then looked to the others. "When you return, the place will be filled with greenery."

Donovan's look of panic caused Wynter to giggle.

"Is that something . . . I mean, should I have . . ." He looked gobsmacked.

"Mrs. Preston handled it as she always does," Meadow shared. "Dukes don't have to remember to send servants out to collect greenery. It is an annual tradition they are familiar with."

Donovan sighed. "Thank goodness."

"Donovan still doesn't understand how important he is," Wyatt observed. "Give him time. He'll become full of himself and be a pain to be around when he does."

"If we weren't at the table, I'd box your ears," Donovan said good-naturedly.

"I would be happy to referee any bouts," Miles volunteered.

"No fighting," Emery said firmly. "It is the Christmas season."

After breakfast, Emery and Miles went up to say goodbye to Ben and then returned downstairs. The three men and Emery left, leaving Wynter and Meadow to meet with Mrs. Preston. The three spoke of how and where the decorations should be placed and soon the house was buzzing as a beehive with activity everywhere.

Meadow rolled Wynter's chair to the foyer, where masses of

greenery had been brought inside. They directed the servants where to place holly, ivy, evergreen, hawthorns, and the hellebores, which were Wynter's favorite. She loved roses but especially these Christmas roses. They supervised the servants decorating the staircase and Meadow continued to wheel Wynter around to various rooms to oversee the decorating in each of them, especially in the dining room where the couples would dine tonight and on Christmas Day.

When the time came, the butler carried Wynter upstairs and a footman brought her reclining chair and she and Meadow monitored the other public rooms, even having bay leaves and laurel placed atop the pianoforte.

"Do you know what we need to make now?" Meadow asked, a conspiratorial smile on her lips.

"A kissing bough?" guessed Wynter.

"Oh, you are too clever," her new friend said. "Let's have Preston bring you back downstairs. That sitting room that had the large table in it would be a good place to work on it."

Downstairs again, the two women had evergreens and mistletoe brought to them and they began shaping the kissing bough. Meadow rang for a maid and asked for apples from the kitchens and for ribbon to be brought. Together, they worked the colorful red apples into the greenery and then used ribbon in red, silver, and gold to tie bows about it.

Wynter looked at the finished bough. "It is beautiful."

"I hope it will be put to good use," Meadow said. "I certainly plan to lure Wyatt to stand underneath it. Where should we hang it?"

"How about in the doorway to the drawing room?" she suggested. "The doors will have to be left open but I think that would be a good spot for it."

They had a footman bring a ladder and put him to work while they retired to a place by the fire.

"The others should be back soon," Meadow said.

The nursery governess appeared with Ben. "Oh, I thought

Her Grace would be here by now."

"I think she will arrive shortly. Might I hold the baby?" Meadow asked.

"Of course, Your Grace," the servant said, handing the baby over.

"Go and have a cup of tea," Wynter suggested. "Ben will be fine with us."

The governess thanked them and Wynter looked at Meadow's cheeks, now flushed with excitement.

"I cannot wait to hold our baby," Meadow declared.

"How are you feeling?" she asked.

"The same as usual. I barely rise from the bed and lean over to the chamber pot, retching as if there is no tomorrow. It ends quickly, however, and I rinse and wash and am as fit as a fiddle until the next morning."

Wynter watched Meadow give her finger to Ben. The baby put it in his mouth, gumming it. She smiled at the two of them.

"Would you like to hold him?"

"Me? Oh, I have never held a baby," she protested, not mentioning she delivered them and quickly handed them over to their mothers. "I wouldn't have any idea how to do so."

Meadow frowned. "Then it is time you did. You can practice on Ben so that by the time my babe comes, you will be an expert."

She took the wriggling baby, worried that she might drop him or do something wrong. Then a feeling of calm descended upon her. Wynter nestled Ben against her and he looked up at her and cooed.

She melted.

All of a sudden, a rush of feelings so strong, so powerful, flooded her. She realized more than anything that she wanted a baby.

*Donovan's baby.*

The feelings overwhelmed her. That thought shocked her.

What if Donovan had spilled his seed inside her last night?

She might have already had a babe growing in her belly.

She sighed. It was ridiculous to even think such things. She wasn't going to wed Donovan or any other man. She didn't need a child. If she pined for one, she would visit Emery or Meadow and play with their children.

Wynter dipped her head and kissed Ben's head. Yearning filled her. She pushed it aside.

"There's my sweetheart," Emery cooed, crossing the drawing room and holding her hands out.

Wynter passed the baby to his mother and then her gaze met Donovan's. Something raw and honest flooded his face and she knew he also wished for a child.

"The house looks wonderful," Miles said.

"I will second that," said Wyatt. "You two have done an outstanding job."

"We merely directed the servants," Meadow said. "They did all the work."

"My house looks lovely," Donovan told them. "Thank you."

"Your home," Wynter prompted. "Hillside is no longer a house, Donovan. The old duke and his cruel ways are gone. This is your home. Where your friends will gather and your family will always be."

He nodded. "You are right."

The others went to their rooms to bathe after a long day in the saddle. Meadow left with Wyatt, a mischievous look in her eyes. Wynter chose to stay in the drawing room and read.

She was still doing so when Donovan came to fetch her for dinner. The other four had already arrived and he allowed them to go first. He paused the chair in the doorway and looked up.

"I see a kissing bough was part of the decorations."

"Yes. Meadow is determined to get Wyatt under it." Wynter chuckled. "As if they needed a kissing bough."

He bent and brushed his lips softly against hers.

Rising, he said, "We should join the others. Perhaps we will take advantage of that bough later."

Later never occurred, much to her dismay. Dinner was full of conversation about the estate and ideas Emery had for several improvements. Afterward, they went to the drawing room and Donovan asked if she was well enough to play for them.

"I would be happy to do so," she told them, taking the cane she had hung on the back of the reclining chair and using it to push to her feet.

"No, it is not too soon," she told Donovan before he could act like a mother hen, though he did take her arm and guide her to the instrument.

Wynter played several pieces, two classical and three folk songs. Then she played a poignant ballad that had always moved her and as she struck the last chord, she saw Donovan brushing away a tear, obviously touched by the song.

He joined her on the bench. "That was very stirring."

"I am glad you enjoyed it."

The others came to stand nearby and Wynter played several more songs, which everyone sang along to.

Finally, Miles said, "It is getting late. We have a big day ahead of us and should turn in."

Donovan carried her from the drawing room, the others in step behind them. They all went up the stairs and since her bedchamber was the first, he opened the door and brought her inside. The same maid from this morning who had helped her dress was sitting, waiting for her.

"Ah, my lady. I hope you had a nice dinner. I'm here to help ready you for bed. I took the liberty of having a bath drawn for you. They just finished bringing up the last of the water."

"That is very thoughtful," Wynter said, knowing she would be busy for the next hour or more.

Donovan set her in the chair. He lifted her hand to his lips and kissed it.

"I wish you a goodnight. You haven't changed your mind about church?"

"No. We will all go," she said with determination.

"Then I will see you in the morning."

He left and she knew there would be no late night visit from him. Not that she had expected it. But a kiss or two would have been extremely nice.

Wynter gave herself over to the maid. An hour later, she tumbled into bed, exhausted.

And dreamed of Donovan.

# CHAPTER TWENTY-ONE

DONOVAN CARRIED WYNTER down for breakfast before they left to go to church. Her reclining chair had been placed at the foot of the stairs and she hung the cane she had been using in her room to get around on its back.

As he wheeled her into the breakfast room, she saw all of his guests already sitting in place.

"Good morning, everyone," she greeted. "What's this?" she asked as Donovan moved the chair up to the table.

Beside each place setting was a package wrapped in brown paper and tied with string.

"A little something from me to commemorate your visit," Donovan said.

"I did not know we would be exchanging presents," Miles said. "We never have in the past."

"Well, we were never dukes," Donovan replied cheerfully. "I suppose something good must come from having such a title hung about our necks."

He took his seat and said, "Well, go ahead. Open them. I even have one I bought for myself."

"You would," Wyatt teased.

Wynter untied the string around the soft package and pushed it aside. Unfolding the paper, she found a shawl of deep, rich blue. She brushed her fingers along it, finding it was of the softest wool.

"Oh, thank you so much, Donovan," she told him, her eyes

misting with tears.

"You are most welcome," he said quietly.

She looked and saw that Emery and Meadow also had received shawls. Both women wrapped them around their shoulders, exclaiming how much they loved the color and feel.

"It was a little hard selecting a gift for people I didn't know," Donovan admitted. "I went by the descriptions of you that I had received in letters. I hope you like the colors."

"You did an excellent job, Donovan," praised Emery. "And it is nice that we have become friends in such a short time."

"I also seem to be cold these days," Meadow added. "It may be because of the baby. I will keep my shawl with me and be able to stay warm now."

Miles and Wyatt expressed delight at their pipes and smoking tobacco. Donovan unwrapped his own gift, which matched theirs.

"Though none of us smokes, I always remember going to see one of the Turner brothers in their study and how pipe tobacco seemed to cling to the room," Donovan shared. "I thought perhaps it was time the three of us tried it." He turned and grinned at Wynter. "Of course, usually smoking is done over port after dinner. Since some women insist upon staying with the men for their after-dinner drinks, perhaps I should have bought everyone a pipe and tobacco."

They all laughed as footmen set down cups of tea and coffee and plates with their breakfast.

"Mrs. Preston suggested we not do our regular buffet this morning," Donovan told the group. "She thought a plated meal might help Cook and her scullery maids, especially since they are preparing for our Christmas dinner."

"What time will we dine?" Wyatt asked.

Donovan laughed. "It is always about the food with you. Mrs. Preston said two o'clock is the usual time. Once our meal concludes, then the servants will be given the remainder of the day off so that they might celebrate their own Christmas dinner in the servants' hall."

They finished breakfast and the carriage was brought around to convey them to church. Wynter allowed Donovan to carry her to the coach but told him she would walk with her cane to the church.

"How far is Wickley?" Meadow asked.

"About four miles from here," she said. "My father and I live three miles the other side of Wickley at Chesterfield."

They arrived and Wynter was grateful the cold day had turned out to be a sunny one. Last Christmas, it had been both cold and wet. She wondered how the weather was in London and hoped her father was enjoying the holiday with his brother.

The carriage door opened and she was the last to leave. Donovan swung her to the ground and handed her the cane, insisting she lean on him as they went inside. The church was decorated with greenery and lit with Advent candles.

"Go all the way to the front and the right. That is the pew reserved for the Duke of Haverhill," Wynter told him.

"I did go to church here once upon a time," he teased. "And I remember that is where my family sat."

Then a shadow crossed his face and she knew he must be thinking of previous Christmases when Sam and the duchess were still alive.

Once the service ended, the congregation spilled outside. In good weather, people would gather and stay for a good half-hour or more, catching up with friends. When cold, though, most left quickly. Today was an exception.

Because everyone was curious about the new Duke of Haverhill and his friends.

As they stepped outside the church, Reverend Ball was the first to greet them. Wynter introduced Donovan and his friends to the vicar.

"My, three dukes at my Christmas sermon!" the clergyman exclaimed. He turned to his wife, standing next to him. "Three dukes, Mrs. Ball. Three!"

"Yes, dear," she said politely. "We are happy to have you, Your Grace, and all your friends."

"Where is Lord Cheston today, my lady?" Reverend Ball asked Wynter.

"Papa went to London to spend the holiday with my uncle and his family."

The observant vicar said, "I see you are using a cane. Is that why you remained behind?"

Rather than go into a longer explanation, Wynter merely said, "Yes, it is. His Grace was gracious enough to invite me to dine with him and his friends so I wouldn't have to be alone on Christmas."

"It was good meeting you, Reverend Ball," Donovan said, trying to ease them along.

Reluctantly, the clergyman said farewell. Wynter then led Donovan and the others down a long line, introducing them to the people of Wickley and beyond.

When they reached Lord and Lady Amos, the viscount said, "It is good to have you in the area, Your Grace. I hope that you will be attending our annual ball on Twelfth Night."

"I look forward to it," Donovan said, surprising her since she hadn't been certain he would attend.

Finally, they had met everyone and entered Donovan's carriage, soon finding themselves back at Hillside. They went to the drawing room and the nursery governess brought Ben down. Miles immediately took the baby, cradling and talking to him. It warmed Wynter's heart to see such a large man go soft in the presence of his son.

She looked around at this group and thought how much a part of them she felt, even after such a short acquaintance. Wynter could picture years down the line, celebrating together with them as their families grew. She tried to forget such a thought, knowing she would never be a wife of a Turner Terror. That she merely was a visitor for this brief interlude. They would continue to meet throughout the years, their friendships growing, expanding as more Terrors took on wives.

This kind of thinking was dangerous. She didn't want to wed. She knew Donovan must in order to have an heir. This would be her only time to be included with these men and women. Yes, she fully intended to remain friends with Emery and Meadow and hoped to see them in London next Season and the Seasons beyond that. But intimate gatherings such as this one at Hillside this year would be a thing of the past.

Wynter needed to look to her future.

Ben went from Miles to Emery and then to Meadow, who passed the baby to Wynter.

"Are you sure you don't want to hold him, Wyatt?" she asked.

"Not a chance," Wyatt said. "I might break him and then Miles would snap me in two. Once I have my own and figure out what to do, I will be more comfortable. For now, I am happy to merely watch and learn."

Wynter cradled Ben in her arms, resting her cheek against his head. He smelled heavenly and again a yearning filled her. Perhaps Papa might consider taking on a ward and she could have a hand in raising a boy or girl.

She glanced up and saw Donovan gazing at her, a wistful smile upon his face.

"You look right with a babe in your arms," he said.

Ignoring his comment, she asked, "Would you care to take a turn with Ben?"

He shook his head. "I belong to Wyatt's school of thought. Until I have my own, I don't want to be responsible for any damages caused by my holding one."

"It's a baby, for goodness' sake, Donovan," Emery said. "You can't harm him."

Preston announced dinner at that moment and Wynter gave Ben back to his nursery governess and then allowed Donovan to roll her to the dining room, where all the household staff had gathered, holding cups of wassail in their hands.

Donovan took a cup and addressed them. "I want to thank all of you for being a part of Hillside. I know I was not the man expected to be Haverhill but I am grateful to each one of you for your service and I hope I will be a good employer. Cheers!"

The servants all called out, "Cheers!" and drank up. Donovan then told them to see Mr. Morris, who had something for them in the foyer.

As the majority filed out, leaving only Preston and several footmen behind, she asked, "Does he have their Christmas gifts? Papa and I usually give our servants a new pair of shoes each year."

"I came so late to Hillside that I thought it best to give them each a crown. That way, they can buy whatever they need. Or want."

"That is very generous of you, Donovan," Miles said.

"It is the least I could do."

Christmas dinner began in earnest then. They had both boar's head and roasted goose and so many side dishes, Wynter lost count. She ate until she thought she might burst.

Donovan called for Cook to come and he thanked her for making his first Christmas home in many years such a special one.

"Go now and celebrate yourself," he said. "Take the footmen with you. All this can be cleared away later. We will retire to the drawing room."

"Thank you, Your Grace," Cook said. "It is a pleasure to have you in the household again."

The six returned to the drawing room and then Emery said, "I think I am going to take a nap while Ben does."

"I will join you," Miles said. "If I stayed here, I would probably go to sleep anyway after such a large meal."

Meadow yawned. "I wasn't sleepy until you started talking about it but a nap sounds lovely. Coming, Wyatt?"

He caught her hand and kissed it. "I go where you do, my love."

The two couples left and Donovan said, "Would you like me

to carry you upstairs for a nap, as well?"

"No, I'm not a bit sleepy," she told him, not wanting to be separated from him since their time together would soon end.

He hesitated a moment and then said, "I was thinking of going back to Wickley and wondered if you might wish to accompany me."

"Whatever for?" she asked, knowing all the shops were closed because of it being Christmas.

"I thought I would visit Sam's grave. I haven't been and today seemed an appropriate time to do so."

At the mention of Sam, a lump grew in Wynter's throat. "Of course."

"With the servants now making merry, we will have to take a cart instead of being driven by coach."

"I don't mind." She tightened her shawl about her. "My new gift will keep me warm."

He lifted her into his arms and stopped for his greatcoat once they reached downstairs.

"We should go out the front door," he said. "If we cut through the kitchens, a servant might see us."

They went to the stables and he placed her on a bale of hay while he went and prepared the horse and cart. She knew how difficult this would be for him to finally see Sam's grave and was glad to be with him to offer her support.

Returning to the village again, he steered the horse toward the graveyard that sat next to the church and then stopped the cart.

"You will have to direct me from here."

She supposed the duke hadn't allowed Donovan to attend his mother's funeral, probably thinking the boy too young. She still didn't understand why Donovan had been sent away after his mother's death, though. He had told her his father blamed him for the duchess' accident—but Wynter had no idea what had occurred. Even in all the years she had known Sam, her friend had not mentioned the cause of his mother's death.

"Go to the left," she told him, directing him as close as they could get the cart.

He helped her down and she used the cane as she led him to the Haverhill plots, coming to stand by Sam's grave.

They stood in silence for several minutes. Donovan's fingers found hers, lacing through them and holding fast.

Finally, he spoke. "I am sorry I did not get to see the man you had become, Sam. I know you were a good one and taken far too soon. I hope you would like how I turned out. In everything I have done, I always tried to model myself after you, thinking how you would handle a situation. I have failed more times than I have succeeded but I will continue to try and be the best man I can be. The best duke I can be."

Donovan dropped to his knees, his hand still holding hers, his free one going to rest on the gravestone. He bowed his head and remained that way for several minutes, a sob bursting from him. Wynter saw his shoulders shake and squeezed his hand, knowing nothing could really comfort him from having been ripped from his beloved brother for so many years.

He rose, wiping the tears away with the back of his hand. "Shall we go?"

"Wouldn't you like to see your mother's grave?" she asked softly.

Pain filled his face. "Yes. I would."

Wynter led him to her plot, one she had visited on numerous occasions over the years with Sam.

Donovan knelt. "I should have thought to bring flowers."

"You can the next time you come."

He went to the headstone and touched it, reverently fingering the inscription with her name and the dates of her birth and death.

"Oh, Mama, how I miss you," he said, his voice breaking.

Wynter's heart went out to him, having the two people he loved the most torn from him.

A long sigh came out and Donovan stood again. He came to

her and kissed her cheek. "Thank you for coming."

"I wanted to be here for you," she told him.

They returned to the cart and he set her on the bench before coming around and taking up the reins. They were quiet the entire way back to Hillside. She didn't mind, knowing he was lost in thoughts from the past.

Sitting on the same bale of hay, she waited while he put away the cart and cared for the horse. Then he joined her and took her hand again.

She wanted to hold this man's hand forever.

"How did the duchess die?" Wynter asked. "You said Haverhill blamed you for her death."

"Sam never mentioned it to you?" he asked, surprise in his voice.

"No. I know Sam loved her a great deal and we visited her grave several times but he never told me what happened."

"Haverhill had Sam as his heir apparent. He didn't need a wife or a second son. Because of that, Mama and I spent a great deal of time together. Something she loved to do was walk. She loved being outdoors, in nature, and passed that love along to me."

His fingers tightened on hers. "That last time we took a long walk, we heard an animal keening. Mama always had a soft spot for animals and she raced ahead. A poacher had set a trap and a doe had been caught up in it." He paused. "There were two traps. Mama stepped into the second one."

"Oh! How dreadful." A sick feeling filled her.

"It was," he agreed grimly. "I was only a boy and not strong enough to free her. I ran as fast as I could for help. Two footmen managed to spring the trap but she was bleeding profusely." His jaw tightened. "Even then, she was pleading for them to help the doe."

"Did they?" she asked, her voice small.

"No. Haverhill crushed its neck with his boot."

Tears sprang to her eyes. "Oh, Donovan."

"It gets worse. Mama was brought home and the doctor said he needed to amputate a portion of the leg to save her life. The duke refused."

"What? Why?"

Donovan's mouth turned cruel. "He didn't want half a woman. He would rather her be buried with two legs than live without part of one."

Nausea filled her.

"She lost a great deal of blood. A fever set in and spiked. She became delirious. And then there was the tremendous pain. Death seemed a blessing after watching her suffer so."

Wynter couldn't fathom such cruelty. She had thought the duke to be a terrible person but had no idea what utter cruelty he had been capable of.

"Of course, Haverhill blamed me. It didn't help that I was her spitting image. He told me Mama had spoiled me and that my selfishness had cost him a wife. He didn't want any reminders of her—and that included me."

"So, that is why you were sent away?"

Donovan nodded, looking so glum that she nearly burst into tears.

Though she knew it was dangerous—knew that she shouldn't do—Wynter still kissed him.

It was a sweet kiss. One that offered comfort.

Until he deepened it.

His kiss would be the most magical thing she remembered about her time spent at Hillside. Donovan was a man she would never forget. Years from now, when she lay dying, her thoughts would turn to this man. This moment. This kiss.

She shivered from the desire rippling through her.

Immediately, he broke the kiss. "You are cold," he said. "We must get you inside."

He swept her into his arms and carried her back into the house, all the way to her bedchamber, where he placed her upon the bed.

"I must return to Chesterfield tomorrow," she told him, refusing to meet his gaze. "Papa is coming back from London. I want to be there to greet him. The servants will also be returning."

"The others are leaving after luncheon tomorrow. Will you stay until then?" he asked, kissing her fingers.

"All right," she agreed.

"I will take you home myself," he promised.

# CHAPTER TWENTY-TWO

"W E MUST MAKE plans to see one another when the Season comes," Emery said as they waited in the foyer for the carriages to come around and the luggage to be placed inside them.

"I would like that," Wynter told her new friend.

"I don't know how much of it we will attend," Wyatt said. "After all, the only reason I went last year was to claim a bride." He twined his fingers with Meadow's. "Now that I have a wife—and one who is expecting our child—I don't really care for going to London."

"Oh, we must go for a brief bit, Wyatt," Meadow protested. "If only for me to get to see Emery and Wynter. And Ben." She smiled at the baby, held as usual by Miles.

"If you insist, my love," Wyatt said. "Perhaps we will do a short Season like last year."

"I find the whole thing utterly boring," Miles said. "I only went last year to show off Emery and let her see a bit of London. If we never went back, I would be happy."

"Speak for yourself," Emery said, laughing. "I enjoyed the parties and the balls. And this year, I can dance more now that Ben isn't in my belly. I do enjoy the museums and lectures, too."

"Oh, so do I," Wynter declared. "I go to as many lectures as I can. And the theatre. I greatly admire how the actors bring their characters to life."

"Then Meadow and I will come for a month or two," Wyatt gave in, "merely to let you ladies visit with one another. Then it is back to country life for us."

"I will invite myself now to Amberwood," Wynter told him. "I have had such fun playing with Ben and I will do the same with your little one."

"You are always welcomed, Wynter," Meadow said. "Perhaps next Christmas, we can host everyone at Amberwood."

"Or you are all welcomed to come to Wildwood," Miles said. "We could rotate sharing the holidays."

Wynter swallowed, a dull feeling coming over her. She adored these women, the first she had ever been close to, and enjoyed being around their husbands. But she couldn't be near Donovan and the wife he would eventually bring to these gatherings.

"Christmas is a year off," she said brightly. "No sense in making plans for it now."

"I agree," Donovan said, the first time he had spoken.

"The carriages are here, Your Grace," Preston informed them.

They all went out to the drive, saying their farewells as both luggage and servants were loaded into the vehicles. Wynter kissed Ben's sweet head one last time, knowing he would grow so much between now and the next time she saw him in the spring. She longed to hold him again but was afraid she might dissolve into tears if she did so.

The two couples climbed into the first carriage, Miles again taking charge of Ben. Both coaches pulled away and Wynter waved, smiling so hard her cheeks hurt.

The last carriage pulled up, one belonging to Donovan. She saw her trunk already attached to it.

"I suppose it is our turn now," she said, using the cane to move toward the carriage. "I have to thank you for use of the cane. I may use it another day or so but then I think I will be fine. After all, I need to exercise my ankle a bit to be ready to dance at

Lord and Lady Amos' ball."

He lifted her over the stairs, straight into the carriage. She took a seat and he climbed in, sitting next to her. She had thought he would sit across from her and had sat more toward the middle. He was so large that he took up much of the seat.

"Am I sitting on your skirts? I'm sorry." He lifted slightly and pulled her gown from beneath him but didn't bother to scoot over any.

She shifted slightly in order to have more room for herself. He still sat far too close to her. She could smell the spice of his cologne, which made her pulse pound. That made her think of the things they had done in his bed and she grew hot all over.

"Thank you for allowing me to accompany you home," he said. "I am eager to see your father."

"Papa may not be home until mid-afternoon," she warned.

"I will wait if need be."

"That isn't necessary. If he is not home by the time we reach Chesterfield, perhaps you would like to come for tea tomorrow."

"I would rather wait. I have something important to discuss with him."

A sinking feeling filled her.

"Donovan," she began, but he held up a hand.

"You said not to offer for you out of guilt. I promised not to offer for you while we were still in my bed."

He took her hand. Wynter tried to pry it away. That only made him hold it more firmly.

She gritted her teeth. "I didn't want you to offer for me at all. I do not have any plans of marrying you or anyone else. Ever," she added emphatically. "So, there is no need to see Papa. No need for him to know what we were up to during his absence. I would prefer he never know."

"We are going to wed, Wynter," Donovan said stubbornly.

"See!" she cried. "That is the very reason I do not want a husband. I have a mind of my own and I enjoy using it very much. I don't want to marry you. You insist we do. If I actually gave in and did wed you, you would be pigheaded and start ordering me about. I won't have it, Donovan. I won't."

Wynter jerked her hand from his and crossed her arms protectively.

"I don't mean to bully you," he said, his tone soft. "But I want you as my duchess, Wynter. We are good together. Even you must admit that."

"Sam and I were good together. We were friends. I enjoy the company of men. I enjoy your company, Donovan. But it doesn't mean I have to marry you."

"You are being obstinate," he stated. "You will come around."

"There you go again," she accused. "Don't think you will tell Papa we are going to wed because he won't make me do anything I don't want to do. I do not want to marry you, Donovan. I beg you, don't cause trouble between us. Don't drag Papa into this mess. Let us be happy we are friendly neighbors and get along so well."

"It is not enough," he said stubbornly. "I want you as my wife, Wynter. It is you—or no other."

She glared at him. "Do not give me ultimatums. I am not responsible if you choose not to wed. But you must, Donovan. You need an heir. A son to pass Hillside along to. It is what Sam would want."

"*You* are what I want."

She would have to hurt him to make him see reason. She bit her lip, wishing it didn't have to be this way.

"But I do not want you."

Wynter allowed her words to hang in the air. She dare not look at him for fear of bursting into tears.

Because she did want him. With all her heart and soul. More than anything she would ever want.

"I do not want to be your mother all over again," she added, setting the stage for what she would tell him. For what would hurt him.

"What do you mean?" he asked quickly. "What does Mama have to do with any of this?"

Wynter braced herself and faced him. "Do you know the only time I ever saw my father cry? It was fifteen years ago. I came upon him in his study, weeping so hard I thought he had learned he was dying. I, too, began sobbing, begging him not to die. Not to leave me. He finally understood what I meant and took me in his lap, assuring me that he was as healthy as an ox and would live to a ripe old age."

She paused. "I asked him why he was so sad. Papa told me that he had lost someone he loved."

Donovan flinched.

"Years later, I learned of the animosity between your father and mine. How my father was smitten with your mother from the first moment he saw her. How he loved her. Worshipped her. Wanted to marry her."

He looked at her dumbly. "Then why didn't they wed?"

"Because she was a woman," Wynter said bitterly. "A dutiful daughter. *Her* father didn't care that she was in love with a good man. Papa was only a viscount at that time. Haverhill was a duke—and he wanted her, too. Your grandfather said his own daughter had no say in whom she would wed. That she was to make the match *he* wanted for her.

"And that was a match with the Duke of Haverhill. He was a duke. That would make her a duchess. Haverhill was wealthy. He held properties across England. He made my papa, a lowly viscount, look like a pauper. Don't you see, Donovan? Your own mother had no control over her fate. No say in the most important decision of her life. She was coerced into marrying a man she cared nothing for, leaving the man she loved—one who loved her—behind."

Wynter shook her head sadly. "It is because of your mother's story that I have chosen I will never wed. I will never be under a man's thumb. I will never, ever be told what to do. I will live my life the way I choose. I will find my own happiness without a man."

Donovan looked at her helplessly. "I would never do that to you, Wynter."

"You say that now—but even in offering for me, you are giving me no choice. No, Donovan, I refuse to marry you. Papa knows what it is like to lose the woman he loved. He has promised never to force me to do anything, especially when it comes to marriage. I must keep my independence. I must stay true to myself."

The carriage rolled to a stop and the door opened.

"Please don't come inside," she said quietly. "Don't try to contact me. I won't keep you from a friendship with Papa but I cannot be your friend, Donovan. I will see your cane returned to you in a few days."

Wynter stood and, using the cane to lean upon, allowed the footman to hand her down as another unloaded her trunk from the carriage. She went inside, deliberately keeping her eyes straight ahead, knowing if she turned back she might give in.

"Ah, my lady, how was your holiday?" their housekeeper asked. She indicated the cane. "I heard about your mishap from young Will."

"I am fine," she reassured the older woman. "I would like to rest now, though. Is Papa home?"

"Not yet, my lady."

"I will be in my sitting room," she said.

Slowly, she made her way there and closed the door. She refused to allow the tears to come. They would do no good and only make her father question her about what had gone on between her and Donovan. Instead, she went to her pianoforte, which always was a source of comfort. Lifting the cover, she folded it back.

And struck the keys with a vengeance.

DONOVAN FINALLY ROSE from his bed after a sleepless night. He still reeled from what Wynter had revealed to him about his mother. He thought back to the many times he had gone to see her in her sitting room, slipping in to surprise her. Too many times, before she was aware of his presence, he had noted the air of sadness that seemed to blanket her. Once he shouted "surprise", though, she would turn and be all smiles, ready for fun and games with him.

Now he knew that during those moments, she had contemplated her life and how unhappy she was, married to a controlling yet distant man who had kept her from the love of her life. What had it been like for her, knowing Lord Cheston was but a few miles away, living his life without her while she did the same?

He shook his head in sorrow. His mother had kept it to herself. Donovan had never heard one mention of Cheston. To think she had been forced to wed Haverhill turned his stomach sour. No wonder Wynter was so opposed to having the same thing done to her. Yet he was nothing like his father. He reflected on how he had become insistent that Wynter wed him. He didn't give her room for argument. Donovan must have seemed as dictatorial to her as Haverhill had been, as well as Donovan's maternal grandfather. He had never known this grandfather since he had died when Sam was a toddler. Donovan knew *ton* matches were made for wealth, power, and position. His grandfather hadn't lived long enough to enjoy the prestige of having a duke as a son-in-law, while Mama had spent the rest of her life stuck with Haverhill. She had probably welcomed her death, knowing she would finally be free from her husband's reach.

How could he convince Wynter that he wasn't like his father? That he hadn't meant to back her into a corner and give her no choice?

He couldn't. It was that simple. He had seen the look on her face. Heard her words. She wanted nothing to do with him. If anything, Wynter was more stubborn than he was. Donovan believed once her mind was made up—especially about rejecting him—she wouldn't change it.

Anguish filled him. He had watched Wyatt and Miles and saw how love had changed their lives. How they were happier than he had ever seen them, fulfilling new destinies with women they cherished by their sides. He would never have that. He would be as other bachelors of Polite Society, marrying a woman he could tolerate long enough to get a son or two off her. They would have their own interests. Go their separate ways.

And he would never have the love and companionship he so desired.

Donovan needed to clear his head. He couldn't do it here, with Wynter only a few miles away. He decided to go to London. Everything at Hillside was running smoothly. Augustus Bagley had told him of two warehouses he owned near the London Dockyards. It was time for him to see them and meet with those who managed these businesses for him.

Ringing for Hall, he told the valet they were immediately heading for London and that he should pack.

"I can dress myself for once. You see to the packing. I'll inform Preston that we are going."

"For how long, Your Grace?" Hall asked. "So I know how much you will need."

"A week or more, I think."

Perhaps by then, the need to race to Chesterfield might be flushed from his system.

Or not.

Donovan shaved and dressed and went to the breakfast room, where he informed Preston of his plans and asked that the carriage be readied at once since he wished to leave after breakfast.

"Right away, Your Grace," the butler said.

Morris sat in his usual spot now that Donovan's guests were gone.

"What is in London that needs your attention?" he asked.

"I wish to visit the warehouses Bagley mentioned. I don't

want to neglect my interests in London. You have things well in hand here which gives me the luxury to do so. In fact, once winter ends and the roads are better, I plan to visit all my estates and see the shape they are in."

"Would you like me to accompany you, Your Grace?" Morris asked.

"I am not sure. Let us see how things are progressing at Hillside before we make that decision. You might want to be here for the spring planting this first time."

They spoke of a few other estate matters and then Morris asked how his visitors' stay had gone.

"Very well. They are longtime friends of mine from our school days. We also attended university and served in the military together as officers. Both recently came into their titles so I had many questions for them. You heard the comments the Duchess of Winslow made when we toured Hillside. She was good enough to compose a list of her suggestions. I left it on my desk. Why don't you look over it and we can discuss the items on it once I return?"

"I will do that." Morris grew thoughtful. "I did enjoy meeting Her Grace. Interesting, a woman running an estate."

"Her Grace is a most capable woman," Donovan replied. "My friend is lucky to have wed her."

"Did Lady Wynter enjoy meeting your friends?"

He supposed Morris had heard of Wynter's mishap and that she also had stayed at Hillside.

"Lady Wynter got along famously with both ladies. I believe they have plans to meet up during the coming Season."

He liked that his tone sounded even. That none of the hurt and anguish which filled him even saying Wynter's name seemed apparent.

"Will you also go for the Season, Your Grace?"

"Possibly," he said. "I don't want to have firm plans just yet. Seeing my properties is more of a priority to me. I can't travel to them and do the Season at the same time."

"You could always partake in the Season at its beginning and then as summer comes, journey to your various holdings."

The thought of being in London at the same as Wynter tore at his gut. He would have to see her dancing with other men. Perhaps even dine with her since they now had mutual friends.

"As I said, I don't wish to make any decisions now," he said brusquely, turning his attention to his food.

They finished the meal in silence.

Once through, Preston notified him that his trunk had been loaded onto the carriage. He accompanied the butler into the foyer and Preston helped Donovan slip into his greatcoat.

"Do you know when you might return to Hillside, Your Grace?" he asked.

"I will be gone a week. Perhaps longer."

"You do remember Lord and Lady Amos' ball on Twelfth Night?" the butler prodded.

Not bothering to hide his exasperation, he replied, "I do. I'll either attend it or I won't. If I have not returned by the day of the ball, have Morris send my regrets to them."

Preston nodded. "Of course, Your Grace. Have a pleasant journey."

Outside, he saw Hall already sitting next to his driver, Peterson.

"To the London docks and my warehouses," he ordered before climbing into the carriage.

Peterson took off and Donovan settled against the cushions, leaning against the side of the vehicle. With his lack of sleep and the movement of the carriage, he soon fell asleep.

# CHAPTER TWENTY-THREE

M ELANCHOLY FILLED WYNTER as she rode back to the stables and handed Onyx off to a groom. She had come from delivering another baby, something which usually brought such pleasure to her. This time, she had stared at the new mother, her baby daughter at her breast, and felt such bitter longing that she had fought to keep from screaming at the top of her lungs to let out the rage inside her.

Thankfully, she managed to keep a smile on her face as she let the father back inside the cottage and gave the mother instructions for the next few days. She also promised to bring around food in a day or two and check on mother and child as was her custom. Her smile evaporated once she set foot outside the cottage.

She wanted a baby. No, not just any baby.

*She wanted Donovan's baby.*

That could never happen. Wynter had pushed him away as hard as she could—and he had stayed away as she suggested. It had been eleven days since she had last seen him. Sat beside him. Inhaled his spiced cologne. Talked to him. Laughed with him.

Obviously, she had done a good job. So good, in fact, that she had heard he journeyed to London and rang in the new year there. Had he found another woman already to replace her? As far as her heart went, it would always be his. She could dance and laugh her way through *ton* events but the shattered pieces of her heart would never mend. Worse, she would have to watch him with other ladies as they fawned over him. Eventually, he would choose one of them to be his duchess. Why, she would even have to be polite to the woman since they would be neighbors. They would see one another in the village and at church and at events such as tonight's Twelfth Night ball.

Wynter didn't even want to go. She suspected Donovan wouldn't attend it. What would be the point of going if she couldn't at least gain a glimpse of him? Even if he had returned from London in time to attend the ball, she had no idea how she could behave in a merry fashion when all she wanted to do was fling herself into his arms. She couldn't. She had made her bed and would now have to lie in it. She reminded herself that she never wanted a man in charge of her destiny. That she was the sole person who made decisions for herself. That should bring satisfaction enough.

Instead, extreme loneliness crept into her soul.

Had she been wrong? Could she live with him trying to dominate her? Should she abandon her commitment to herself because she was so desperately in love with him?

Love. Such an odd thing. Wynter had never experienced it before. She had seen how it broke her father in two. Then she had witnessed it between Emery and Miles. Meadow and Wyatt.

And for a brief moment, she thought it flared between her and Donovan.

It hadn't. At least on his part. If he had loved her, he would have fought for her. Torn down her walls. Let nothing she said or did stop them from being together. Committing to one another.

But hadn't he tried to change her mind about marriage? Oh, she was so confused. She hoped he wouldn't be present tonight. That she could lose herself in the dances and pretend that the gaiety surrounding her amused her. She would hope in the new year she could forget him, if only for a little while.

She entered the house through the kitchens and Cook shouted, "She's back! Take the bath water up now." To Wynter, she scolded, "My lady, where have you been? Your maid has been beside herself. You've a ball to attend."

"I know, Cook. I was delivering a baby. Some things simply cannot wait, ball or no ball."

Sighing, Wynter left the kitchen, servants scurrying past her, toting buckets of water up the stairs and to her bedchamber. Her maid immediately took charge, stripping Wynter's clothes from her and forcing her into the bath, scrubbing her.

"We can't have you smelling like a horse at the ball, my lady."

Adding more of the lemon oil to the bathwater, the maid stirred it and took up her brush again.

"We won't have time to wash your hair and let it dry. I will have to style it simply," the maid said. "I've laid out the silver and blue gown for you. And your sapphire earrings."

"Thank you," she said perfunctorily.

An hour later, Wynter was dressed and her hair arranged in a simple chignon. She joined her father downstairs.

"Sorry I am running late, Papa. A baby decided it had to come today and the midwife is off visiting her sister."

He kissed her cheek. "You look lovely, my dear. Fear not, I wouldn't have left without you though we may be a few minutes late."

"Lord Amos won't mind. Lady Amos will notice but she is too polite to say anything about it."

"The carriage is waiting."

They rode to the Amos' estate, going through Wickley and then turning east for three miles. The village looked deserted and Wynter knew a majority of its inhabitants would be at tonight's ball. Lord Amos always extended an invitation to all his neighbors and tenants, as well as those who lived in Wickley.

No receiving line was evident, as Lord Amos despised them and said all those invited knew everyone in attendance. She bid Papa goodbye and found Lady Amos.

"Good evening, my lady. I think you have outdone yourself

with this year's decorations but, then again, I seem to say that to you every year."

"Oh, thank you, Lady Wynter. I do so enjoy supervising the servants as they set up for our ball. Don't you think it looks like a winter wonderland?"

"Very much so. Thank you again for having Papa and me."

"I heard you recently sprained your ankle. I hope that will not interfere with you dancing."

It was something she knew she wouldn't be able to keep from others. Gossip was a mainstay not only in London but the countryside, as well.

"It has healed nicely. Thank you for asking."

"I heard you spent Christmas with Haverhill. We barely spoke to him after church on Christmas Day. What is he like?"

*A marvelous kisser. Even more marvelous in bed.*

"He is most impressive, my lady. More reserved than his brother, Lord Pickford."

"I always did think that strange, Haverhill sending a son away like that. I suppose he didn't like the boy for some reason. Hopefully, the new duke has grown into a decent fellow."

Wynter leaped to Donovan's defense. "Oh, he is very charming, Lady Amos. Handsome and intelligent."

The viscountess eyed her. "Hmm. They say he entertained friends over Christmas. Two dukes. Is that correct?"

"Yes, the Dukes of Winslow and Amesbury and their wives. Both couples were most amiable."

"Hmm," the viscountess repeated. "I hadn't thought dukes or duchesses to be amiable. There's no need for them to be so because of who they are."

"They were most agreeable," she emphasized. "As was His Grace."

Lady Amos sniffed. "Well, he isn't here yet. I do wonder if he is coming or not. I heard he went to London."

"I am certain he will be here if he can," Wynter said. "If you will excuse me."

Normally, she was able to tolerate Lady Amos' snobbery in small doses. Tonight, however, she wanted to avoid her hostess for the rest of the evening.

A stranger approached her. "Might I introduce myself, Lady Wynter? I am Morris from Hillside."

She brightened. "Oh, His Grace mentioned you several times during my stay. He was quite gleeful to have stolen you away from Mr. Bagley. I am sorry we did not meet while I was there recovering from my sprained ankle."

"Are you recovered fully?" he asked.

"I believe I am."

"Then would you join me in the first dance?" He glanced toward the musicians, who were now tuning their instruments.

"I would be delighted, Mr. Morris."

Since it was a country ball, no programmes had been passed out. She would be free to dance—or not—as she chose. Everyone lined up, the women in one line facing the men opposite them, and the music began.

As she whirled about, Wynter promised herself not to look for Donovan—and not to be disappointed if he did not show.

⟫⟫⟩⟨⟨⟨

DONOVAN SAID, "ENOUGH, Hall. You have fussed over me far too long. I am going to be late to my neighbor's ball as it is."

The valet finished tying the cravat. "Now you may go, Your Grace. This is your first appearance in the neighborhood beyond church. Everyone will be curious about you. I want you to look your absolute best."

He took a deep breath. "Well, thank you, Hall. I appreciate your efforts."

Going downstairs, Preston placed the greatcoat about Donovan. "Have a wonderful evening, Your Grace."

In the carriage, he thought it would be anything but wonderful.

Donovan was downright miserable.

He had spent time in London merely to avoid being at Hillside. Once he had seen his warehouses and met with Bagley for good measure, he could easily have returned several days ago. He hadn't because he didn't want to rush to Chesterfield and beg forgiveness from Wynter.

Pride was in the way of doing so.

He had never displayed pride of any kind. Not when he excelled in school. Not when he graduated with highest honors from university. Never in the army because all his thoughts had been for keeping his men safe.

But pride now oozed through him. He admitted that Wynter had hurt him. Deeply. He had been miserable without her. He told himself he wouldn't return early from London and go see her. Though he could have called upon Lord Cheston and spent time with the earl, Donovan had chosen instead to stay far away so that he wouldn't be tempted.

He could do without her. It was important he prove that to himself.

In London, though, he had failed miserably in that regard. Going to a nearby tavern when he left the docks one evening, he drank heavily. The barmaid, a comely wench, had made it obvious she was his for the asking.

Donovan had kept silent.

He didn't want the buxom brunette. He didn't want any woman. Wynter had ruined him for all others. He recalled her sweet curves. The breathy noises she made as he touched her. Her enthusiasm in learning about the art of lovemaking. How her body had responded to his and his to hers. He had never made love to a woman the way he had Wynter.

Thoughts of her, even now, brought him to his knees.

That was why it was important he show up at this neighbor's ball. Because she would be there. He had to learn to go out into society and act as if he didn't care a thing for her. It was especially important that he didn't constantly look for her. Donovan would be polite if their paths crossed. Polite and distant. He would keep their conversation to a minimum. Else he'd drag her from the room and kiss her as if there were no tomorrow.

For him, there would be no tomorrows with Wynter.

The coach ground to a halt and Richards opened the door.

"Have a nice evening, Your Grace," the footman said.

Donovan mumbled and exited the carriage, hurrying through the cold into the Amos house. He was late and knew it. It would be important to make his apologies.

A footman took his greatcoat and Donovan followed the sound of the music.

Entering the ballroom, he saw dancers in full swing. He glanced across the floor and couldn't help but spy Wynter. She wore a gown of silver and blue, which complemented her hair and made her stand out from the entire crowd.

"Good evening, Your Grace," said a voice to his left.

Turning, he found Lord Cheston at his elbow.

"Good evening, my lord."

"I must thank you for taking care of my daughter during my absence. She told me she had taken a spill from Onyx and twisted her ankle. That you came along and brought her back to Hillside."

"With Lady Wynter having dismissed your servants, I couldn't take her back to an empty household. It was no trouble having her at Hillside. I had friends visiting for the holiday."

"Yes, she mentioned them. She seems quite fond of the two ladies." The earl smiled, looking pleased.

Donovan looked at Cheston with new eyes now, knowing his mother had loved this man.

"There you are!" a voice cried.

Glancing up, Donovan saw a couple in their forties approaching him and recognized them from their brief meeting after the Christmas church service.

"Ah, Lord and Lady Amos." He took the viscountess' hand

and kissed it and then shook with the viscount.

"We are delighted you could make it, Your Grace," the viscount said.

"Yes. We heard you had gone to London," Lady Amos said. "It was very good of you to make it home in time to come to our little ball."

He forced a smile. "I see nothing small about it, my lady. It looks as if you spent many hours decorating the ballroom. I am happy to be here and meet more of my new neighbors."

"Lady Wynter said you were charming. She was right," the viscountess purred. "Perhaps we could dance the next number, Your Grace. I would love to tell you all about our neighborhood."

Donovan groaned inwardly but nodded. "I would be honored, my lady."

The music ended and Lady Amos led him to the dance floor. As they danced a reel, he continually caught sight of Wynter. It was obvious she loved to dance. Her face was flushed with happiness and her eyes sparkled. She was grace personified. He wanted her more than anything.

But he refused to ask her to dance.

He partnered with several women, eventually finding himself with Mrs. Ball, the vicar's plump wife.

"We have missed you at church, Your Grace," she told him.

"I had business in London," he said vaguely, his eyes again searching for Wynter.

The music ended and Mrs. Ball said, "I thought you and Lady Wynter looked splendid together. You are meant to be, Your Grace."

He shook his head. "No, Mrs. Ball, you are mistaken."

She studied him a moment. "Don't be so proud that it leads to your downfall, Your Grace." She curtseyed. "Good evening."

He watched the woman walk away, his gut twisting.

"There you are, Your Grace," Lord Amos said, throwing an arm about Donovan. "Come and eat. The musicians are taking a short break. Lady Amos has a beautiful buffet laid out."

"Of course," he said, accompanying the viscount to another room.

They went through the buffet together and Amos insisted Donovan join him at his table. It was full of the nobility of the neighborhood and the viscount went around it, introducing him to all present.

At the far end sat Wynter and her father. His heart lurched.

"I believe you already know Lord Cheston and his daughter, Lady Wynter."

"Yes, we met the first day I arrived," Donovan managed to say. "You are looking lovely tonight, my lady," he said evenly.

"Thank you, Your Grace," she replied, giving him a tight smile and then turning to speak to the baron on her right.

Donovan and his host took a seat and Amos began a discussion with those at the table, which Donovan tuned out. He was deliberate in his movements, not turning his head once in Wynter's direction. Yet he was more than aware of her, hearing the tinkle of her laughter waft through the air.

A footman arrived at the table with a small, silver tray. "A message for you, Lord Cheston."

Donovan watched the earl open it. His lips thinned.

"It is as I suspected. My brother has fallen ill again and is calling for me. He had been in poor health before I visited at Christmas but had seemed to rally. My nephew says his father is sick again and wishes me to visit and raise his spirits."

The earl stood. "I fear I must leave our happy gathering."

Wynter rose. "I will go with you, Papa."

"No, my dear. Stay and enjoy yourself. As you know, Edward has done this before. If things grow dire, I will send for you. For now, I will leave for London."

Donovan spoke up. "I will see Lady Wynter safely home, Lord Cheston."

"Thank you, Your Grace. That sets my mind at ease."

Cheston went and kissed his daughter's cheek. "I will write to you in a day or so and let you know how Edward is doing."

"Goodbye, Papa," she said. "Safe travels."

Once the earl had gone, conversation resumed at the table. Wynter ignored him, as Donovan suspected she would.

But she wouldn't be able to ignore him during the carriage ride home tonight. It might be his last chance with her.

Donovan planned to make the most of it.

# CHAPTER TWENTY-FOUR

Wynter sensed the smoldering looks Donovan tossed her way. She was unhappy he had spoken up so quickly, offering to see her home. He was the last man she wanted to be alone with in a dark carriage. She would have to make sure he understood her position hadn't changed and she wouldn't accept him courting her in any way.

Not that she could see a man like Donovan courting any woman. He was too important. Too large. Too full of himself, thinking he was always right and telling others what to do. He would assume any woman would fall at his feet merely because he was a duke.

She refused to be any woman. She was her own woman. One who didn't need a man. Especially one like Donovan.

At least she kept telling herself that.

Wynter returned to the ballroom and danced every dance. She didn't want time to think. Instead, she lost herself in the rhythm of the music. Or tried to. Her thoughts continued to be filled with one man, though.

Finally, she decided to ask him to dance since he hadn't made any move in her direction. The last number was to be a waltz and she wanted to be in his arms.

She found him and smiled pleasantly. "Have you enjoyed your evening, Your Grace?"

"Moderately so," he replied. "I am not much for social occasions but it has been nice to make the acquaintance of others in the neighborhood."

"Since you are escorting me home, would you care to partner for the final number? If we are together, it will be easier to leave in the crush that ensues."

One brow arched. "Is that so?"

"Dance with me," she ordered.

He offered his arm and she placed her hand atop it, feeling the solid strength that lay under his evening wear.

The musicians began to play and Wynter found herself twirled about the floor by a master. It shouldn't have surprised her. Donovan did everything well. She didn't look him the eyes, though. She averted her gaze and looked out across the floor, at the dizzying colors that flew by. When the music ended, a small part of her withered as he released his hold on her.

They joined the queue of those waiting to get their cloaks and coats but a servant brought theirs directly to them. She knew Lady Amos had seen to that and nodded at the viscountess in appreciation as they left the manor house.

The air was cold and crisp as they moved to Donovan's ducal carriage. Lamps had been lit and hung on both sides of the carriage to help light the way home.

"Peterson, we are taking Lady Wynter to Chesterfield first," Donovan called up.

"Yes, Your Grace."

Richards opened the door for them and the footman handed Wynter up. She sat on the bench facing forward, wondering which seat Donovan would take.

He sat beside her.

She tried to tamp down the thrill that moved through her. It would only be for five miles or so and then she would be home. She would remain quiet and doubted he would try to force any conversation upon her. The inside of the coach was dark so she wouldn't have to look at him.

The vehicle went into motion and she closed her eyes. Suddenly, Donovan lifted one hand from Wynter's lap.

"I love being near you," he began and then fell silent.

She held her breath.

Finally, he spoke. "I thought I wouldn't say anything as we drove to Chesterfield because I was afraid I would foolishly offer for you again—and that you would turn me down." He sighed. "I have missed you so much, Wynter. I have thought about nothing but you. And my mother."

She heard his anguish.

"Mama always tried to put on a happy face around me but even at a young age, I could see that Haverhill made her miserable. To learn after all these years why she was perpetually sad almost broke me."

He paused and she sensed he looked at her.

"I could never do that to you. I know you think I am obstinate and unyielding but I want to change. For you. I love you, Wynter. I would never try to make you into something you don't want to be. I went about asking you to marry me in all the wrong way. Forgive my clumsiness. I have been at war for too long and don't always remember the social niceties I was taught at Turner Academy."

Donovan squeezed her fingers. "All I know is that I cannot be the duke I am meant to be if you are not by my side. Yes, I want you as a wife. As the mother to my children. More importantly, though, I need you to be my partner. To teach me. To be with me. To share in my victories and help me understand myself the times I fail."

His voice broke. "Please, Wynter. Tell me that we still have a chance. That I don't have to live in misery or fear for the rest of my days. That I can live with you. With love."

Something crumbled inside her. The walls she had erected to keep Donovan out came crashing down.

"I love you, Donovan. So much it hurts," she admitted. "I have been wretchedly unhappy ever since we parted."

Her free hand went to his face and she stroked it. "I know

you are a good man. That you will make for an excellent duke. You will be the best of husbands and a wonderful father to our children."

He sucked in a breath. "Have I heard you say what I have longed to hear or are my ears playing tricks upon me?"

"I am yours, Donovan. I always have been. I will forever be yours. I love you."

"Wynter!" He gasped her name as if he were a man dying of thirst and she was the water that would save him.

His hands framed her face and his lips met hers in a searing kiss. The magic was still there between them. An electricity sparked, igniting flames of desire. Donovan pulled her into his lap, kissing her, kissing her, over and over. She clung to him, tears cascading down her cheeks as she drank her fill of him. He did the same, his tongue finding hers, mating with it, as his hands stroked her throat.

"I love you," he murmured against her lips.

"I love you more," she said, feeling his smile against her mouth.

"More," he said. "I want more. I can never have enough of you, Wynter. You are a balm to my soul."

His searing kiss branded her. Wynter began to chuckle.

"What?" he asked, his lips hovering over hers.

"I was a fool to think I could live without you. Without your kiss," she told him.

"Yes, you were," he cheerfully agreed.

She swatted him playfully and he devoured her mouth again.

Suddenly, the carriage lurched forward as they moved down a hill. It caused them to break the kiss.

"What is—"

Wynter never finished her sentence. The vehicle rocked again and suddenly tilted to the side, causing them both to fall onto the floor. She screamed as the carriage began turning in the air, slamming her against the side. She struck her cheek and felt it tear, searing pain shooting through her.

The door flew open and Donovan fell out part way. Wynter reached for him as the carriage crashed into something, coming to a stop on its side.

"Donovan!" she shrieked, falling onto him.

He grunted and she quickly scrambled off him as she tried to get her bearings.

The vehicle shifted some and she held her breath. Then she heard a voice above her.

"Are you all right?"

It was Richards, the footman.

"No," she shouted, looking at Donovan. He lay in the open doorway, pinned to the ground. His left arm was partially hidden by the carriage itself.

"His Grace is trapped. Do something!"

"Cover yourself, my lady. I'm going to break the window."

Wynter turned away from the window, trying to shield a moaning Donovan as the footman broke the glass. She felt pieces of it rain down upon them. When it stopped she looked up and saw Richards had dropped himself into the carriage's interior.

"I'll get you out, Your Grace," he said.

"Get . . . her out . . . first."

Wynter tugged on him and he screamed in pain. Panic filled her.

"How do we free him?" she asked frantically as Richards joined her.

"Get . . . her out," Donovan said through gritted teeth.

Richards hesitated a moment and then said, "Come, my lady. You'll only be in the way. Let me boost you up and you can crawl through where the window was."

"I don't want to leave you," she told Donovan, her voice rising in hysteria.

"Go," he commanded, his voice sounding weak and far away.

"Donovan," she said, her voice breaking.

"Come, Lady Wynter," Richards said forcefully, lifting her elbow and pushing her away from Donovan and boosting her toward the opening.

She reached out and grabbed the ledge of the frame, allowing Richards to push her out. Glancing back, she could see Donovan's arm trapped underneath the carriage. Her weight only added to his discomfort so she scrambled down.

Moments later, Richards joined her, a worried look in his eyes.

"We won't be able to lift the carriage. We need to go for help."

"I cannot leave him!" she said, her voice panicked. "You go. Get the driver, too. I will stay with him."

"Peterson is dead," the footman said. "The axle broke, causing the wheel to come off. If we hadn't been going down a hill, it might have been all right. But we crashed into a tree. Peterson was thrown from the vehicle. I think he broke his neck."

"The duke will die if we don't do something soon," she insisted, pulling herself together. "Are any of the horses still left?"

"I don't know."

They both went to the front of the carriage. Two of the horses had escaped from their harnesses. Two others lay dead. The final pair struggled to move.

"We must free these two," Wynter said. "I will ride to the village for the doctor and try to rouse others to come and help. We are almost at Chesterfield. You go there and bring back as many men as you can, along with a cart and blankets. We will take His Grace there once he is freed."

"Yes, my lady."

She hurried to the other side of the carriage. Though she couldn't see Donovan, she shouted, "Richards and I are going for help. We will be back soon."

*No reply.*

Wynter prayed Donovan had passed out from the pain and that he wasn't dead. He couldn't be. Not when they had finally found each other.

She returned to the horses and helped Richards free the first one. Hiking up her gown, she had him lift her onto it, bareback. Clinging to the horse's mane, she rode off, returning to Wickley. She wouldn't think of anything but saving Donovan. He would live. He would live. He would live. She said the words over and over as she rode to the doctor's house.

Leaping from the horse's back, she hurried to the door and banged upon it, shouting, "Wake up! Wake up!"

Moments later, the door flew open. Dr. Freeman stood there in his shirt sleeves.

"You must come at once. Haverhill's carriage crashed. His arm is trapped beneath it. We need as many men as possible to come and help free him."

Mrs. Freeman appeared. "I will help you knock on doors. We just arrived home from the ball as did so many others. Hopefully, they are not asleep."

Wynter ran from house to house, gathering men to come with her. Horses were saddled and she was surprised to find the carriage horse she had ridden still standing in front of the Freemans' cottage. With sheer determination, she clasped the horse's mane and threw her leg over, nudging it. The horse took off and she once again took up the same prayer in her mind.

*Let him live. Let him live. Oh, please, God in heaven, let him live . . .*

She reached the site of the accident. Some of the men she had summoned were already there, along with Richards and a few footmen and grooms who had come from Chesterfield. Together, they shouted in unison, Miraculously, they lifted the carriage a few feet, straining to hold it in place. Richards scrambled beneath it and latched on to Donovan, dragging him out and away. Once they were clear, the volunteers released the carriage and it slammed back to the ground.

Wynter ran to him and fell to her knees as Dr. Freeman began examining him. As he held a lantern up, she saw Donovan's mangled forearm and knew it couldn't be saved.

"Can you save his life?" she asked, her eyes blurring with

tears.

"I will do my best, my lady."

The cart from Chesterfield arrived and Wynter had them spread out a blanket. Several men lifted Donovan, who was unconscious, and placed him in the center of it. Then they held the edges and carried him to the cart. She climbed into the back of the vehicle, cradling his head, murmuring soothing things as she stroked his hair.

When she looked up, they had arrived at Chesterfield. She barked orders at the butler and Donovan was carried inside to her father's bedchamber. It had the largest bed in the house. She was afraid Donovan, with his height, wouldn't fit comfortably into any of the others.

Their housekeeper appeared with a stack of clean cloths. Water had been boiled and was brought up, as were herbs.

"You should leave, my lady," Dr. Freeman said. "I cannot save the arm. I will have to amputate it below the elbow."

"I am not going anywhere," she said firmly. "He is my betrothed. I will stay."

Dr. Freeman nodded. "Of course. Then hold his hand. Try to comfort him the best you can."

The physician cut away Donovan's clothes from the chest up, tossing the material aside. He began ordering several of the men who had come upstairs to hold Donovan down, warning he might be unconscious now but that he was bound to awaken when the sawing began.

"It is imperative that you hold him so he cannot move. His life depends upon it," the doctor instructed.

Wynter knelt beside the bed, her hands holding Donovan's. She closed her eyes and kissed it, willing her strength to flow into him.

A piercing scream erupted from him and she could feel him trying to buck. Thank God they had so many men to keep him in place.

"Be strong, my love," she said over and over until he had

once more passed out from the pain.

Quickly, the doctor cleaned the limb as the blood flowed freely and then asked the men to hold Donovan again.

"I must cauterize it to give him any chance to survive," he explained.

Wynter would never forget his screams. The smell of burning flesh. The awful silence of those who watched.

Finally, Dr. Freeman finished by pouring brandy over the seared flesh and then bandaged it as the others silently filed from the bedchamber.

"What now?" she asked, her throat swelling with grief.

"We wait. For fever. For infection. And we fight."

"He is a fighter," she assured the physician. "He is a warrior."

"His Grace is in excellent physical condition," the doctor noted. "It will help." He shook his head. "I was new to practicing medicine when Her Grace had her accident in the forest. I should have fought the duke harder. Instead, I bowed to his wishes and she died." He took a deep breath. "I will not let the same thing happen to her son."

Dr. Freeman then said, "I must attend to your cheek, my lady."

"What?" Wynter put a hand to her face, which only now seemed to be filled with pain.

"Sit here," he instructed.

She did and he cleaned the slice with both water and more of the brandy, which made her feel as if her cheek had been lit afire. The physician then stitched up her cut before soaking a cloth in brandy and cleaning her face again.

"We must also watch you for infection, Lady Wynter. Even the smallest of cuts can result in death."

"I will stay by his side," she said firmly.

The physician nodded. "We will stay together."

And so the vigil began.

# Chapter Twenty-Five

T HE FEVER CAME with a fury in Donovan. Thankfully, Wynter never got one. She only felt a dull ache in her cheek after the initial heat and throbbing. Dr. Freeman warned her she would bear a scar. How could she complain about that when Donovan had lost part of a limb?

Three days had passed, with Wynter never leaving his side. Their housekeeper and maids brought her clean cloths to bathe him with. His body, already like a furnace when he was healthy, now raged with heat. Wynter constantly dipped a cloth into basins of water and stroked his face. His chest. His other arm.

Sometimes, he would kick at the bedclothes, murmuring things she didn't understand. Other times he trembled with cold and she covered him to his chin. She asked for feverfew to be brewed in hot water and made into a tea for him, trying to use it to lower his fever. Though never fully conscious, Wynter would hold a cup to his lips and somehow, by instinct, Donovan would drink.

Dr. Freeman came twice a day, changing the bandages on his arm and checking Wynter's cheek.

"You are healing nicely, my lady," he told her now as his eyes went to the duke, still and prone in the bed.

"That is good news," she said, not actually feeling it good or bad. She was indifferent to everything except Donovan.

The physician said, "His fever seems less today. Keep up what you are doing, my lady."

"I will," she promised, knowing she would go to the ends of the earth to help Donovan recover. They had already wasted enough time as it was. She was ready to start her life with this man as her husband. Her lover. Her friend.

As Dr. Freeman left, a maid came in and handed her a letter. Wynter thanked her and saw it was from her father. She had received one yesterday that told her Uncle Edward was recovering from his latest health crisis. Her father expected to return to Chesterfield in another two days.

She opened this letter and found things to be much the same. Wynter knew she should write her father about what had happened to her and Donovan but couldn't muster the energy to do so. It would involve leaving the sickroom and she refused to be parted from Donovan for even a minute.

His fever rose again as day turned into night, a steady pattern that Dr. Freeman had predicted. Each night, though, it increased less. Hopefully, by tomorrow morning, his fever would break.

She accepted a tray from a maid and only picked at the food before setting it aside. She closed her eyes to rest them for a moment.

Something woke her.

Wynter's eyes flew open. The candle burned low. She glanced to the bed and saw Donovan's eyes open and close several times. She sat up, taking his hand in hers.

Pressing a kiss to it, she said, "How do you feel?" With her other hand she felt his brow and noted it was cool. Finally.

"Where am I?" he croaked, his eyes finally remaining open.

"You are at Chesterfield," she said soothingly. "There was an accident."

"Accident?" he echoed.

"Yes, when we were coming home from Lord Amos' ball. You were injured," she gently explained. "But you are fine now." She held his hand against her uninjured cheek.

"I hurt."

"I know, my love. But you are alive. That is what is important."

Donovan frowned. "What happened to you?"

Self-consciously, she touched her bandaged cheek. "I hit against something sharp in the carriage as it flipped onto its side. An axle broke, causing the wheel to come off. We were coming down a hill and your driver lost control, crashing into a tree."

He winced. "How is Peterson?"

She swallowed. "Dead, I'm afraid."

He fell silent. She didn't say anything more, waiting for a cue from him, not really knowing how to tell him that Dr. Freeman had removed part of his arm.

Donovan began to struggle, trying to sit up. His brow furrowed in confusion. He looked down and his eyes widened. She gripped his hand.

"What . . . what . . . where . . . oh, God."

"You are fine," she said firmly. "Your arm was pinned by the weight of the carriage. Richards helped pull you to safety."

"My arm . . ." His voice trailed off.

"Dr. Freeman had to remove part of it," she said, eyeing him steadily. "No infection set in, however. You are going to make a full recovery."

"What?" he roared. "He did what?"

Donovan jerked his hand from hers. It went to his other side, where his hand and forearm were missing.

"How dare he!" he roared. "He has mutilated me!"

Wynter heard the anger and shock in his voice.

"Dr. Freeman saved your life, Donovan."

She tried to take his hand again but he pushed her away.

"I am missing half my arm!" he shouted. "I have no hand. No hand," he echoed, anguish obvious in his voice.

She stood. "I know you are surprised. Hurt."

He laughed bitterly. "You know nothing. You still have both your arms. Get out!" he raged. "This was your doing. Get out!"

Wynter felt as if she had been slapped. She backed away.

"I knew you would be upset. Even angry. But you are wrong to take this out on me. It was no one's fault, Donovan. No one could have predicted the axle would break and what that would lead to." She paused. "At least you are alive. It is more than Sam can say."

He snorted. "Sam died a whole man. I am only part of one."

Anger filled her. "That is where you are wrong. You are hurting, both physically and emotionally. Yes, you are sad. Frustrated. Of course, you will grieve the loss of a part of you. But you—"

"I said leave. Now. I don't want to see you. I don't want to see anyone."

Donovan reached for the basin of water resting upon the table next to him. He picked it up and flung it through the air. It hit the wall with a loud crash, shattering.

Wynter fled the room.

THE NEXT TWO days were almost more than Wynter could bear. Donovan raged as a lunatic in the madhouse whenever anyone tried to enter the bedchamber, especially Dr. Freeman or her. The physician told Wynter it was a natural reaction.

"His Grace woke up to a different world, one he doesn't understand," the kindly doctor told her. "He is shocked. Angry. Disgruntled. He will experience sadness. Despair. Eventually, he will come around."

"It can't happen soon enough for me," she declared.

What she didn't tell the physician was how horrible Donovan had treated her when she did remain by his bedside. His ugly words clung to her, making Wynter feel horrible and small.

"Let us go in and see him together. We will bolster one another."

"All right," she agreed reluctantly.

As they entered the bedchamber, Donovan sat glumly, staring out in the distance.

"How are you today, Your Grace?" Dr. Freeman asked.

"How do you think? I cannot sleep. I have no appetite. Oh, and I have no arm, thanks to the two of you."

"You are only missing part of your arm, Your Grace. Your feelings of anger will pass," the doctor said reassuringly.

"Will the pain also pass?" demanded Donovan.

"Describe it to me, please."

Donovan frowned. "It varies. It begins as a shooting, stabbing pain. Where my arm used to be. Sometimes it throbs or burns."

"I have heard patients experience these phantom pains."

"They are real," Donovan insisted. "And they only grow worse."

"Once you are up and about, you will get past them," Dr. Freeman said.

"Up and doing what, might I ask?" he sneered. "I cannot ride. Dress myself. I can't even dance. Not that I would want to. I don't care about anything, Doctor."

"These feelings will change, Your Grace, as you adjust to your new situation. True, you are experiencing anxiety now. Your appetite will eventually pick up. I can give you something to help you sleep."

"I don't want anything from you," Donovan said stubbornly. "I am already self-conscious enough about missing an arm. The rest of my life will be a challenge."

"I will leave you now," Dr. Freeman said. "My lady."

The physician exited the room and Wynter turned to Donovan.

"He is right, you know. You are in a world of pain now. A world unfamiliar to you. You will get through this. We will get through this. Together."

"We?" he asked, his lips snarling. "There is no *we*, Wynter."

"What . . . what do you mean?" she asked. "I thought when we came home from the ball that things were finally settled between us. I told Dr. Freeman you were my betrothed."

His eyes narrowed. "You were wrong. We are not going to wed. Ever."

"Donovan," she pleaded. "Why are you being this way?"

"Why?" he growled. "Perhaps it is because I am half a man now. I wouldn't want the vivacious Lady Wynter Day to be saddled with a mere shadow of a man."

"You are wrong," she told him. "I love you. I—"

"Well, I certainly don't love you," he stated.

Her eyes filled with tears. "You don't mean that."

"I do. In fact, I am tired of looking upon you. Seeing you hover over me." He tossed the covers back with his only hand. "I want to leave. Now."

"But Dr. Freeman said—"

"I don't care what that fool has said. I want to be home. I am going to Hillside. Have my carriage . . ."

He stopped, realization dawning upon him that he no longer had a carriage.

"Have yours readied for me."

"Father has it. He is still in London with my uncle but he is expected later today."

"When he arrives, I want use of it, do you understand?"

"No," she said truthfully. "I don't. Why are you pushing me away, Donovan? We love one another despite what you say. We can face this together."

"I no longer want to marry you, Wynter."

"Why not? I suppose it is because of this."

She ripped the bandage from her face and marched up to the bed, leaning over so he had a good look at her face.

"Is this why you no longer wish to wed me, Your Grace? Because my beauty is marred? I suppose I am no longer your perfect woman. You might be missing a piece of your arm but you are a duke. Nothing will be said of it. I, on the other hand, will have people judge me left and right because my face is the first thing they will see."

Wynter stared hard at him, seeing the anguish fill his face. She had yet to see what her cheek looked like. She knew, though, it had to be bad. It hurt too much and the slice had been too deep. Dr. Freeman had to take a good number of stitches to close the wound.

"Look at me, Donovan, and tell me this is the reason you choose not to marry me."

His jaw tightened and he averted his glance. "Yes. It is the reason, Wynter. I don't love you anymore. Are you satisfied?"

"I said look at me!" She paused until he did so. "Say it again to my face. That I am too ugly to become your duchess. That you don't love me."

His gaze finally met hers and he shrugged. "You have said so yourself." His look was cold and distant and he said, "Your scar is hideous. I could never make love to a woman who looked like you, much less make you my duchess."

"I don't believe this," a voice said.

She turned, relief sweeping through her as Miles and Wyatt walked through the doorway. She had written to them, begging them to come, hoping that if Donovan saw his friends, his depression would lift.

Donovan glared at her. "Why did you send for these two?"

"Because we are your friends," Miles said solemnly.

"We want to be here with you," Wyatt added.

"Did you come in a carriage?" Donovan demanded.

"We did," Miles said, frowning at the question.

"Then take me to Hillside. I want to quit this place and never return."

The two men looked to Wynter.

"Take him," she said. She moved toward them and quietly said, "Try to talk some sense into him," before exiting the room.

Immediately, she went to her sitting room. She didn't believe him for a second. Donovan wasn't a man who was only interested in surface beauty. He had been just as attracted to her mind as he had been to her looks. He'd lied to her.

And she wasn't having it.

If anyone could tear down the walls her beloved had erected about him, it was William Finchley.

Wynter thought back to when Donovan had spoken of his special friendship with Finch, the only Terror who had remained in England as the other four went away to war. She thought of the wisdom Finch had possessed for a boy his age and the advice he had imparted to Donovan the very first day the pair had met. How Finch had been the one to always calm Donovan and keep him from trouble. How Finch had taught Donovan to be considerate of all, not just those of the ruling class.

Her hopes rested on bringing Finch here. She prayed he would come. That somehow, Finch might work a miracle where others had failed.

Seating herself at the desk, she removed a fresh page of parchment—and wrote to a man she had never met.

*Dear Reverend Finchley,*

*We have not been introduced but I know all about the Turner Terrors and your membership in this tightknit group. I have met Miles and Wyatt and now count them and their wives among my friends.*

*I am in love with Donovan. He was also in love with me, at least until a recent carriage accident. His arm was trapped under the weight of the vehicle and our local doctor had to amputate just below Donovan's elbow. After a bout with fever, he is now recovering and extremely bitter. He claims he no longer loves me. He isn't interested in anything. I fear for his health as well as his sanity.*

*I know the two of you were especially close and I beg for you to come at once to Hillside and offer him the guidance he needs. Wyatt and Miles are here now but Donovan has grown depressed and I fear they will not be able to talk any sense into him.*

*Please come, Reverend Finchley. He needs you more than he would ever admit. He may have lost part of an arm but it is as if he has lost the best of himself. I refuse to give up on him—or on us. I pray that you will visit and help Donovan find himself again.*

*Sincerely,*
*Lady Wynter Day*
*Chesterfield, Surrey*

Wynter sealed and addressed the letter and took it downstairs. She went to the stables and gave it to her favorite groom, charging him to deliver it straightaway. Returning to the house, she prayed this friend of Donovan's would come and help the man she loved find himself again.

# CHAPTER TWENTY-SIX

DONOVAN REACHED FOR the crystal decanter and didn't bother pouring the remaining liquid into his tumbler. Instead, he drank straight from the bottle, draining it. He tossed it aside, too drunk to stand and cross the room to get another bottle. He had come home wearing only Lord Cheston's banyan and asked for Preston to see to its return. He now wore his own banyan over a pair of loose trousers and hadn't changed from them in the three days he had been back at Hillside.

He hated himself. He hated everything about his life now.

Most of all, he hated lying to Wynter.

It hurt him to see the gash on her face. But it didn't take away from her beauty. Nothing could ever do that. She was—and forever would be—his ideal woman. The scar that would form would be a slight physical imperfection but it did not diminish her radiance. Still, he had told her the scar was the reason he no longer desired her.

The truth was he doubted she desired him. She was clinging to the idea of the old Donovan, the one who was whole. If anything, Wynter was as loyal as any Terror. She couldn't possibly want him anymore but she would never reject him, especially now that he was crippled.

It didn't matter. If he couldn't have her, he would never wed. Let the dukedom go to whichever relative was next in line. He didn't care for the land or the wealth or the position. He didn't care for anything anymore.

A knock sounded on the study's door. He certainly didn't care for any company and so he refused to acknowledge it. When he had arrived home, he thanked Miles and Wyatt for coming and then told them he was not inviting them inside and that they could leave. Wyatt had begun to argue with him heatedly, while Miles merely stood and observed. When it had almost come to blows, Miles stepped between them and told Wyatt they were leaving. Though Wyatt protested, Miles had always been the leader among them. What he said, went.

His friends climbed back into their carriage without even a goodbye.

In the three days that followed, Donovan had sunk into a deep depression. He had barely eaten. Only slept for short bouts. He had allowed Dr. Freeman admittance for a short while each day so that the physician could change Donovan's bandages. He had seen too many men die of their injuries at war; long, lingering, painful deaths. He didn't want any kind of infection to set in, which was why he tolerated Freeman's presence for brief spells.

The rest of the time, he sat in his study and drank. Heavily. He had always enjoyed a few drinks, especially the wines in Spain during the war, but for three days, he drank himself blind. If he was too drunk to think, then Wynter couldn't haunt him.

The knock sounded louder. Still, Donovan ignored it. Finally, it became a pounding.

"Go away!" he shouted, though the words came out so slurred that he doubted anyone would understand them.

Collapsing into the chair behind his desk, he shut his eyes and willed whatever servant was there to leave him in peace.

A sudden crashing noise startled him and he sprang from the chair, swaying, dizzy from the drink and moving too fast.

Finch stood there, glaring at him.

Donovan hadn't seen his old friend for several years now, not since he and the other Terrors had left for war after university.

Finch hadn't changed much. He still wore his blond hair a little longer than was fashionable, which probably caused a stir among some of the more conservative members of his parish. His eyes, always bright blue, now bored into Donovan.

Without a word, Finch strode toward him and grabbed hold, pulling and then dragging Donovan from the room. He sputtered, first with indignity and then because of the ache where his missing limb had once been now burned with pain.

"What are you doing?" he roared—or rather slurred—the effects of the copious amounts of brandy he had consumed affecting his speech.

Finch took him past a wide-eyed Preston. A jaw-dropped Mrs. Preston. A shocked Hall.

"Have a bath readied for His Grace!" Finch shouted. "He will need one once I am done with him."

Before Donovan could protest, they were out the front door. The cold January wind struck him full force. Immediately, he tried to draw inward to protect himself from it. Worse, a light dusting of snow covered the ground and Finch paraded him through it, despite the fact that Donovan's feet were bare.

"Where are we going?" he demanded, seeing the black carriage sitting in front of Hillside. He doubted vicars had the funds to possess so fine a carriage, much less the horseflesh that stood harnessed to it.

Finch turned them toward the stables.

"Ah, so you want to ride my new estate," Donovan said. "Well, you will have to do it on your own. I can't mount a horse in my condition, much less hold the reins in one hand."

That brought Finch to a stop. "Do you mean you shouldn't mount a horse because you are blindingly drunk? That is the only condition I concede. As for holding your reins in one hand, you always have been reckless. Perhaps even more so than Wyatt. I suppose you will tell me that you can no longer dance either."

"I can't," he said stubbornly.

Finch spat upon the ground. "The last I witnessed, dancing

was done with two feet and two legs. No arms necessary. Or in your case, brains."

Once more, his friend latched on to Donovan and maneuvered him through the snow. His feet now burned with the cold, hurting even more than his phantom limb did. He wanted to protest but his lips were already numb from the cold. The thin banyan offered precious little protection against the fierce wind.

They reached the stable area and Finch released him. Donovan wobbled as Finch lifted his foot and slammed his boot in a trough, cracking the thin veneer of ice which had formed on its surface. Before Donovan could question why, Finch physically lifted him in the air.

And dropped him into the trough.

The icy water enveloped him and Donovan shouted an obscenity, trying to scramble up and finding himself trying to push against a hand which was no longer there to support him.

Then Finch latched on to Donovan's hair and forced his head back under water. He struggled, whipping his body back and forth. Finch released him and he broke through to the surface, gasping for air which only burned his lungs as it entered.

"Get out," Finch ordered, stepping away.

Donovan fought to do so, knowing if he asked for help that Finch might very well dunk him again. Rising, he stepped one bare foot over the trough and brought the other behind him.

"What the bloody hell did you do that for?" he demanded.

"If I'm going to talk to you, I need you sober. It was the fastest way to accomplish that."

The freezing water might have done a small part in sobering Donovan up but the rest of Finch's actions had him shivering. His teeth chattered so loudly it sounded as if he snapped at his friend. Which he should.

Without a word, he stormed back to the house, Finch keeping pace next to him.

"I suppose Miles wrote and begged you to come. No, more likely it was Wyatt that rode to Marbury and insisted you make an appearance at Hillside."

"I can barely understand a word coming from you," Finch replied nonchalantly. "The chattering is affecting your speech too much. Kindly shut up, Donovan."

Finch strode ahead and opened the door, leaving Donovan to trail after him.

In the foyer, Finch said, "Bathe, shave, and dress His Grace. Pour a good amount of coffee down him as you do so."

"Yes, Vicar," Hall said meekly.

"I want you gone," Donovan ordered.

Ignoring the comment, Finch said, "I will be waiting to talk with you once you are decently dressed and you no longer smell like a distillery. I think I'll check out your library while I am waiting." He looked to a footman. "Take me there."

The two left as Hall and Preston rushed to a swaying Donovan. He probably passed out from cold or fatigue because the next thing he knew, he was in a bath. A very hot bath. Scalding, in fact. But he didn't care. He never wanted to be as cold again as he was earlier. Donovan wiggled his toes and felt relief sweep through him. At least he wouldn't lose his feet to frostbite.

He saw his clothes had been removed, as well as the bandages around his stump. God, how he hated that word. Hated what had happened. Hated that he was now only a shadow of his former self.

Donovan leaned his neck against the tub's edge and closed his eyes as Hall scrubbed him. He was too tired to fight. Too tired to think.

Except about Wynter.

He saw her clearly and moaned.

"Be careful," Preston said. "Don't hurt His Grace."

His hurt wasn't physical, though. It was deep within his heart.

The two men finished bathing him. Preston held him upright as Hall toweled off Donovan. He was placed in a chair and kept his eyes closed as his face was lathered and Hall shaved him.

He heard Dr. Freeman's voice and knew the physician had

come for his daily visit. Donovan was too weary to argue with the man. He could feel fresh linen being wound about his stump. Freeman said something to him about things looking extremely well. Then clothes started being placed on him. Still, he was too exhausted to open his eyes. All he finally wanted to do was escape into sleep.

They must have realized it because the next thing he knew he was on the bed. Someone placed a blanket over him. The muted voices grew softer and then only silence filled the air.

Donovan tumbled into sleep.

When he awoke, it was to the smell of roasted chicken. His stomach gurgled noisily. He couldn't remember the last time he'd eaten. At least he was right-handed so he could feed himself without any problems. Where his left hand and forearm should have been tingled with pain. He knew what Dr. Freeman had said about it but the false pain seemed more than real to him.

Finally opening his eyes, he looked into the sitting room and saw a table there with plates and stemware. Finch was saying something to Mrs. Preston and then she moved from his sight. Finch walked to the doorway.

"Ah, I see the smell of your cook's chicken has done the trick. Come along. I've waited to eat with you and I'm starving."

Finch didn't ask if Donovan needed help. He turned around and returned to the sitting room.

Anger boiled within him. With his hand—his only hand—he tossed off the blanket covering him and saw he wore trousers, a shirt, waistcoat, and cravat. The shirt had been altered. Cut and stitched in some manner to end where his arm did. He supposed Hall or someone had gone in and butchered all his shirts in such a manner and hadn't had time yet to remake his coats.

Bitterness filled him as he swung his legs to the floor. He was weak from lack of eating and being lethargic for so long. Slowly, he made his away across the bedchamber to the doorway.

Finch glanced up. "You can sit on the settee. I will push the table up to you."

The last time Donovan had sat on this settee, it was with Wynter in his lap. They had kissed for an eternity before he had taken her to his bed. Where he had made love to her. Where he had known he would love her for all eternity.

Blinking rapidly, he moved toward the settee and sat. Finch pushed the table close and picked up his knife and fork, carving into the chicken on his plate. Donovan stared dumbly at it.

"How am I supposed to eat this?" he asked, realizing he wouldn't be able to cut the meat up and too proud to ask his friend to do so for him.

Finch didn't reply.

He lifted his fork and began sampling the other items on his plate. Thank goodness nothing else needing cutting into pieces. When he had finished, he dipped his butter knife into the crock of butter and managed to get more butter on the bread than his plate. Not bad for one hand.

The bread done, his stomach gurgled loudly.

"Sounds like you need some roasted chicken," Finch commented blandly.

Donovan picked up the chicken with his fingers and devoured it. It tasted better to him than anything he'd ever eaten.

Except Wynter. The taste of Wynter would always linger in his mind and in his heart.

He rubbed his hand against his napkin, trying to get the grease from it. At least his belly felt full now. Hopefully, this meant he had regained his appetite.

"I told you to leave."

Finch shrugged. "I heard you. I chose not to obey." With a wry smile, he added, "I was never much on obeying rules, if you recall."

Donovan sighed. "Why are you here, Finch?"

"Perhaps because I am a fellow Terror and I was concerned about you?"

"I am fine."

"You don't seem to be."

"Who made you the judge of me?" he snapped.

"I am not judging you, Donovan. I am here as your friend. What you have undergone is a terrible tragedy but it is not the end of the world."

"It is for me," he hissed.

Finch crossed his arms. "Is that so? You've proven you can still eat. I'm sure you can also piss. Talk. Think. Walk."

"What is your point, Finch? Should I be grateful to be alive?"

"Yes. That would be a start."

"I will never be whole again," he pointed out.

Finch studied him. "No, you won't. But you are still Donovan Martin, Duke of Haverhill. You have responsibilities to uphold. You have friends that still care for you. And you have a woman who loves you."

He sucked in a breath. "What do you know of Wynter?"

"I know that she's too good for you," Finch said. "Just as Emery is too good for Miles and Meadow is much too good for Wyatt. The Terrors seem to attract amazing women."

"There is nothing between Wynter and me."

"Yes, there is," Finch insisted. "You simply are not acknowledging that there is. Or is it true—that because Wynter was permanently scarred in the same accident that you no longer love her?"

"No!" he objected vehemently. "She could be bald and blind and I would still . . ." His voice faded.

"Then why have you rejected her, Donovan?" Finch asked softly. "Love is a rare thing. You are fortunate it came into your life. You love Wynter. She loves you. Why are you pushing her away?"

"Because she deserves a whole man. Not part of one," he said harshly.

"You sound just like your father," Finch accused.

"Don't say that!"

"You cannot control what I think or say, Donovan. What I am saying is true. Your mother was injured. Haverhill refused to allow the doctor to amputate a small portion of her leg. Tell me this. Would you have loved her any less had she been missing her lower leg and foot?"

"Of course, I would have loved her," Donovan said. "She was my mother. It wouldn't have mattered to me one whit."

"Nothing would have changed between you?"

"No."

"Then why should things change between you and Wynter?" Finch countered. "So you can only fondle one breast at a time since you only have one hand. I doubt she would mind that."

"You are a man of the cloth!"

"Even men of the cloth have needs. And we understand the needs of other men. You loved your mama because of who she was, not because of one of her limbs. It is the same with Wynter. She loves your mind. Your spirit. Your dedication and honor. She probably even loves that ugly face of yours.

"The point is that you are essentially the same person you were before a random accident caused a small part of you to go away. If the roles were reversed and Wynter had lost her hand and forearm, would you stop loving her?"

"Never," he said fiercely.

"Yet you have done a grave injustice to her, Donovan. Your mother died and you were left alone. You have forced Wynter to be alone—and you aren't even dead. She has to exist in a world without you because you forced that choice upon her. You are deciding what you think is best for her when she should be making that decision for herself."

He reeled hearing Finch's words. He hadn't listened to Wynter. He hadn't given her a choice to reject him on her own. Instead, he had done what he thought was best for her and made the decision for the both of them. He was just as bad as his father and grandfather had been. His grandfather hadn't allowed Mama to wed the man she loved. His father hadn't given her the chance to live after her accident. Donovan knew Mama could have lived many years longer. She could have seen him and Sam become men. She could have seen him wed and played with her grand-children.

Donovan had placed Wynter in a box and put her away upon a shelf, never consulting her about something that concerned the both of them. But Wynter was a woman with her own mind. She had the heart of a lion. It should be up to her to decide and not have that decision taken from her. Even if she now rejected him after how horribly he had treated her, it would be a choice she made.

Not one he made for her.

A sob burst from him and he broke down. Finch was there, his arm coming about Donovan, comforting him. Donovan cried for all the years he had been without his mother. For how he had treated Wynter. For the missing limb he would never regain. Finally, his tears subsided.

"I have been a fool, haven't I?" he asked.

"You've been a bloody fool," Finch agreed, grinning. "But even God can forgive a bloody fool for doing bloody idiotic things."

"Spoken like a true clergyman." He paused. "I must see her."

"Not now," Finch said. "Hall tells me today is the first time you have really slept. You need more rest, Donovan. Tomorrow, you can go see Wynter."

"The woman I love."

"The woman you love."

"You will love her, too, Finch. She is an amazing woman."

"I know."

He frowned. "I don't understand."

Finch said, "It was Wynter who sent for me, Donovan. Per-haps she thought since God is on my side that the two of us would help you see the light. I stopped at Chesterfield before I came here because I wanted to meet the remarkable woman who would write to a complete stranger. Wynter wasn't ready to give up on you—even when you wanted to give up on yourself."

Donovan smiled, his eyes misting with tears. "I told you that you would love her."

"She is special. And again, much too good for the likes of you."

"Emery and Meadow adore her."

"I can see why. Now, let's get you into bed. Tomorrow, you may go see Wynter and grovel at her feet. You need to ask for forgiveness first."

Resolve filled Donovan. "I will do whatever it takes to win her back, Finch."

# CHAPTER TWENTY-SEVEN

WYNTER ROSE AND slipped the brief note from Finch from under her pillow, reading it again, telling her that he was staying overnight at Hillside. Finch had sent the carriage back, along with the note, yesterday afternoon. She hoped it was a good sign that Donovan had not tossed his old friend from the house. She wished Finch had written more but she supposed he was being cautiously optimistic and not trying to give her too much hope.

She had liked the clergyman from the moment he arrived yesterday morning. She could definitely see why he was a Turner Terror. They all had something their eyes. An air of mischief, she supposed, as well as the fierce loyalty they displayed toward one another.

Finch had asked her to share everything she could with him before he confronted Donovan. Wynter had explained how she and Donovan had fallen in love and why she had been reluctant to wed him, even telling the vicar about the unrequited love between her father and Donovan's mother. She explained how she had abandoned her stance on never marrying because she knew Donovan to be a good man and she believed they had a wonderful future ahead of them.

Discussing the accident had been painful, of course, but not as painful as relating the hateful things Donovan had said to try and drive her away. She admitted his words hurt but she understood he pushed her hard because he thought to save her from a life with a cripple. Donovan would never be that to her.

He was simply the man she loved.

Once Finch heard the entire story, he was ready to go to Donovan. Papa had insisted that Finch take their carriage since his horse was exhausted from the journey from Marbury.

Today, she would know whether or not Donovan accepted her and if they would have a future together. She only hoped a miracle had occurred and that Finch had gotten through to Donovan.

Wynter rang for her maid and dressed in blue because Donovan liked her in that color. She kept her hair simple, once again knowing he liked it arranged that way. Dismissing the maid, Wynter stared into the mirror for a long time.

She might want Donovan—but would he desire her?

The stitches ran vertically down her cheek for about two inches. Dr. Freeman told her a scar would form and never leave but that it would fade in time. Donovan led her to believe it was why he did not wish to marry her but Wynter held out hope that wasn't the case.

The thought of breakfast didn't appeal to her. Instead, she went to her sitting room and sat at her pianoforte. She had pounded the keys for several days now, in anger and frustration. Today, though, a calm had descended upon her. Either Donovan would want her or he wouldn't. Once the verdict was in, she would have to move on with her life.

She decided to go with Beethoven and began playing *Piano Sonata No. 24*. She played the entire piece through, ten minutes of intense concentration which ironically soothed her. As she lifted her hands from the keys, she was aware she was no longer alone.

*Donovan had come.*

Wynter glanced up and saw he stood in the doorway. Immediately, she noticed the modified coat, which had been altered to accommodate his missing hand and forearm. Her gaze went to his. She saw a range of emotions dance across it. Hesitation.

Yearning. Fear.

And hope.

She rose from the bench and Donovan closed the door, giving them privacy. She stopped in front of him.

"How are you?"

He smiled wryly. "As well as a man with a missing limb can be, I suppose."

Humor was a good sign.

"Better yet, how are you?" He reached and smoothed her injured check with his thumb.

"It itches," she said. "My cheek. Dr. Freeman said that is part of the healing process." She paused. "There will always be a scar, though."

"There will always be a scar on my heart, Sunshine. That is, there will be one if you choose not to take me back."

She caught her breath. Then she reached out and wrapped her fingers about his wrist.

"I was a damned fool. I thought I was saving you from having to reject me. Or worse, keep you from thinking you still should honor any kind of commitment to me."

"But I—"

His fingers moved to her mouth, silencing her.

"I didn't want you to be forced to be with someone so flawed. I thought you deserved better than that. Scar or no scar, you will always be the most beautiful woman in the world to me. I didn't think it fair to hold you to me. To an unspoken promise between us. I hadn't formally offered for you but you are full of honor. I didn't want you to feel any obligation to marry a man who was at such a disadvantage."

Donovan cupped her cheek. "But the decision should have been yours. Once again, I was insensitive and trying to make it for you instead of allowing you to make it for yourself. I see now that I am hopeless at this without you."

He smiled wistfully at her. "I need you, Wynter. In so many ways. Most of all, I need you to kick my arse when I do something arrogant and foolhardy. I need you to keep me in line. Make me the best man I can be." He sighed. "I am afraid I am going to need a lot of work. I have regressed in the past week without your good influence. What I am trying to say is I was a bloody fool who should have trusted you. Trusted in your love for me—and mine for you."

Tears brimmed in her eyes. "Do you love me, Donovan? I most certainly love you."

She saw tears form in his eyes, as well. "I love you more today than I have on any day leading up to this one. If you give me a chance, I will love you a little more with each day that follows. That love will deepen over the years and bind us together. We will be able to meet any challenge because we have one another and stand strong together."

Donovan dropped to one knee and took her hand in his. He pressed a fervent kiss against her fingers.

"Wynter Day, my love, my life, my everything—will you have me as I am? Will you marry me and make me the happiest man on this earth?"

Tears cascaded down her cheeks. "I would have no other, Donovan. You are my light and my life. You are the man I want by my side for the good and the bad and everything in-between that we might face. To me, you are perfect and always will be in every way."

He rose and slipped his arm about her waist, bring her close. "I will spend every day loving you, Wynter."

She beamed radiantly. "I know. And I will love you back, Donovan."

His mouth covered hers and she lost herself in his kiss.

When they emerged from her sitting room an hour later—after a bit of repairing clothes gone askew and hair which had come undone—they went to the drawing room where Finch and her father sat before a roaring fire, sipping tea.

"We have good news, Papa," Wynter said. "Donovan and I are going to be married."

Her father kissed her cheek and then offered Donovan his hand. "I know my daughter has shared with you how much I loved your mother."

"She has, my lord," Donovan said.

"I am sorry she won't be here to see the two of you joined in holy matrimony. I am glad, however, that I am gaining a son. Her son. I see much of her in you, Donovan."

"All the good in me comes from her," Donovan said.

Finch stood and kissed Wynter's cheek. "Congratulations, Wynter." He threw his arms about Donovan. "Well done, my friend. When is the wedding?"

Donovan looked to Wynter. "I think we would like it to occur as soon as possible."

Knowing they had made love just minutes ago and that he had emptied his seed inside her, she thought she could even be carrying his child now. The sooner they wed, the better.

"You know I have performed the marriage of two other Terrors," Finch pointed out. "As long as I am here, I would be happy to do so again."

"Will you ride with me to London then so that I may purchase a special license?" Donovan asked.

"I would be happy to," Finch agreed, and Wynter saw the Terror finally smile for the first time since she had met him.

"We better send word to my fellow Terrors then," Donovan said. "I cannot be married without Miles and Wyatt taking part in the ceremony."

"I will send messengers to each of them while you are in London," she said. "I will stress they and their wives should come at once."

"Tell them to come to Hillside. I would like for us to be married there," he told her. "In what will be our home." Donovan pulled her to him. "Who knew I would find my duchess in the neighborhood? Now I have no need to peruse the Marriage Mart."

He kissed her, despite Papa and Finch being present.

"We are still going for the Season," she informed him when he broke the kiss. "Emery and Meadow and I have plans, you know."

Donovan grinned. "The Duchess of Haverhill will be the one in charge of everything, I suspect."

"Because I am so clever?" Wynter teased.

"That—and because you hold my heart."

Donovan kissed her again and Wynter knew each day with this man would be a day spent in love.

# EPILOGUE

*Hillside—February 1812*

DONOVAN WAITED PATIENTLY as Hall finished tying the cravat and stepped away.

"There, Your Grace. You are as ready as you'll ever be," the valet said.

He moved to the mirror and took in his reflection. The dark morning coat. The crisp white shirt and white brocaded waistcoat. The adjusted sleeves on the left side where the lower part of his arm once rested.

It didn't matter. He understood that now. What was important was he felt more whole than he ever had.

Because in a few minutes, it would no longer be just him. He would have claimed Wynter as his wife and Donovan knew the Duchess of Haverhill would never leave his side.

"Get the ring, Hall," he instructed and the valet retrieved the small box sitting on a table, opening it and removing the ring.

"I'll take it," Wyatt volunteered.

"No, I will. You would probably lose it between here and the drawing room," Miles quipped.

"Miles is right," Donovan said. "He is more responsible."

"Well, I have been a duke longer than the two of you," Miles said drolly, his eyes mirthful.

Hall handed Miles the ring and excused himself, leaving the

three Terrors alone.

"This is a big day for you," Wyatt said. "You will soon be a married man."

"Every day will be a bigger and better one," Donovan said. "Because I will be wed to Wynter."

"Wait until your first child arrives," Miles said. "Your love for Wynter will explode. And you'll find even more love in your heart for the babe."

"He's right," Wyatt said. "Our child won't even be here until summer and already I love it and Meadow so much that I walk around with a perpetual smile on my face."

A knock sounded and Miles answered it, admitting Finch.

"Everything is ready downstairs," Finch told them. "I need the groom in place and then Wynter will be summoned."

"Before we go, I must say something," Donovan began. He waited a moment and then continued. "You three—along with Hart—have been my brothers for many years. You saved me then, all those years ago, and you have saved me now."

He thrust out his only hand. Miles set his atop it. Wyatt came next and Finch placed his last.

"Terrors forever," Donovan said and the others echoed his words. "Now we can head for the ceremony."

They went to the drawing room and Donovan's heart began beating faster at the thought of seeing Wynter. Moments later, she entered the room on her father's arm. Lord Cheston led his daughter straight to Donovan, whose gaze never left his bride. She was more beautiful than ever, scar and all, and he knew the life ahead of them would be one of joy and filled with love.

Wynter joined him, her face radiant.

Donovan leaned down and whispered in her ear, "I love you."

They both blinked back tears as Finch began to speak.

When it came time to present Wynter with a ring, Miles stepped forward and handed it to Finch, who blessed it and passed it to Donovan. As he slipped the ring onto her finger, he swallowed the lump in his throat. Lord Cheston had given this ring to Donovan when he learned of his daughter's betrothal. The ring had been the one the earl was going to give to Donovan's mother when they wed. Lord Cheston had kept the ring locked away all these years and had told Donovan it was fitting for it to be used as the wedding ring that symbolized the love Donovan and Wynter had for one another.

Finch concluded the ceremony and as he did, Donovan thought how thrown into disorder his life had been in the last few months. He had left the army. Become a duke. Taken on a massive amount of responsibilities. And found the one woman who made him whole.

He would take that disruption any day, as long as it included Wynter. His Sunshine.

Finch pronounced them man and wife and Donovan gazed into the beautiful eyes of his wife. His duchess. The woman he would love and cherish every day going forth.

His lips met hers.

And their life together began.

# About the Author

Award-winning and internationally bestselling author Alexa Aston's historical romances use history as a backdrop to place her characters in extraordinary circumstances, where their intense desire for one another grows into the treasured gift of love.

She is the author of Regency and Medieval romance, including: Dukes of Distinction; Soldiers & Soulmates; The St. Clairs; The King's Cousins; and The Knights of Honor.

A native Texan, Alexa lives with her husband in a Dallas suburb, where she eats her fair share of dark chocolate and plots out stories while she walks every morning. She enjoys a good Netflix binge; travel; seafood; and can't get enough of *Survivor* or *The Crown*.

CPSIA information can be obtained
at www.ICGtesting.com
Printed in the USA
LVHW080952151021
700543LV00022B/425

9 781956 003062